HER LIEUTENANT PROTECTOR

Lara Lacombe

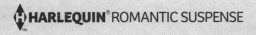

HARLEQUIN® ROMANTIC SUSPENSE

Recycling programs
for this product may
not exist in your area.

ISBN-13: 978-0-373-40218-2

Her Lieutenant Protector

Copyright © 2017 by Lara Kingeter

HARLEQUIN®
www.Harlequin.com

Printed in U.S.A.

Lara Lacombe earned a PhD in microbiology and immunology and worked in several labs across the country before moving into the classroom. Her day job as a college science professor gives her time to pursue her other love—writing fast-paced romantic suspense with smart, nerdy heroines and dangerously attractive heroes. She loves to hear from readers! Find her on the web or contact her at laralacombewriter@gmail.com.

Books by Lara Lacombe

Harlequin Romantic Suspense

Doctors in Danger

Enticed by the Operative
Dr. Do-or-Die
Her Lieutenant Protector

The Coltons of Shadow Creek

Pregnant by the Colton Cowboy

The Coltons of Texas

Colton Baby Homecoming

Deadly Contact
Fatal Fallout
Lethal Lies
Killer Exposure
Killer Season

Visit the Author Profile page at Harlequin.com for more titles.

This book is for my friend Shayla Swift, in honor of her work as founder and director of Speak Truth to Sexual Violence Nebraska

Prologue

Peterson Shipyard
Norfolk, Virginia

"You heading out, Cam?"

Cameron leaned back and glanced at his watch. "A little early, isn't it?"

Frank shook his head. "Boss told us to knock off at four for the holiday weekend. Didn't you see the announcement posted in the elevator?"

"I must have missed it."

Frank shifted his thermos to his other hand and pushed his hard hat back off his forehead. "So are you coming, or what?"

"Yeah, just gimme a minute." Cameron began to gather up his tools, stuffing them into the tough canvas bag that served as his carryall. He was done installing this toilet, and the others would keep for the weekend.

The boss didn't give them a break very often, so he wasn't about to pass this one up.

Frank waited patiently while he got his tools in order, then the two of them set off, joining the steadily growing stream of workers headed for the main exit of the ship. She wasn't a huge ship, by industry standards, but Cam had caught a glimpse of the master plans and knew she was going to be overflowing with features and amenities galore. Her beauty was already starting to take shape in the clean lines of the cabins, the elegant scrollwork adorning the walls of the common areas, and the large, open spaces scattered throughout the ship for guests to congregate and socialize. Even the toilets he was installing were top of the line. There was no way a man of his salary would ever be able to afford a voyage on this ship, but he felt a quiet pride at the knowledge he had helped build her.

Cameron and Frank chatted amiably as they walked until they reached the parking lot. Both men paused, each one searching for his respective vehicle in the lot.

"A bunch of us are getting together down at the Crow's Nest," Frank said. "Want to join us?"

Cameron thought of his small apartment and the frozen TV dinner waiting for him there. Not the most appealing way to spend a Friday night. "Sure thing," he said, patting his pockets for his keys. His stomach dropped as he realized they weren't there. "Damn," he muttered.

"What's wrong?"

"Left my keys inside."

"That's a bummer," Frank said, shaking his head in sympathy. "Want me to wait?"

It was a nice offer, but Cameron could tell by the way

Frank glanced toward his truck that he was anxious to get going. "Nah, you go on ahead. I'll meet you there."

"Thanks, man," Frank said, the relief in his voice confirming Cameron's suspicion. "I'll save you a seat at the table."

Cameron gave him a wave, already turning back to the gangplank that led to the ship. It didn't take long to make his way back on board; the crowd of workers had thinned substantially, all of them eager to get home to their families or to head to the bar to unwind.

The keys were exactly where he thought they'd be, sitting on the floor next to the last toilet he'd installed. They must have slipped out of his back pocket while he was on the floor working; he really should just clip them to his belt…

He scooped them up and began to retrace his steps, heading back for the parking lot and the promise of a relaxing evening with the guys. He was halfway down the hall when the shadow of a movement caught his eye. He stopped and leaned back, glancing into the cabin he'd just passed. Was it just the dying rays of the sun shifting through the window, or perhaps something else?

At first glance the cabin appeared empty. Then he caught a glimpse of a boot dangling from the ceiling and did a double take. Who was working, and why were they in the duct above the room? As far as he knew, that work had already been completed.

Cameron stepped inside, craning his head to try to catch a glimpse of what was going on. "Hello?"

The man in the room froze, and Cameron had the sense he'd startled him. "Everything okay in here?" He glanced around, noting the absence of a ladder. How did the man get up there, and more important, how was he going to get down?

"Hello?" he repeated, stepping fully into the room. "Need any help? Your ladder seems to have wandered off."

The man didn't respond, which was odd. Cameron felt the fine hairs on the back of his neck rise as he glanced around the cabin. The small black box that should have been mounted near the ceiling was lying in pieces on the built-in dresser. It was the in-room hub for the ship-wide Wi-Fi network, and he hadn't seen any electricians on board today...

Was someone trying to tamper with the ship? The thought sent a jolt through him, and he was suddenly very aware of the fact that he was alone in the room with an unidentified worker, one who probably shouldn't be here.

He took a step back, keeping his eye on the man's dangling leg to make sure he didn't move. Best to get off the ship and call security, let them deal with this. He took another step, feeling his way toward the door.

The blow to his head came without warning. A flash of pain, an explosion of light. A last, desperate gasp. And then nothing.

"What did you do?"

Harvey lifted one shoulder in a dismissive shrug, his gaze locked on the floor and the body at their feet. "He was snooping. Thought he'd seen something."

"Did you know that for sure, or was it just a guess?" Terrence didn't bother to hide the impatience in his voice. This wasn't the first time Harvey had caused trouble, but he couldn't get rid of the man. Blood ran thicker than water, and since Harvey's brother was a well-connected member of the Organization, Terrence was stuck with him.

"Couldn't take that chance, now, could I?" He sounded

a little indignant, and Terrence decided not to press the issue. Arguing with Harvey wasn't going to change the fact that there was now a dead body to deal with, and since Terrence was in charge of this little operation, it was his problem to solve.

It wasn't supposed to be like this. The project was simple and straightforward: go throughout the ship and "enhance" some of the black boxes, adding a few chunks of gray, putty-like material before sealing them back up. He'd been given a set of plans marked with the locations of the boxes to be altered, several bags of the mysterious substance and a bag of unmarked bills. His instructions had also included a list of suggested precautions, ominous statements that warned he shouldn't directly touch the material or breathe in any of its dust. It was almost enough to give him pause, but then he'd counted the money and decided the risk was worth the reward.

Things had started out well. The team had come aboard in the late afternoon to familiarize themselves with the layout of the ship and the location of the target boxes. When quitting time rolled around and the crew had started to leave, they'd made themselves scarce so as not to draw attention to the fact they were staying behind. Now they were making their way through the ship, going from room to room to modify the boxes on the plan.

At least they *had* been, before this nosy guy had stumbled across something he wasn't supposed to see.

"What should we do with him?" Harvey nudged the body with the toe of his boot, as if he expected the man to stand up and walk out of the room. He glanced up at the ceiling, nodding at the dark opening where Terrence had been only moments before.

Terrence answered his unspoken question. "No. There's not enough room." The body would also begin to stink and leak fluids soon, which meant it wouldn't stay hidden for long. Maybe they could weigh it down, sink it in the water? But no, there was so much boat traffic in the harbor nothing stayed under for long.

Terrence glanced around the room, wishing the answer was written on the walls. Thick plastic sheeting hung from the ceiling and covered part of the floor, a protective barrier that would soon be removed as the cabins were finished. Would anyone notice if it came down a little early?

"Pull that down," he instructed Harvey. "Lay it flat on the floor."

"This?" Harvey tugged at the plastic tarp dubiously. "Why?"

Terrence ground his teeth together. "You're going to wrap the body in it."

"Oh." Harvey wrinkled his nose. "Are you going to help?"

"Nope." Terrence crossed his arms and stared hard at the other man. "You killed him. You get to clean it up."

It took several minutes, punctuated by Harvey's mumbled complaints, but eventually the body was arranged on the thick layer of plastic. "Hand me that duct tape."

Terrence picked up the silver roll, glancing dubiously from it to the body. "Won't he smell?" He had no idea how they were going to dispose of the man, but he did know the coming stench would only make life more difficult.

Harvey rocked back on his heels, considering the question. "Yeah. Give me a minute."

He stood and walked out of the room before Terrence could protest. *What the hell?* This was not going well at all. And now the idiot had left him here with a dead body at his feet. What if someone walked in and saw? How was he going to explain the situation?

He needn't have worried. Harvey returned a few minutes later, lugging a large bag on his shoulder. He dropped it to the floor, and Terrence read the label: Ice Melt.

"Are you kidding me?"

Harvey spared him a glance. "It's basically salt. It will keep him from stinking."

Terrence swallowed a surge of disgust. "How do you know that?" He immediately regretted the question. The less he knew about Harvey's activities, the better.

Harvey merely raised one brow. "I just do." He started tugging at the laces of the man's boots, loosening them.

"What are you doing?"

Harvey didn't look up as he pulled the boots off the man's feet and set them to the side. "These are nice boots. Be a shame to waste them."

Terrence shook his head, wondering why he'd even bothered to ask. At this point, he shouldn't be surprised by anything Harvey did.

It didn't take long to spread the white pellets of ice melt over and around the body. Terrence rose, dusting his hands on his pants. Harvey stayed crouched by the man's head and began folding the plastic over the body. He stuck out his hand, silently asking for the tape.

Terrence handed it to him, then began to pace around the room while Harvey completed the gruesome task, his thoughts a tangled knot of worry and frustration. The man who had hired him would know how to get rid of a body, but Terrence didn't want to tell him about this little hiccup. Even though Harvey had been the one to kill the interloper, Terrence knew he would be held responsible.

Harvey stood up and put his hands on his hips, eyeing

his handiwork with a critical expression. "Think that'll hold him?"

A small shudder ran through Terrence, and he closed his eyes, trying to clear the image from his brain. "I don't know. I don't have a lot of experience in this."

"I say we put him in the wall."

The sheer insanity of the statement nearly made him laugh, but he choked off the sound. "Which wall?"

Harvey pointed at the back wall of what would someday be the closet. "Why not there?"

Terrence glanced at it and shrugged. It was as good a plan as any, provided they could patch things up enough that no one would notice.

Harvey removed a section of drywall with surprising delicacy, revealing the curve of the ship's hull. They worked quickly, maneuvering the body into the space and propping it against a steel beam. Terrence stood back while Harvey sealed the wall up again, patching the seams with some putty a worker had left behind. It was all very neat and tidy, and Terrence felt a grudging respect for Harvey as he finished disguising the cuts he'd made. Apparently the man had some skills after all.

"What do you think?" He stood back from the wall, tilting his head as he studied it.

Terrence did the same. "Looks good," he admitted. "You really can't tell."

Harvey nodded. "Not bad for a quick job. Once they spray the texture on and paint it, no one will ever know."

"Let's get going," Terrence said. They couldn't stand here all night admiring Harvey's construction work. "We're behind schedule."

"We'll catch up," Harvey said confidently.

"Only if you don't kill anyone else."

"I'm not making any promises."

Chapter 1

*P*ressure.

No, that wasn't right. Mallory searched her brain, trying to find the right word to describe the unsettling sensation. Something pulled at her, an insistent tugging at her shoulders and hips that made it hard to focus. She tried to lift her hand to brush away the annoying feeling, but her arm wouldn't obey her brain's command.

Her heart kicked hard against her breastbone, panic rising in her chest as she fought against the unexpected paralysis. What was happening to her?

She tried again and managed to shift her leg to the side. It was heavy, the movement sluggish and difficult. But it was a start.

Her eyelids were twin weights trapping her in darkness. Opening her eyes proved too much of a challenge, so she tried to call for help instead. Her tongue was a thick obstruction in her mouth, but she managed to make a sound—a moan, really, but hopefully it was enough to draw attention.

The tugging stopped and a blast of cool air hit her skin. Another strangled sound escaped her throat, and suddenly there was warmth spreading across her torso.

"Shh." The whisper was hot against her ear, an urgent command that made her catch her breath. Someone was here! They were going to help her!

A split second later a weight descended on her body, pressing her flat. Mallory tried to move away, to ease the pressure on her chest that made it hard to breathe. But the effort was like trying to swim through syrup, her limbs stiff and uncoordinated.

"Just relax. It's okay."

It was a nice thought, but her body refused to consider it. She thrashed around as much as she was able, trying to dislodge the crushing burden pinning her down. No matter what this voice said, something was very, very wrong.

"Stop it." Sharp pain at her wrists cut through her confusion, and she froze. The pain eased, leaving behind a dull ache that throbbed in time with her heart.

"That's good. Just like that. We'll be done soon."

The words swam in her mind, mixing and churning together until she almost lost their meaning. The fumbling started up again, a new hint of violence in the clawing and pulling. She heard the unmistakable sound of fabric ripping, and the noise made her heart stall.

She tried to move, but it was too late.

"No!" She screamed the word over and over again, but all that came out was a muffled sob...

Mallory jerked awake with a roar of protest, limbs flailing as she fought off the imaginary assailant. She blinked several times, trying to clear her vision and shake off the fog of the dream that clung to her mind like sticky cobwebs.

I'm okay. It was only a dream.

She lifted a trembling hand to brush her hair back from her face. The tendrils clung to her cheek and neck, damp with sweat. A vile, bitter taste coated her tongue, and she reached for the glass of water beside her bed, drinking deep in an effort to wash it away. She focused on the cool liquid as it filled her mouth and slid down her throat, using the visceral sensations as a lodestone to help her navigate back to reality.

Her heart fluttered like a panicked bird against her rib cage, the feeling unpleasant and troubling. Mallory took a deep breath, trying to recall the meditation techniques she'd learned over the years in therapy. *Clear your mind*, her therapist had said. *Empty it of all thoughts and just breathe.*

"Easier said than done," she muttered to herself. She pictured a bathtub, imagined herself pulling the plug and watching the water drain. But that reminded her of the aftermath of the rape, when she'd spent what had felt like days in the tub, scrubbing and soaking in a desperate attempt to wash the stain of her violation away...

Nope, don't go there. She shied away from the memory as if burned, searching for an image that didn't carry so much emotional baggage.

Her gaze caught on the red numbers of her alarm clock, and she focused on the color. Red was a nice, bright, happy color. The color of apples, of roses.

Of the marks on her body, and the bloodstains on her...

Stop it!

Another deep breath, another attempt to walk back

from the cliffs of panic. It was too early to call Avery and Olivia, so she shoved off the bed and began to pace. The carpet was soft under her feet, and she curled her toes into the fibers with every step. There wasn't a lot of room—it was seven steps from one wall to the other—but she made do.

Fuzz built up under her toes, a testament to the newness of the carpet. Of everything, really. The *Abigail Adams* was hot off the assembly line and was the most luxurious ship to sail in recent memory. She was also the first ship to have been constructed in the United States in years, which meant she would sail under the US flag, a rarity among cruise ships. It was an honor for Mallory to have been selected to work as the ship's doctor on the *Abigail*'s maiden voyage. She closed her eyes, picturing the spacious sick bay with its state-of-the-art equipment, gleaming counters and crisp, white linens. It was a wonderful facility, befitting this crown jewel of cruise ships.

She let her mind wander, reviewing supply lists, protocols, storage locations. It was always a bit of a challenge coming onto a new ship; it took her several days to get familiar with the staff and the facilities. But the people she'd met today had seemed professional and polite, and she knew they were the best of the best. With so many VIPs scheduled to come on board, the company wanted everything to be perfect.

And they picked me.

The reminder filled her with pride and banished the last vestiges of the dream. She was no longer a helpless, scared college student. She was Dr. Mallory Watkins, chief medical officer for the most exclusive ship on the seas. She had overcome the tragedy in her past to rise to the top of her field, and she wasn't about to let an annoying dream shake her confidence now.

Another glance at the clock told her it was too late—or too early—to go back to bed. She knew from experience she wouldn't be able to fall asleep easily again, so she might as well start her day. The gym on board was open, and it would be good to get a workout in before the day truly started and she got too busy. Not only did she have a long prelaunch checklist, but her best friends, Olivia Sandoval and Avery Thatcher, were arriving today for the cruise.

Mallory was excited to see them both and to meet the new men in their lives. She was happy her friends had found love, even though it did make her feel a little wistful. In the years since her assault, she'd worked to overcome her fears regarding men and dating, but with limited success. She'd made a few awkward attempts to connect, but it hadn't worked out. The men she'd tried to date had started out patient and understanding, but they'd all grown tired of her issues with physical intimacy. Her therapist had told her not to stress about it, but that was easier said than done.

"Don't force yourself to engage in sex until you're ready," Dr. Givens had said, her brown eyes warm and kind behind the rims of her tortoiseshell glasses. "Everyone recovers at their own pace, and you can't judge your progress against artificial benchmarks."

The logical part of Mallory understood and agreed with Dr. Givens, but her emotional side wondered if she would ever feel safe enough to sleep with a man again.

"Someday," she muttered, shaking her head as she pulled a T-shirt and yoga pants from the built-in dresser. "I just haven't met the right man yet."

It was a juvenile fantasy, the idea that there was some kind of Prince Charming out there for her. Nevertheless, it gave her comfort to think that she wasn't permanently broken, that she would be able to enjoy intimacy with someone out there.

Avery and Olivia seemed to have found their happily-ever-afters. Maybe it was time Mallory started looking for hers.

Everest LeBeau slowed his pace for a moment and reached for the water bottle, keeping one hand on the elliptical machine for balance while he twisted off the cap. Once upon a time he wouldn't have had to throttle back his workout, but thanks to his war injuries those days were behind him.

He replaced the bottle and kicked things up again, gritting his teeth at the ache in his lower right leg. The prosthesis he wore just below his right knee was shifting a little, rubbing the skin of his stump with every step. It was a new prosthesis, and he knew from experience it would take a little time for calluses to build up. Until they did, he was just going to have to deal with the discomfort.

He was used to handling pain. He'd pushed himself to the limit at the army basic officer course, wanting to test his physical capabilities. His classmates had thought he was crazy—everyone knew boot camp was easier for officers, and they thought he should take advantage of the more relaxed standards. They'd laughed at him, right up until the two-week field training exercise when all his extra work had paid off. He'd passed with flying colors and had set a few new records for his efforts. Not bad for a guy from the backwaters of Louisiana. The army had shipped him off to Iraq with a pat on the back and a smile.

The heat of the desert had been uncomfortable, but nothing he couldn't handle. The dry, oven-like atmosphere had been a novel change from the hot and sticky weather he was used to, but as long as he stayed hydrated, things were bearable, if a mite stifling. The desert wasn't his favorite place, but it didn't take him long to settle into a routine with his team. He had this war thing figured out, or so he'd thought.

Until it all came crashing down on a lazy summer day seven years ago.

The IED had done its work with brutal efficiency. The explosion had thrown him clear of the Humvee, and the shock of it had kept him from feeling much of anything at first. It wasn't until the medics arrived and began to move him that the pain had registered: a white-hot agony radiating from the stump below his right knee... Everest closed his eyes for a second and could almost smell the stale, chalky odor of the desert. He brushed sweat off his forehead, half expecting to feel the fine grit of sand under his fingertips. The stuff had been everywhere, a kind of fine, powdered sugar–like particulate that hung in the air and clung to skin and hair and clothes with ferocious tenacity. Just stepping outside was enough to make a man want a shower, but bathing was a luxury. Even then, Everest hadn't truly felt clean until he'd been home for a while. Weeks after his return he'd still been sloughing off grains of sand, little reminders of his tour. Of course, it hadn't helped he'd spent so much time in a hospital bed. Sponge baths were no match for all the layers of desert funk he'd accrued during his tour.

That first real shower, though? Heaven. He could still feel the warm rivulets of water cascading over his shoulders, down his chest and back. It had been so damn amazing to feel clean again, it was enough to make him forget about his leg. Or rather, the missing parts of his leg. The strangest part of all was that he had felt the water on the soles of his feet—both of them. In fact, if he'd kept his eyes closed, he'd been able to feel the shower spray on both legs, not just the one he still had. He mentioned it to the doctor, and the man had nodded knowingly, a small, sad smile on his face.

"It's a phantom sensation," he'd explained. "We don't know why it happens, but it's not uncommon for amputees to still feel their missing limb."

The pain had come later, a wrenching, bone-crushing sensation that nearly took his breath away. Even now, he still wasn't used to the intensity of the sensation, or the incongruity of it. How could the ghost of a limb cause so much agony? More important, why did his brain insist on betraying him like that?

Fortunately, the attacks of phantom pain had grown less frequent over the years. Physical therapy had helped, as had the prosthetic legs he'd used. His limb felt somewhat whole again when he wore the prosthesis, and apparently that was enough to convince his brain that things were working as they should. It had been a long, hard road to reclaim his mobility, but he wasn't going to dwell on the past. He'd left the desert behind, and he had no desire to go back. He much preferred the beach sand he encountered now while working on a cruise ship.

The glass door of the gym swung wide, and a curvy redhead walked in, pulling up short when she saw him. She clearly hadn't expected to find anyone here, and he noticed the brief flicker of alarm that passed over her face, there and gone in an instant. *Interesting*, he mused. *What was she afraid of?*

Everest nodded at her and tried for a friendly smile. She gave him a guarded wave and headed for the treadmill at the far end of the row. He watched from the corner of his eye as she hopped on and began to warm up, her stride graceful as she moved.

Who was she? As head of security, he made it a point

to know all the staff on the ship, even if only on a superficial level. Since this was the *Abigail Adams*'s maiden voyage, most of the crew was new to him, which meant he had a lot of catching up to do. He would meet everyone, though. He always did.

He slowed his pace as the woman ramped up hers, her footsteps beating out a steady cadence on the tread of the machine. After a few moments of cooldown, he stepped off the elliptical and fought the urge to bend down and rub his leg. He didn't like people to know about his injury or prosthesis.

Especially not beautiful women.

Even though she was at the opposite end of the row of equipment, Everest could feel her eyes on him as he wiped his face and gathered his water bottle and keys. She reminded him of a cat his family had owned when he'd been a kid. Mittens had spent hours lying in the windowsill, his eyes trained on the birds and squirrels that frequented the backyard feeder. He'd never once lunged or swiped at any of the critters, but he'd known where every visitor was located. Everest got the sense now that this woman was taking his measure in much the same way. He stood a little straighter, his ego demanding he put his best foot forward.

Or his real foot, as it were.

She didn't try to hide the fact she was watching him. In his experience most women played it coy, glancing away when he met their eyes. Not this one. She kept staring at him, her expression open but with a hint of wariness, like she was trying to assess what he might do. Her eyes widened when he started walking toward her, but she didn't miss a step.

He stopped in front of her treadmill and placed his right shoe on the engine cover, easing his weight onto his left leg. He glanced down to see if his prosthesis was exposed, but the fabric of his pants kept it hidden. Good.

"Hello." He raised his voice, hoping it was audible above the noise of her workout.

"Hi." She didn't sound thrilled at his interruption, which was an understandable reaction. He'd just have to make it quick, and perhaps he'd get a chance to have a longer conversation with her another time.

"My name is Everest LeBeau. I'm the head of security on the ship, and I wanted to introduce myself, as I don't remember meeting you."

She relaxed as he spoke, the fine lines of strain around her eyes and mouth softening as she realized he wasn't there to bother her. "I'm Mallory Watkins," she offered. "Ship's doctor."

"Nice to meet you," he replied. He studied her face for a moment, committing her features to memory. It wasn't a hardship—she was a beautiful woman. Pale skin, auburn hair, dark brown eyes. Not to mention killer cheekbones, accented by the ponytail she wore now. It bounced playfully with every step she took, at odds with her serious expression. She had a kind of girl-next-door quality about her that he found appealing. In another time, she was just the kind of woman he would have wanted to date.

Now? Not a chance. Not only was he still finding his way back to himself again after the injury, but he wasn't about to mix business with pleasure.

"I won't bother you any longer," he said, stepping back. "Enjoy your workout."

"Thanks," she replied.

He started to walk away but stopped and turned back after a few steps. "If you don't mind, I'd like to drop by the sick bay later today. Will you be there?"

"Yes," she said, a little breathless from her run. He

could see the questions in her eyes, but she didn't say anything else.

"Great. I'll see you then."

What are you doing? he chided himself as he headed for the door. He didn't need to see her again—now that he'd met her, he'd recognize her. It wasn't like he had any business with her.

But there was something about the way she watched him that piqued his curiosity. Even now, he felt the weight of her gaze as she tracked his movement toward the exit. It wasn't lust that kept her eyes glued to him; there was no heat in her gaze. If he didn't know better, he'd say she was afraid. But why? Was she trying to hide something?

Mallory Watkins was a woman who had secrets, that much was clear. And despite his better judgment, Everest wanted to know more.

Chapter 2

Mallory sat at the bar, her eyes glued to the entrance in the hopes of catching sight of Avery and Olivia. They were supposed to meet here at noon, but she was so excited to see them she'd arrived a little early.

"Can I get you anything?"

She smiled absently at the offer from the bartender. Technically, she was on the clock, which meant she couldn't drink anything stronger than tea. "Coke, please."

He nodded, and she turned her focus to watching him select a glass and prepare her drink. Ever since the attack in college, she'd been vigilant about keeping her drinks in sight at all times, lest someone try to slip her something again. The logical part of her knew the odds of her being drugged twice were infinitesimally low, but it was a chance she didn't want to take. *Fool me once, shame on you*, she thought. *Fool me twice...*

The bartender slid her drink across the polished wood

surface with a smile. She dug in her pocket for some cash, but he held up his hand. "No charge," he said, nodding at her ID badge.

"Thanks," Mallory replied. She slipped a bill into his tip jar and turned back to the door, taking a sip of her soda.

The bubbles slid down her throat in a tickling cascade, the sensation pleasant and soothing. Coke was her vice; she loved everything about the sweet, fizzy drink. She knew it was bad for her, but since she had worked out this morning she figured a little indulgence wouldn't hurt. Besides, after her encounter with the security officer, she deserved a treat.

What was his name? She frowned a bit as she tried to recall it. Something unusual… Everett? No, Everest. Like the mountain. *Probably a story there*, she mused. Even though she'd blanked on his name, she had no trouble recalling his face. Dark blond hair and eyebrows, a square jaw and the most piercing blue eyes she'd ever seen. He was definitely a handsome man, and the rest of him wasn't too bad to look at either. Even though his workout clothes had been a little on the large side, she'd seen the way the fabric of his T-shirt moved as his muscles shifted underneath. His long legs had eaten up the distance between them in easy strides, his gait a little stilted but still graceful.

Her first response to his approach had been alarm. It was an instinctive reaction now, thanks to her past. She'd tried to overcome the flare of panic that sparked whenever a man drew close, but her body wouldn't listen to her mind. And maybe that was for the best. After all, it had been her mind that had ignored the little warning signs all those years ago…

She'd gotten better at controlling her reaction, though.

In the weeks following the attack, she couldn't stand to be in the same room with a man she didn't know. Over time, and with the help of her therapist, she'd been able to work through the initial burst of fear that came with meeting someone new. Statistically speaking, the vast majority of people were decent and had no interest in harming her. But she still kept an eye on them all the same.

Everest was just the kind of man she normally stayed away from. Tall and strong, his body was a constant reminder of her comparative physical vulnerability. But there was something about him that had put her at ease and quelled her nerves. Maybe it was his deep voice and the calm manner of his words. Or the quiet confidence in his gaze, as if he was sure he could handle anything. She couldn't quite put her finger on it, but she'd been drawn to him, had felt her wariness ease as he'd stood there talking to her. She hadn't felt so relaxed around a man in ages, and the fact that a relative stranger had had such an effect on her left her a little shaken.

Was it just a one-time thing? Or would she have the same reaction when she saw him again? She'd find out soon enough. He had mentioned stopping by sick bay today, and while he hadn't made good on the remark yet, she was sure he would at some point. Everest didn't seem like the type of man to forget an appointment, even one as loosely made as his earlier suggestion. A shiver of anticipation ran down her spine, and not for the first time, she wondered why he wanted to visit.

"There she is!"

The excited exclamation cut through Mallory's thoughts, and she focused on the door to the bar. Olivia and Avery stood at the entrance flanked by two men. As soon as she made eye contact, her friends dashed forward, leaving the men behind. The guys exchanged bemused looks and stepped inside, trailing in the wake of their girlfriends.

Mallory set her empty glass on the bar and stepped forward to meet her friends, her arms raised high so she could hug them both.

"It's so good to see you!" said Olivia.

"I've missed you so much!" said Avery.

Mallory closed her eyes and let their voices wash over her, happiness welling in her chest. Avery and Olivia were her best friends, her confidantes. The sisters of her heart. Thanks to their demanding careers—Olivia was a plastic surgeon in DC, and Avery worked as a disease investigator for the Centers for Disease Control and Prevention in Atlanta—they didn't get to see each other in person nearly as often as Mallory would like. Not for the first time, Mallory wondered if she should move from Miami to Baltimore, just to make it easier to see her friends. She missed them so much at times it was a physical ache in her chest. But they were here now, and she was determined to enjoy every minute of this trip.

Even though she *did* have to work.

"I'm so glad you could both come," Mallory said, leaning back so she could look at her friends. They both looked good. Olivia's dark eyes practically glowed, and there was a spark in Avery's blue gaze Mallory hadn't seen before. She glanced beyond her friends to the men standing a few feet away. They must be the reason for her friends' newfound joy.

"Hello," she said, nodding to them both.

"Hi," said the man on the left. He stepped closer to Olivia and put his hand on her shoulder. "I'm Logan."

"Nice to meet you," Mallory replied with a nod. Both Olivia and Avery held her hands, so she couldn't offer to shake his. They were protecting her, giving her a socially acceptable excuse for not touching the men. They knew how much she dreaded physical contact, and she felt a flash of gratitude for their efforts.

Logan looked nice enough. He was tall, with dark brown hair and angled eyebrows over intelligent green eyes. He smiled, revealing twin dimples that made him look a little boyish, in a charming sort of way.

"So you're the one who saved Olivia in Colombia," Mallory said, referring to Olivia's misadventures on her last medical charity trip.

Logan snorted. "I think it was the other way around," he said, giving Olivia's shoulder a squeeze. She lifted her free hand to cover his and looked up at him, love shining in her eyes.

"I'm just glad you got home safely," Mallory said. "Both of you."

She turned to the other man who was standing next to Avery. "And you must be Grant."

He offered her a quick smile. "Guilty as charged."

Mallory nodded, taking in his slightly curly hair and hazel eyes. There was a humorous slant to his mouth, and she could tell by the fine lines at the corners of his eyes that Grant was a man who laughed a lot.

"Have you thawed out from your stint in Antarctica yet?"

He wrinkled his nose. "Oh, yeah. Atlanta gets downright steamy in the summer."

"Told you," Avery said softly.

Grant put his arm around Avery's shoulders and drew her close. "It's a small price to pay to be with you," he said, pressing a soft kiss to her temple.

Mallory couldn't help but smile at her friends and their partners. Olivia and Avery had both chosen well, it seemed. They'd both been through a lot, and it was good to see them so happy.

"Let's grab a table," she suggested. People were starting to trickle in, wanting before-meal drinks. It wouldn't take long before the bar was packed.

"Do you have time?" Olivia asked. "I know you're on the clock."

Mallory glanced at her watch. "I said I'd be back by five, so we're good. Besides, they can page me if they need me." She led them to a round table in the corner, away from the growing bustle of the room.

The women sat down while the men remained standing. "Ladies, what can we get you to drink?" asked Grant.

Olivia and Avery both requested a fruity cocktail. Grant nodded, then looked expectantly at Mallory.

She hesitated only a second. "Water for me, please."

Olivia and Avery exchanged a shocked look, but if Grant noticed it, he didn't react. "Sure thing," he said.

Avery waited until Grant and Logan were out of earshot. "Okay, now I know you must like them," she said, leaning forward with a smile. "That's the first time I've seen you order a drink from someone who wasn't me or Olivia."

Olivia nodded in agreement, her expression hopeful. "She's right. Does that mean they get your seal of approval?"

Mallory smiled and shook her head. "You guys don't need me to tell you they're great."

"Yeah." Avery leaned back, a dreamy smile drifting across her face. "We're really lucky."

"Tell me about the new house," Mallory prompted. Avery and Grant had recently bought a house and moved in together. She'd seen a few pictures, but it would be good to hear about the details firsthand.

"Oh! It's fabulous!" Avery dug in her purse and pulled out her phone, talking excitedly as she pulled up photos.

The men came back just as she handed her phone to Mallory. Olivia leaned over to view the images, as well.

"Is she showing you pictures of the house?" Grant asked. "Did she tell you about the table she wouldn't let me bring inside?"

Avery rolled her eyes, but it was clear from the look on her face she wasn't upset. "I told you, baby. That thing is hideous." She leaned forward and addressed Olivia and Mallory. "A bottle-cap tabletop, can you believe it? He thought it would make a good coffee table."

Grant shrugged and looked at Logan. "The guys and I made it in college. It's still got a lot of life left."

Logan nodded and took a swig from his bottle. "Sounds legit to me."

Olivia glanced at him in horror, and Mallory couldn't help but laugh. "Where is this table now?"

"The garage," Grant and Avery said in unison.

"Seems like a fair compromise," she said.

"For now," Grant replied. He leaned forward, a conspiratorial glint in his hazel eyes. "I'm just biding my time until we move to a bigger house and I can have a man cave. Then I'm bringing it inside."

"As long as I don't have to look at it," Avery remarked.

Mallory held up her glass of water, capturing the attention of the table. "A toast," she said. "To new beginnings."

"And to friendships," Olivia added. "Old and new."

"Hear, hear."

Their glasses touched with a delicate clink, and everyone took a sip. Then the conversation started up again, an easy back and forth between them all. Mallory relaxed into the flow, enjoying the comforting push-pull of talking with her friends. She felt revitalized by their company, and the knowledge that she could let her guard down and speak freely about anything; Olivia and Avery were her support system, and she knew they wouldn't judge her. They all managed to stay in touch via the phone or the computer, but seeing them in person was a huge boost to her mood.

She had just started to tell them about her last cruise when the pager on her belt began to vibrate. "Sorry, guys," she said, pulling it free to examine the display. Crap. It was an emergency. Her heart sank as she stood to take her leave. "I have to go. I'll catch up with you later."

The group called out a chorus of goodbyes, but she was already headed for the door. Adrenaline thrummed through her system as she raced back to sick bay. What could possibly be going on? The ship had launched a few hours ago, and so far the sailing had been smooth. Still, it did usually take time for the passengers to adjust to walking around on a moving vessel. Had someone fallen and injured themselves?

She rounded the corner just in time to hear an eruption of voices from sick bay. Mallory broke into a run, covering the remaining distance in a few seconds. The voices grew louder as she approached, and she skidded to a stop in front of the door. Whoever was inside sounded angry and scared, a bad combination. She took a deep breath to regain her composure, then pushed open the door and walked into the chaos.

Everest clenched his jaw and tightened his grip on his temper. The two young men in the sick bay were loud and obnoxious, and he could tell by their body language they were on the verge of getting physical. It was his job to make sure that didn't happen, but the men weren't interested in listening to reason right now.

"You don't understand! The walls are melting—we have to get off the ship!"

The other man eyed the porthole window at the far end of the room. "Why is the sun in here?" He shuddered and took a step back, running into a gurney. "We're going to burn up!"

They began to talk over each other, their exclamations growing more and more agitated. One of them began to pace, his steps jerky and uncoordinated. He came dangerously close to crashing into one of the nurses, and Everest held up a hand, trying to stop him. He jerked away with an incoherent yell.

Before Everest could respond, a new voice cut through the fray. "What is happening here?"

Everyone turned to view the new arrival, and Everest felt a surge of relief when he saw Dr. Watkins standing in the doorway. These men were obviously psychologically disturbed, and if anyone could help them, it was her.

The men stared at her in silence, jaws gaping. A nurse stepped forward and spoke in low tones. "They were brought in a few minutes ago, ranting and raving. We haven't been able to examine them, so I don't know their vitals yet. They might be having a psychotic break of some kind."

Mallory's gaze drifted over her two patients while the nurse gave her report. She nodded once, then walked forward until she was only a step away from one of the men. Everest moved to stand next to her, wanting to be close just in case the guy became violent.

Mallory stared up into her patient's eyes. "I'm Dr. Watkins. Can you tell me your name?"

"Jeff."

She nodded. "Okay, Jeff. What's going on with you today?"

"The walls are melting." His voice had calmed compared with his earlier distress, and now he sounded almost earnest. "Don't you see it?"

"Which walls?" Mallory asked. Her voice was soothing as she used a penlight to examine the man's eyes.

The second man drifted closer, apparently drawn in by her calm presence. Everest shifted a bit, using his body to make sure the doctor had some space. She seemed to be making progress with the men, and he didn't want to break the spell she'd cast on them.

"All of them!"

"And the sun," said the second man. He stood in Everest's shadow, cowering behind him. "The sun is in the room right now!" He pointed at the porthole and glanced quickly away, squeezing his eyes shut as if in pain.

"Okay," Mallory said, nodding as if this was the most natural observation in the world. "I need you both to get on the gurneys. It's the only way to protect you from the walls and the sun."

The men scrambled to comply, both of them leaping onto the exam beds with more enthusiasm than grace. Mallory walked over to the nearest bed and began to fasten Velcro straps around the man's ankles and wrists. "I'm just going to make sure you're attached, so you don't float away." She nodded at one of the nurses, who hurried over to do the same to the other man.

Everest watched her quietly, his respect for her growing by the minute. She'd walked into a chaotic mess and hadn't hesitated to act. But rather than adding to the confusion, she'd taken charge and applied a calm, cool response that had served to de-escalate a volatile situation. It was a mark of her leadership, a skill he knew not everyone possessed; his time in the army had taught him that much.

"Have you taken anything today?" she asked, glancing at each man in turn.

"No," said Jeff.

Mallory merely raised one eyebrow and stared him down. He squirmed a bit, his cheeks going pink under her scrutiny. "I mean," he amended, "maybe I did. I can't remember."

"Uh-huh," she replied. "I can't help you if you don't tell me the truth."

Jeff closed his eyes with a sigh, and his head lolled back. "Special K." He stretched the words out like taffy, grinning like a loon.

Mallory nodded, his answer plainly confirming her suspicion. She turned to the nurses and began issuing orders. "Start an IV and give two milligrams Versed to each, please."

The women nodded and left the room, ostensibly to gather supplies. Mallory caught Everest's eye and angled her head, silently asking him to join her.

She walked over to the corner of the room, and he met her there, careful to angle his body so he could keep an eye on both men. They were quiet now, but that could change in an instant.

Mallory gestured for him to lean forward, clearly wanting to keep their conversation private. Everest dipped his head and caught a whiff of her shampoo. It was a light, floral scent that made him think of spring. She tilted her head up to meet his gaze, and he noticed her dark brown irises were shot through with flecks of gold. It was the kind of observation he hadn't made in a long time, and he shouldn't have noticed it now. *Keep it professional.*

"I'd like to post a guard here, if you don't mind," he

said. "Just to make sure these two don't cause any trouble for you or your staff."

She nodded. "I appreciate it. The sedative should take effect quickly, but it will be nice to have someone here in case they get agitated again."

Everest pulled the walkie-talkie from his belt and called up Wesley, his right-hand man. He relayed the request for a security officer and glanced at the men as he clipped the handset back into place. Jeff was talking to himself, muttering and shaking his head. His friend still had his eyes closed, as if he was afraid to open them. "How long until the drug is out of their system?"

Mallory lifted one shoulder. "No idea. It depends on how much they took, and that's not something they're likely to know. The street pills don't exactly come with dosage instructions."

"You think it was a pill?" Everest knew that ketamine, their drug of choice, could be ingested, injected or inhaled. He hadn't smelled any smoke on the men, but they may have used a needle.

"I didn't see any injection marks on their arms, but they could have used another site. Regardless of how they took it, it might take a while for them to come down. They're experiencing some pretty powerful hallucinations, so they likely took the drug fairly recently." She shifted to glance at them, then looked back at Everest. "I want to keep them here for observation until they're back to normal."

Everest frowned at the suggestion. Even though Mallory had displayed a no-nonsense, take-charge attitude, there was something almost fragile about her that made Everest want to shield her from the likes of these two party boys. He knew the likelihood of them causing more trouble was low, especially since he was going to station a guard here. But he just didn't like the idea of Mallory being around them for long; he'd feel much better if he could transfer them to the room that served as a make-shift jail cell on the ship.

His reticence must have shown on his face because she let out a small sigh. "This is the best place for them. They're restrained, and they're about to be sedated."

"I suppose," Everest said, conceding the point. "But I want you to page me if they so much as look at you funny."

She nodded. "Will do. Where are you going?"

He felt the barest hint of flattery at her interest in his plans but brushed it aside. *She probably just wants to know if I'll be nearby in case there's any trouble*, he told himself. "I'm going up to the bridge to inform the captain of this development," he said. "And to call the police in Jacksonville so they can take custody of these two when we make port in the morning."

Mallory nodded thoughtfully. Jeff chose that moment to let out a yelp, and Everest glanced over in time to see one of the nurses taping the IV in place on his hand. "If it's all the same to you," Mallory said, her voice draw-ing his attention back to her, "I'm not going to tell them what's in store when we dock in Jacksonville."

"Good thinking," Everest said. He didn't imagine these two would take kindly to the news their vacation was about to be cut short, and in such dramatic fashion.

"Thanks for your help," she said softly.

His stomach did a little flip, and he shook his head. "I didn't do much. It was all you."

She smiled, and his heart thumped hard against his breastbone. When was the last time he'd noticed a wom-an's smile?

"I'm glad you were here, though. Just in case." A

shadow crossed her eyes, there and gone in a blink. *That's interesting*, he thought. Maybe she wasn't as calm as she'd appeared to be. But was it just the stress of the situation bothering her, or was something else going on?

"Hey, man," Jeff called out.

Everest glanced over and met his eyes. "Are you talking to me?"

Jeff nodded. "Yeah. Are you the police or something?"

"Or something," Everest said easily. "Why?"

Jeff sat up as much as the restraints would allow, trying to get closer to him. "There's a problem with my room. You've gotta fix it."

"Oh?" *This ought to be good*, Everest thought. What kind of issue had Jeff's drug-addled brain concocted? "What's wrong?"

Jeff met his gaze, his eyes serious even as he struggled to focus. "The body," he whispered, real fear in his voice. "There's a body in my room."

Chapter 3

The exam room fell silent in the wake of Jeff's announcement. After a second, every head in the room swiveled to face Mallory, each person looking to her for guidance. The two nurses wore identical quizzical expressions, clearly wanting to know how they should respond to the patient's latest delusion. Jeff and his friend looked at her imploringly, wanting her to acknowledge the legitimacy of their claim. And Everest? He looked astounded, confusion and disbelief warring for dominance over his features.

Under any other circumstances, his expression would make her laugh. Even though she had just met him his morning, Mallory got the impression Everest was a sober, composed man. To see him so flabbergasted now struck her as funny, and she bit her lip to keep from smiling.

"A body?" she said, keeping her tone neutral. "What kind of body?"

Jeff frowned at her, apparently taken aback by her question. "A dead body. Is there any other kind?"

Mallory sighed. "Okay, fair enough. But what type of animal was it?"

The young man shook his head vigorously, his eyes wide. "Not an animal. A person." He nearly whispered the last word, as if he was afraid of summoning a ghost.

Everest shot her a questioning look, and Mallory subtly shook her head. Jeff and his buddy must have gotten their hands on some pretty potent stuff to be experiencing such vivid hallucinations. She might need to up the dose of sedative to get them through the next several hours…

"Okay," she said soothingly. "Everest will take care of it."

"That's good," Jeff said. He rested his head against the pillow, his voice growing dull as the drugs took effect. "Have him patch the walls, too." He kept talking, but it was the jumbled nonsense of intoxication, a last-ditch effort before he succumbed to sleep.

Mallory waited until both men were unconscious before she turned to Everest. He regarded her with a bemused expression. "So…" he began. "Is this something I need to take seriously?"

She shrugged. "I doubt it. I think it's just another effect of the ketamine—the drug is known for triggering hallucinations, and some of them can be quite disturbing."

"That's true," he said. "Still, I should probably have one of my men check it out. Just to be on the safe side."

It was the responsible thing to do, and Mallory couldn't help but approve. Most people would have been content to dismiss Jeff's words as the unhinged ramblings of a man under the influence, but she liked that Everest was going to dot all the i's and cross all the t's. It was the kind of thing she herself would do, and she appreciated the fact he seemed to share her sense of duty.

The sick bay door opened and two men stepped inside. Both wore the dark slacks and pale blue polo shirts sported by ship security officers, and Everest nodded approvingly. "Dr. Watkins, allow me to introduce two members of my team. This is Wesley Tatum, my right-hand man." He gestured to the stocky, dark-haired man on the right, who acknowledged her with a nod. "If you ever need anything and you can't get me, Wesley is your man." Everest then turned to the second man, a tall red-head with kind brown eyes. "And this is Taylor Higgins, one of the newest members of my team."

Taylor smiled and offered his hand. Mallory's stomach turned over, and she hesitated. He was only being polite, but she couldn't bring herself to touch him.

"Ah, I'd better not," she said, shaking her head. "I haven't washed my hands yet. Don't want to spread anything around." It was a weak excuse, but it was the best she could do. She glanced over to find Everest watching her, the look in his eyes far too knowing. Did the man miss anything?

If he was curious about her refusal to shake Taylor's hand, he didn't mention it. Instead, Everest turned back to his men and briefed them on the situation. "Wesley, I need you to go check out the room. I'm sure it's probably nothing, but I want to be able to assure the captain we've followed up on everything."

Wesley nodded, apparently unfazed by the order to search a guest's cabin for a dead body trapped in the wall. Maybe it wasn't the strangest thing he'd ever done in his line of work. Mallory certainly understood there were some odd things that happened on cruise ships. Or maybe Wesley's immediate acceptance of Everest's order came more from his respect for his boss. She studied Everest as he spoke to his team, noting the way he laid out a clear, concise plan and made it sound like he had every confidence his employees would succeed. It was no wonder he was the head of security for the ship—his manner seemed to inspire loyalty and trust, and even though he wasn't asking these men to do anything terribly difficult or dangerous, Mallory had no doubt their reaction would have been the same if he'd proposed they storm a bunker carrying only water pistols for protection.

"Taylor, I'd like you to stay here and keep an eye on these two. Make sure they don't cause any more trouble for the medical staff."

The young man nodded eagerly, clearly excited for his first assignment on the ship. He reminded Mallory of a puppy, and she glanced discreetly at the seat of his pants, half expecting to find a wagging tail protruding from his slacks.

"And you, sir?" asked Wesley.

"I'm going to brief the captain. Any questions or issues, you can reach me on channel three."

The men nodded, and Wesley walked over to Jeff's side, where he proceeded to search the man's pockets, presumably for his room key. Taylor took up a post between the two beds and assumed a parade rest stance. Mallory wondered if he planned to stand all night, or if he'd relax enough to sit down.

Everest's voice cut into her musings. "You have my pager number?"

"I think so—we have a form by the phone with contact information listed for various people." Mallory waved a hand in the direction of the wall-mounted unit where she'd seen the information sheet posted. She hadn't checked lately, but she was willing to bet Everest's number was on it.

Everest frowned. "Let me give you my personal cell number, as well." He pulled a business card from his pocket and snagged a pen off the table. "If anything comes up, don't hesitate to call me." He passed her the card, and Mallory tucked it away. The paper was still warm from his body, and she felt the heat of it through the cotton of her pants. It was an odd sensation, this almost-contact between them.

"I think we're in for a quiet night now, but I'll let you know if that changes."

He nodded and turned to go. For some reason, Mallory was reluctant to see him leave, and she called out before she could think twice about it. "Hey."

He turned back, one eyebrow lifted in silent question. *Great, now what?* "Um," she stalled, her self-consciousness threatening to swamp her. "I want to thank you. For being here."

The corner of his mouth curved up in a smile. "I didn't do anything. You had things well under control."

Mallory felt her cheeks heat and hoped her blush wasn't too obvious. "Well, I still appreciate your backing me up."

"It was my pleasure," he said. A spark of heat flared in his blue eyes, and Mallory was shocked to feel an answering tingle in her stomach. "Like I said, call me anytime."

Was there a hint of innuendo in his voice? Mallory dismissed the possibility almost instantly; Everest seemed far too professional for that. Even so, she felt a little wistful at the thought that he might flirt with her. She was quite out of practice as far as dating went, but the idea of spending more time with Everest was...appealing.

"I will," she replied. God, did he hear the quaver in

her voice? *Get it together!* She was turning into a mess, and all because the man in front of her had somehow slipped past her defenses. But there wasn't time for her to worry about that now. She'd think about it later, when she was in the privacy of her own room.

Everest turned and walked out of the sick bay, closing the door quietly behind him. The room seemed to deflate with his exit, another sign that he'd gotten under her skin.

Part of her wanted to celebrate; this was the first time in years she'd felt any kind of attraction to a man. She was curious to see how it would develop. Of course, there was no guarantee he had noticed her in that way, and perhaps that was for the best. If her attraction was one-sided, she could indulge in a little crush without having to worry about getting hurt. This might turn out to be a great opportunity to shake the dust off her emotions and finally put the rape behind her, once and for all. If she could see herself with Everest, she was one step closer to having a real relationship someday.

But the small, scared girl inside wanted to slam the door on any kind of attraction. It wasn't worth the risk. He was a physically powerful man—tall, broad-shouldered, his hands large enough to wrap around her arm in a painful grip. And she'd seen the evidence of his muscles earlier in the gym and knew he was in excellent shape. If he decided to hurt her, she wouldn't stand a chance.

"Dr. Watkins?"

She shook her head slightly and focused on the nurse in front of her, grateful for the distraction. "Yes?"

The woman launched into a question regarding drug dosages for Jeff and his friend, and a sense of calm descended as Mallory turned her thoughts back to work. Medicine was her refuge, and no matter how upset or emotional she felt, tending to patients was a surefire way to push the reset button on her inner turmoil.

For now, anyway.

Wesley slipped into the room and was immediately assaulted with the stale, slightly sweet stench of weed. Apparently, Jeff and his buddy hadn't limited themselves to only one drug tonight…

Sure enough, two fat stubs lay discarded on top of the built-in dresser amid a scatter of pills. He poked at the display with his fingertip, searching for any marks that would indicate what the different-colored pills were. The blue ones were easy enough—the star shape stamped onto the surface made it clear he was looking at ecstasy. But the oblong white pills and the yellow tablets sported no such identifiers. He scooped a few into an empty plastic baggie and tucked it into his pocket. Maybe the doctor could figure out what these were. If not, the police in Jacksonville would probably know.

He glanced around, a sense of disgust rising in his chest as he took in the mess. Two open suitcases sat on the desk, vomiting clothes onto the floor. Towels sat in damp piles on the bed and the recliner, and empty beer cans littered almost every horizontal surface.

Wesley shook his head. The *Abigail Adams* was a premier ship, and what she lacked in size, she made up for in luxury. How had these two classless idiots gotten on board?

Mommy and Daddy, he thought, taking in the expensive watches lying on the bedside table, the designer sunglasses tossed on the floor, and the roll of cash peeking out from one of the suitcases. All telltale signs of the "easy come, easy go" attitude exhibited by spoiled rich kids.

"I wonder if Daddy can buy you out of this mess," he

said softly to himself, smiling as he imagined the fate in store for these two. They'd dock in Jacksonville in the morning, and it wouldn't take long for the police to come aboard and take them into custody. Given the amount of drugs on display here, Jeff and his friend were looking at some very serious charges.

"I hope the high was worth it." Wesley gave the room a final glance. Despite the mess, he saw no signs of any kind of body. But they had said it was in the wall…

With a sigh, he turned his attention to the walls. Everything looked fine as far as he could tell—nothing was out of place. Perhaps they had mistaken a shadow in the room for a body? He checked the bathroom with no results. Finally, he opened the door to the closet.

He saw the hole first, a foot-sized punch through the drywall about twelve inches above the floor. One of the guys had probably kicked the wall for God only knew what reason. Was this the source of the problem?

Wesley crouched down to peer inside the dark hollow and caught a glimpse of something shiny inside. Holding his phone up for light, he discovered he was looking at some kind of thick plastic. Remnants from the construction of the ship, maybe?

He leaned closer to get a better look and realized the plastic was wrapped around something that looked an awful lot like… But it couldn't be…

Realization hit him like a slap to the face, and he jerked back, his stomach churning. The plastic was wrapped around a human foot.

He sat on the floor for a moment, his mind racing. This certainly complicated things, to say the least. If word got out that there was a body in the wall of this room, the response would be immediate. The police and possibly the FBI would swarm the ship, turning her inside out in their search for evidence.

And he knew they'd find more than what they bargained for.

He couldn't let that happen. His mission was clear: he was to ensure that the *Abigail Adams* did not deviate from her planned itinerary. It was imperative that she arrive in New York Harbor in time for the Fourth of July celebrations. After all, she had a starring role in the show, and it was his job to make sure she did not disappoint.

He felt a small pang at the thought of destroying such a beautiful ship, but he dismissed it quickly. The *Abigail* had a greater purpose to serve, and if he was successful, the Organization would reward him handsomely for his efforts. It would all be worth it in the end.

But for now, he had to deal with this unexpected wrinkle.

Gritting his teeth, he gingerly stuck his hand inside the hole and pushed against the plastic. The foot underneath was firm and unyielding, and he nearly threw up as he felt it through the artificial shroud. Whoever this was, the person had been in here awhile.

Moving carefully, Wesley maneuvered the macabre bundle so that it was no longer easily visible to anyone looking through the hole. Then he stood, wiping his hands on his slacks and eyeing his handiwork critically. It would do for now, but he was going to have to patch things up soon, before housekeeping caught sight of the problem. The last thing he needed was someone else making this gruesome discovery.

First things first, though. He pulled his walkie-talkie from his belt and called up Everest.

"Go ahead."

"I'm in the guest room. No sign of anything unusual."

"That's what I figured," Everest said with a sigh. "Thanks for checking."

"No problem. Over and out."

Wesley carefully shut the closet door, then turned and walked through the room. He paused by the desk, the open suitcases gaping up at him. With a shrug, he reached down and plucked a wad of bills free from a tangle of clothes and slipped it into his pocket. Jeff would have no need of money where he was going, and it would be a shame for it to wind up in a police evidence locker.

With that, Wesley stepped into the hall and set off for the maintenance supply room. He'd rig up a patch for the wall, and that would be the end of it. No one, especially not any member of the Organization, need ever know how close two spoiled addicts had come to wrecking everything.

Chapter 4

The night passed without incident. The sedatives kept Jeff and his friend quiet, and they slept off their high in the relative comfort of the sick bay. The two men woke, groggy and hungry, but no worse for wear.

Until the police showed up.

Everest nodded a greeting to Mallory as he led the officers into her clinic. "Dr. Watkins, these gentlemen are from Jacksonville PD. They're here to escort our guests off the ship."

She smiled at the uniformed men, but before she could say anything, Jeff started shouting.

"I'm not going with them! You can't make me leave!"

The noise stirred his friend into action, and soon the two men were hollering their displeasure at a volume that made Mallory's ears ache.

Everest tried to talk over the men, but they merely

shouted louder. The two policemen exchanged a look and started forward, but Mallory held up a hand to stall them.

"That's enough," she said, glaring at Jeff. When he continued to yell, she raised her own voice. "I said, that's enough!"

Jeff and his friend stared at her, apparently shocked into silence by the temper in her voice. "Calm down, both of you. I won't tolerate this kind of behavior in my sick bay."

"But Doc, you can't let them take us! We didn't do anything!"

She aimed a level stare at the men, and Jeff squirmed a bit under her regard. "You confessed to using ketamine last night. And when a security officer entered your room to investigate your claims of seeing a body in the walls, he found pills scattered around the room."

"You can't search our stuff without a warrant!"

"You gave the man probable cause," she shot back. She cast a quick look at Everest to verify she was correct, and he nodded subtly. Warmth shone from his eyes and a small smile played at the corners of his mouth as he watched her. *He's enjoying this.* The realization made her feel a little self-conscious, but she shook off the sensation and returned her focus to the job at hand.

"C'mon, we were just having a little fun," Jeff whined. "There's no need to involve the cops."

Everest stepped forward. "You've both proved to be a danger to yourselves and possibly the other passengers on board. Your cruise ends here. If I were you, I'd go with these officers quietly. Wouldn't want to add resisting arrest to your list of problems."

The two policemen stepped forward, one walking to Jeff's side and the other to his friend. Their voices were low but clear as they arrested the men and recited their rights.

Everest drifted closer, coming to stand near her. Mallory felt herself leaning toward him, pulled as if by some invisible force. "Almost done," he murmured, nodding at the scene unfolding before them. "Hopefully this is the most exciting thing we'll have to deal with on this cruise."

Mallory nodded in agreement. She always had mixed feelings about her job. She loved helping people and taking care of them, but at the same time, she hoped no one would need her services. Her patients were people on their honeymoon or on vacation, enjoying a trip they had planned and anticipated for months, if not longer. No one ever wanted to be sick, but to fall ill or get injured while on a cruise seemed to make things even worse somehow.

"It's strange," Everest said conversationally. "I love what I do, but I wake up every morning and wish for a boring day."

Was the man a mind reader? Or were her thoughts that transparent? "I know exactly what you mean," she said.

"I have yet to make it through a cruise without some kind of incident. I was hoping this would be the one, but then these two showed up." He tilted his head in the direction of the men, whom the officers were now helping to stand.

Mallory stepped back to give the procession space to walk to the door. Jeff shot her a nasty glare as he moved past. "This isn't over," he warned. "Do you have any idea who my father is?" He lurched forward, and her heart shot into her throat. Logically, she knew he couldn't do anything with his wrists in cuffs—he was simply trying to intimidate her. Even though her mind refused to cower, her body reacted. She forced herself to stay put, but her legs began to tremble involuntarily.

The next thing she knew, Mallory was staring at a wall of blue. She blinked, taken aback by the sudden change to her vision. Then she realized what had happened—Everest had stepped in front of her, placing his body between her and Jeff. "No one cares about your daddy." He spoke calmly, but there was a sharp edge to his voice that sent a shiver down Mallory's spine. She didn't know the head of security all that well, but it was clear he was not a man to mess with.

She peered around his body to see that apparently, Jeff realized it, too. His eyes widened and a stunned look crossed his face. Clearly, he hadn't expected Everest's reaction to his threat. Then he was gone, the officer urging him out the door.

Everest waited until both men had left the room. Once the door shut behind them, he turned and offered her an apologetic smile. "I'm sorry about that," he said.

Mallory's heart began to slow, and she shrugged off the young man's actions. "Not your fault."

Everest studied her a moment, his bright blue eyes seeming to see right through her. "I'm going to follow the officers, make sure they don't need me for anything after they escort our guests off the ship. After that, would you like to grab a bite to eat?"

His invitation flustered her, and Mallory's thoughts jumbled together as she searched for a response. "Um, that sounds nice. But I'm supposed to meet my friends for breakfast. They're on board, and I'm trying to spend as much time with them as I can." It was the truth, but it was also a convenient excuse.

Everest nodded, but she caught a glint of what might have been disappointment flash in his eyes. "Sure thing," he said easily. "Another time, maybe."

"You could join us," she blurted. As soon as the words

left her mouth, Mallory wondered what she was thinking. She didn't know this man. And she didn't strike up friendships with men. She had no business socializing with him.

But there was something about him that made her curious to know more. And really, what could it hurt? Olivia and Avery would be there, along with Logan and Grant. She'd have a table full of buffers to keep Everest from getting too close. Maybe it would be good to learn more about him. Hopefully, she wouldn't need his help again, but anything was possible.

"Yeah? You don't think they'd mind?" He sounded a little hopeful, and Mallory was surprised to find she actually wanted him to come. She was happy for her friends and their newfound loves, but having Everest at the table would keep her from feeling like a fifth wheel.

"Not at all," she assured him. "I'm meeting them in the Yorktown dining room. I'll save you a seat."

"Thanks," he said. "I'll try not to take too long."

Mallory watched him leave, her gaze drawn to his legs and the subtle hitch in his gait as he walked away. For the first time in a long time, she actually felt safe around a man. Maybe it was his quiet, calm manner. He seemed to see everything in the room, and she had the sense that no matter what happened, he could handle it.

As evidenced by the way he'd physically intervened to keep Jeff from getting closer to her.

He hadn't hesitated to act, and looking back on it, Mallory was impressed by how smoothly he'd handled the situation. Everest could have simply ignored Jeff—after all, the man was in handcuffs and being escorted by a police officer. Objectively, he didn't pose much of a threat to anyone. But rather than let the arresting officer handle the situation, Everest had quickly and calmly placed himself in a position to make sure nothing happened. Mallory had never experienced such a gesture of protection before, and she had to admit, it felt…nice.

"Don't read anything into it," she muttered to herself. Everest had likely acted on instinct; he would have done the same thing if Jeff had lunged at one of the nurses, or anyone else, really. His action was simply that of a professional who worked in the security field. It was his job to keep the ship's passengers and staff safe. That was all.

She glanced at her watch. It was time to head to the dining room so she wouldn't be late for breakfast. Hopefully she would be able to explain the situation to Avery and Olivia before Everest joined them.

Assuming she was able to figure things out for herself first.

It didn't take long to escort the troublemakers off the ship. The Jacksonville officers were quick and competent, and Everest had already emailed the relevant reports to the police department before the ship had docked this morning. All that was left was for him to walk with the group as they made their way down the gangplank and onto shore. Even though the Jacksonville police had already arrested the men, Everest still felt like they were his responsibility as long as they remained on board. Once their feet hit the dock, he could wash his hands of them.

"Thanks for your help today," he told one of the officers. "It's appreciated."

"This isn't over," Jeff said. It was clear he wanted to say more, but his jaw snapped shut as the cop escorting him gave his arm a rough-looking tug and pulled him toward the waiting police cruiser.

The other officer rolled his eyes and sent Everest a

knowing nod. "Our pleasure. Hope the rest of the voyage is quiet."

"You and me both."

He stood there for a moment, not sorry to see them go. He'd dealt with some crazy incidents while working on cruise ships, but for some reason, last night's shenanigans had worried him more than he was used to. And as much as he hated to admit it, he knew why.

Mallory.

There was something about the ship's doctor that intrigued him and made him want to get to know her better, both personally and professionally. It was an unfamiliar urge, and the intensity of it was surprising. It had been a few years since he'd had any kind of interest in a woman. His ex-fiancée had done a number on his confidence, and so he'd thrown his efforts into building a career outside the military. There simply hadn't been time for romantic entanglements. But more important, he hadn't felt up to dealing with all the rejections.

Leah had tried to be supportive after he'd been shipped home, battered and bruised. But as the weeks had dragged on, it had become apparent to both of them that he was missing more than just part of his leg. The IED had ripped through his group, killing two of his men and shattering any illusion that he'd had about his ability to keep his team safe. He'd been plagued by survivor's guilt, and the grueling challenge of learning to walk again had very nearly pushed him over the edge. He had changed, and not in a good way.

Looking back, he couldn't really blame Leah for leaving. Working through his grief and pain had been a long, messy process. And as the days had passed and her smile had grown more forced, he'd felt her slipping away. So he'd released her from her promise.

"You don't have to stay." He focused on the end of the bed, on the small bump his one remaining foot made under the thin hospital blanket. Maybe if he stared at it long enough, he'd get used to the visual reminder of his loss.

"I don't mind," she said. She pushed a tendril of honey-blond hair behind her ear and shifted in the chair. *"Your physical therapy appointment isn't for another hour."*

Everest winced at the thought of the upcoming torture session. He knew it was for his own good, but the exercises were downright painful. To make matters worse, the physical therapist was an unnaturally cheerful person who seemed to revel in his suffering like a born sadist. He just wanted to be left alone so he could cry in peace, but Scott refused to let him wallow in self-pity. It was annoying, to say the least.

"That's not what I meant."

Leah didn't respond right away. When she spoke, she sounded hesitant, as if she was afraid of saying the wrong thing. *"I don't understand."*

Everest sighed and met her eyes for the first time. *"We both know you didn't sign up for this."* He gestured at the bed, his hand sweeping down to indicate his missing limb. *"I can tell you don't want to be here. Not really. You should go. Find someone whole. Someone who can make you happy."*

"You don't mean that." But there was doubt in her voice, along with something else. Hope.

In that moment, he knew he was doing the right thing. Leah was nothing if not loyal. She'd stick with him; that much he knew. But she would hate it. And eventually, she'd grow to resent him for it. He didn't want that kind of life, that kind of marriage. Better for her to leave now, before the cement of these new circumstances hardened around them.

"I do. I want you to leave." It was the truth. The war had changed him, and she was no longer the woman for him. It wasn't her fault—it wasn't anyone's fault. In the weeks since he'd been back, he'd tried to find the man he'd used to be inside the man he was now. But that wasn't going to happen, and it was time to end things so Leah could move on with her life. God knew he wanted to do the same.

She shook her head. "I can't do that."

He was going to have to push her, then. Fine. He could do that. "Why? Because you don't want to be the girl who dumped a cripple?"

She flinched but didn't respond. Ah, he'd hit the nail on the head.

"Don't worry about it," he said. "Just tell everyone I walked out on you. I still have my good leg, after all."

It was a bad joke, and she didn't laugh. "Are you sure?" she said softly.

Everest felt a little jolt at the realization she wasn't going to put up much of a fight. Wasn't their relationship worth more than a moment's deliberation? But he quickly pushed the hurt aside. He was giving her an out. He couldn't be angry with her for taking it, especially when it was what he wanted her to do.

"I'm positive. I want you to be happy." And he did. He'd once thought they would grow old together, but now he knew their time had ended. It was just as well. He'd rather be alone than be faced with the evidence of her growing unhappiness. And the last thing he wanted was to be a burden to the people in his life.

Leah was never going to look at him the same way again. She tried to hide it, but he could tell that every *time she saw him, she compared him with a memory of when he was whole and uninjured. He couldn't live up to the ghost of his former self, and he didn't want to spend the rest of his life trying.*

"I don't know what to say." *Her eyes glimmered with unshed tears—of happiness? Or was she truly sorry about the way things had worked out? Hopefully the latter. He liked to think the woman he'd planned his life with would at least mourn the death of their future. But maybe she simply felt relieved.*

"You don't have to say anything," *he told her gently.* "Goodbye is traditional, but not required."

"Why are you doing this?" *She frowned at him, her features twisting in confusion.* "I don't understand."

Everest ran a hand over his head, distracted by the feel of his hair against his palm. He hadn't had a haircut in weeks. One of the perks of being in the hospital, he supposed.

"Do you want to stay?"

Leah blinked at him, as if he'd asked the question in a foreign language. "What?"

"Do you actually want to stay here?" *he repeated.* "Do you really want to deal with my recovery and all that it entails? It's going to be a long, drawn-out process. And we both know I'm not the same man I was before, mentally speaking."* He paused, letting his words sink in.* "The war changed me, Leah. I'm still figuring out how. I just don't think we're the right people for each other anymore."

She sighed, her shoulders slumping as the breath left her body. "I'm so sorry," *she whispered.* "I thought I could handle it..."* She trailed off, shaking her head.* "But it's too hard. I don't think I can do it."

"You don't have to."

"How can you be so nice about it? Why aren't you angry with me?"

Everest searched his heart for an answer that would make sense, but came up empty. "I don't think I have the energy for that right now."

She stared at him, her blue eyes wide as she digested his response. Finally, she nodded. "Okay."

He tried to smile, but his mouth wouldn't cooperate. Leah stood and gathered her sweater and purse. She twisted the ring off her finger and held it out to him. He hesitated a moment, then took it from her and placed it in the drawer of his bedside table. "I guess this is goodbye?" she asked.

"Looks like it," he confirmed.

Leah leaned over his bed and pressed a chaste kiss to his cheek. "Promise me you'll take care of yourself?"

Everest felt like he was having an out-of-body experience. This situation was so strange—they were breaking up, and yet he still cared about her and she still cared about him. Maybe this is how adults end things, *he mused. All his previous experiences had been full of hurt feelings and a few tears. It was a novelty for him to end a relationship on such a positive note.*

"I'll be fine," he assured her. He didn't know if it was the truth, but he knew that's what she needed to hear right now.

She straightened and tucked her hair behind her ear again. It was a nervous gesture, something she did when she was feeling uncertain or uncomfortable.

She didn't know how to leave, he realized. And he didn't know what to tell her to ease the way.

He was saved by the entrance of Scott, his physical therapist. The man charged in wearing a big grin, but stopped short when he saw Leah standing by the bed.

"Oh, excuse me," Scott said, taking a step back. "I didn't mean to interrupt."

"You didn't," Everest said. "It's okay."

"I was just leaving," Leah said. She gave Everest a small smile and squeezed his hand. "Have a good session," she said.

He nodded, and she turned to go, nodding at Scott as she slipped past him and out the door.

Scott was silent for a few seconds after she left. "Please tell me I did not see what I think I just saw."

"Depends," Everest said lightly. "What do you think you saw?"

Scott rocked back and forth on his heels, clearly uncomfortable. "I know this is none of my business," he began, "but did you two just break up?"

"How'd you guess?"

Scott's face fell. "Oh, man. I'm so sorry." He walked to the bed and perched on the side of the mattress. "Do you, uh, want to talk about it? I can get a psychologist or something if you don't want to talk to me."

Everest shook his head, touched at the other man's concern. "I'm okay. But thanks."

Scott looked at him dubiously, clearly doubting his words. "Really. It's fine," Everest assured him. "It's for the best. She wasn't happy. I wasn't happy. It was time to end things."

Scott snorted. "No one is happy to be here."

"Except you," Everest said slyly. He appreciated Scott's efforts to help, but he didn't want to wallow in the aftermath of Leah's departure. He'd thought now that he was back in the States the war couldn't take any more from him. But he was wrong. It was time to move forward, to reclaim some control over his life.

The physical therapist grinned. "Well, yeah. But that's

because I get to give you a hard time." He stood and placed his hands on his hips. "Do you want to push your session back a bit, in light of what just happened?"

Everest shook his head. "Nope. Let's get to it." The pain would be a welcome distraction and would keep him from dwelling on Leah.

"I'll get your chair," Scott said. "We can have a light day."

"No," Everest said. "Taking a break isn't going to help me walk again. I can't stay in this bed forever."

Scott nodded at him, a glint of respect in his eyes. "That's the spirit, man. We'll have you back on your feet in no time."

"You mean foot."

Scott arched a brow. "They don't pay me enough to laugh at your bad jokes."

"I thought that one was pretty good," Everest said.

Scott shook his head. "You've got a long way to go before you're funny."

Everest smiled at the memory of Scott's words. The image of Leah faded back into the recesses of his mind as he focused fully on the present. It was funny he'd thought of her now, when his mind was so preoccupied by Mallory. The two women were nothing alike, physically speaking. Leah was petite and blonde, her hair always styled, her makeup always perfect. Mallory was tall and had a no-nonsense quality to her appearance he found appealing. Both were beautiful women, but he found himself drawn to Mallory.

She was a study in contrasts, he mused as he headed back into the depths of the ship. Mallory's looks made her seem very approachable, but she had a do-not-disturb manner about her that he was certain she used to keep people at arm's length.

"Why is that?" he murmured to himself. What had happened to the good doctor to leave her so skittish around people? She had a story, he was sure of it.

And he wanted to hear it.

Chapter 5

Breakfast was going surprisingly well, all things considered.

Mallory hadn't known how her friends would react to Everest's presence. She hadn't had more than a minute to announce he would be joining them before he walked over to the table, which meant she hadn't been able to explain her invitation to Olivia and Avery. The women had taken his presence in stride, though, and Logan and Grant had welcomed Everest with enthusiasm. They sat at one end of the table now, talking about football. Or maybe it was basketball. *Some kind of sport or team*, she thought, smiling a little as the men laughed in unison.

Whatever the topic, it was clear the guys were getting along well. Which created a small degree of privacy for the conversation at Mallory's end of the table.

And Olivia and Avery weren't wasting any time.

"Spill," Avery ordered, her voice low so as not to break the conversational spell the men were under.

"I don't know what you mean," Mallory tried, but Olivia shook her head.

"Nice try, but you know what she's asking. Is there something going on between you and him?" Olivia nodded ever so slightly at Everest, who was currently telling Logan and Grant some kind of story that had the other two men listening quietly. Mallory wondered what he was saying, but she didn't want to appear to be paying too much attention to the man. It would undermine what she was about to say to her friends.

"We work together," she said. "That's all."

Avery leaned back in her chair. "Sure." Her voice was heavy with doubt. "If you say so."

Olivia offered her a small smile. "This is the first time you've ever invited a man to join us," she said. "You can see why we're curious."

Her friend made a good point. Avery and Olivia both knew about the assault she'd suffered as a college senior, and in all the time they'd known each other, the two women had never pushed her when it came to men. They had respected her boundaries and supported her as she'd struggled to overcome the aftereffects of the trauma. She felt like she'd made good progress, but there was still work to be done, as evidenced by her recent nightmare.

Given her past history, Mallory had known inviting Everest to breakfast would send a signal to her friends. But she had hoped to have a little more time to figure out how to explain her interest in him.

The problem was, she couldn't explain it to herself.

She was definitely attracted to him. But it wasn't just his looks that appealed to her, though they were nice enough to study. No, it was the glimmers of personality she'd seen that made her want to stay close, to get to know him better. She liked the way he carried himself and the way he responded when tensions were running high. He seemed like a dependable man, someone who would be good both in a crisis and in calm times. Exactly the kind of man she would want by her side, if she could handle being so close to him.

Normally, just the idea of being in close physical proximity to a man was enough to make her break out into a sweat. But the thought of being around Everest didn't bother her. In fact, she found it rather appealing.

Which made her wonder—was she truly attracted to Everest, or did she just like the way he made her feel almost normal again?

"It's complicated," she admitted to her friends. "I'm not quite sure what's going on."

Avery leaned forward and laid her hand over Mallory's. "That's okay. Just take your time. We're here if you need to talk things out."

Mallory smiled, tears pricking her eyes. "Thanks, guys. I appreciate it."

A sudden silence descended over the other end of the table, and Mallory, Avery and Olivia looked down to find the men watching them, the three of them wearing identical expressions of concern.

"Everything all right?" Grant asked.

Olivia nodded while Mallory dabbed at her eyes. "We're fine," she said.

"Girl talk," Avery said.

Grant and Logan nodded and returned to their conversation, but Everest wasn't so quick to look away. His gaze lingered on Mallory, concern shining in his bright blue eyes. Only after she gave him a nod of reassurance did he rejoin the men's conversation.

"Oh, my," Olivia murmured. "Did you see that?"

"I sure did," Avery said quietly. "Mal, you might be confused, but I'd say your friend knows exactly how he feels."

"You might be right," Mallory admitted. Everest's obvious concern made her stomach flutter pleasantly, and for a second, she wished she was alone with Everest.

She watched him talking with Grant and Logan, admiring the easy way he interacted with her friends' partners. He seemed very relaxed, with a quick smile and a ready laugh that only heightened his appeal.

Would it be so bad to indulge in her attraction for Everest? This was the first time since her rape she had been drawn to a man. Why shouldn't she explore these feelings more and find out where they led? The timing really couldn't be better—with Avery and Olivia on board, she'd have her friends close if she needed them. But she didn't think Everest would give her a reason to cry on their shoulders. From everything she'd seen, Everest was a calm and patient man. He didn't seem like the type to try to pressure her into moving too fast or doing anything that made her feel uncomfortable.

And if the worst should happen? If she put herself out there and Everest rejected her? They would simply part ways once the cruise was over. Even if they were assigned to the same ship in the future, it would be easy to limit their interactions to professional concerns.

Everest glanced over, apparently feeling the weight of her gaze on him. Mallory met his eyes and held them, then smiled. Her flirting skills had atrophied from years of disuse, but Everest's answering smile told her that her message had been received.

She turned back to her friends in time to see Avery and Olivia exchange a knowing glance. "She doesn't look so confused anymore," Avery said, amusement lacing her words.

"No," Olivia agreed, smiling as she took a sip of her mimosa. "I'd say she's made up her mind."

Mallory was paged just as she popped the last bite of pancakes into her mouth. She glanced at the number, not surprised to see it was the clinic calling. But rather than the emergency number the nurse had used yesterday to notify her of the situation with Jeff and his friend, this time it was the routine code that flashed on the screen.

"Time for me to go," she said, taking one final swig of juice. She dabbed at her mouth with the napkin and shot her friends an apologetic smile. "Sorry to run like this. Again."

"Don't worry about it," Avery said. "We all know what it's like to be on call."

Olivia and Grant nodded, and Logan shot her a sympathetic smile. "Hopefully we can meet up with you again soon."

"I hope so," she said. She placed her napkin on her plate and stood.

Everest's chair scraped back a second after her own. "I'll walk you back," he said easily. He nodded at her friends. "It was nice to meet you all. Thank you for letting me join you."

"Our pleasure," Olivia said.

"Come back anytime," Grant added.

Mallory smiled, happy to see her friends had enjoyed Everest's company. She knew it had been a risk inviting him to breakfast, but fortunately, the meal hadn't been awkward at all.

With a final wave at the table, she and Everest set off.

He fell into step beside her, as if they had been walking together like this for ages.

"Thanks for the escort," she said. It was nice to have his company, if only for a few minutes.

"My pleasure," he said. "You know, we didn't really get a chance to talk at breakfast. At the risk of making a pest out of myself, would you like to meet for lunch?"

"That would be nice," Mallory said. "Provided I don't have any patients at the time."

"I'll keep my fingers crossed," Everest said. "Hopefully the rest of your cases will be easy compared to last night."

"No kidding," she replied. They arrived at the clinic and stepped inside. The curtains were drawn around three of the gurneys, giving a modicum of privacy to their occupants.

A nurse approached, holding several charts. She nodded at Everest, then looked at Mallory. "Dr. Watkins, we have three cases of acute GI upset."

Mallory's stomach sank at the news. Everest took a step back. "Sounds like you have your hands full here," he said. "I'll get out of your way."

"Thanks," Mallory said. "I'll page you later."

He nodded and turned to leave, and Mallory returned her focus to the nurse. "What are their symptoms?"

The nurse rattled off the usual symptoms of a gastrointestinal illness, and Mallory nodded grimly. "Any fever?" she asked. The nurse shook her head, confirming her suspicions.

Mallory sighed and ran a hand through her hair. "Sounds like norovirus," she said, naming a common scourge of cruise ships. The highly contagious virus could sweep through the passengers in a matter of days.

It didn't discriminate between staff and vacationers, so if it got out of hand it could affect the crew's ability to safely operate the ship. She'd heard of ships that had been forced to cut voyages short because of the overwhelming number of patients on board, and the possibility of the *Abigail Adams* being affected to such an extent was one of the things that kept her up late at night.

She performed a quick exam of the patients, to confirm for herself what the nurse had told her. All three passengers reported identical symptoms, which wasn't surprising since they shared a cabin. There wasn't anything she could give them to treat the virus, but she prescribed some medication that would make them feel better while the sickness ran its course.

"And don't forget the sunscreen," she said, gesturing to one woman's sunburned neck.

"I know," she replied. "The thing is, I haven't been in the sun that much. I've mostly stayed inside, shopping and watching the shows."

Mallory nodded. "I understand. But it doesn't take long to get burned, especially if you're not used to being outside."

She drew the curtain around the woman's bed and stepped into her small office, where she reached for the phone. She dialed the bridge and asked to speak to the captain. It took only a second for him to come on the line.

"What can I do for you, Dr. Watkins?"

"I've got three patients in the clinic presenting with signs of norovirus."

The man swore softly, recognizing the seriousness of her words. "Do you need me to start decontamination procedures?"

"I think that's best," she said. "If we move fast enough,

we might be able to get on top of this before it becomes a shipwide outbreak."

"Roger that," the captain said. "I'll alert the crew and get the ball rolling."

"Thank you, sir."

"Keep me posted," he said. "Let's hope you don't see any more cases."

Mallory hung up and reached for her cell phone. She hesitated only a moment before texting Avery and Olivia.

Possible noro on board. Be careful.

Technically, she shouldn't talk about her concerns with any of the passengers. But Avery and Olivia were both doctors, and she knew they wouldn't panic unnecessarily. She just wanted her friends to stay healthy so they could enjoy their vacation—she knew they didn't get much time off, and she would feel terrible if they spent the cruise sick in their cabins.

Oh no, Olivia texted back. Sorry to hear that!

Yuck, Avery replied. Thanks for heads-up.

Mallory tucked the phone back into her pocket and logged into her computer to update her records. With a mental sigh, she realized she was probably going to miss lunch with Everest. Now that she had possible cases of norovirus on board the ship, her schedule had gotten a lot more crowded. Maybe he'd let her take a rain check on lunch. If the virus didn't spread, she'd have time to eat with him later.

That's a big if, she thought. But it was important to stay positive. She'd dealt with this illness before; anyone who worked in the cruising industry had experience with it. None of the ships she'd sailed on in the past had suffered from large outbreaks, and she was determined the *Abigail Adams* wasn't going to be the first. She would keep this bug at bay, no matter how hard she had to work to do it.

Chapter 6

The pager on Danny's belt buzzed to life. He propped his mop against the wall and glanced down at the display.

Code Red. Initiate protocol.

He clipped the pager back into place and reached for the mop handle, anxiety spiking through him. Code Red meant there was a health concern on the ship. It wasn't an unusual page, but he hadn't expected to receive it so early in the voyage. Normally, this kind of thing didn't happen until several days into a trip.

A Code Red page was a signal that the housekeeping staff should initiate a deep-clean protocol, in an effort to prevent the spread of whatever contagious disease had appeared on board. Almost always, it had to do with norovirus, but he'd once worked a voyage where there had been an outbreak of flu among the passengers. Whatever this was, he'd find out at the next staff briefing.

A quick glance at his cart showed he had everything he needed, saving him a trip to the supply room. *Might as well get started now, then.* He'd already wiped down the bathroom sinks and toilets, and he was almost done mopping the floor. All that remained was to disinfect the walls.

He sprayed cleanser on the tiled walls, wrinkling his nose as the acrid scent of bleach burned his sinuses and made his eyes sting. Working quickly but competently, he affixed a clean mop head and began to scrub the wall, reaching up to stroke from ceiling to floor.

It was on his third pass that he hit the black box affixed high on the wall in the corner. The cover of the box fell to the floor with a clatter, and a second later there was a splat as something else hit the tile.

Danny's heart leaped into his throat, and he winced. The boxes were mounted all over the ship, and he knew they had something to do with the shipwide communications network. He wasn't sure how it all worked, and he hoped he hadn't inadvertently knocked out the system.

He picked up the cover and examined it closely, checking for cracks or any other signs of damage. It looked fine; maybe he hadn't really broken anything after all...

At his feet sat a lump of gray material. He knelt and poked at it with a finger, trying to figure out what it was. It didn't look like anything he'd seen before, but it had definitely come out of the box. He glanced up to find the innards of the box exposed, a tangle of wires and some blinking lights. Everything was green, though, so that was a good sign. Right?

Danny scooped the gray stuff off the floor and cupped it in his palm. It had a clay-like consistency, and it reminded him of the stuff his kids used to play with when they were younger. Maybe it was some kind of adhesive to help hold the cover of the box in place. He rolled it around in his hands, shaping it into a ball so he could tuck it back inside the nest of wires. If he was lucky, he could put everything back together without causing any issues, and no one ever needed to know about this little mishap.

Keeping the ball of putty in one hand, he used the other to remove the stepladder from his supply cart. He maneuvered the ladder into the corner behind the toilet and popped it open, then started to climb.

His palm tingled while he moved. The sensation started out innocuously enough, but in a matter of seconds he felt like hot needles were driving into his skin. He shook his hand, hoping to dispel the feeling, but it was no use.

When he reached the top of the ladder he opened the hand holding the putty. The skin underneath the ball was red and angry looking, almost as if he had burned it. *My God*, he realized. *It's the ball.*

What *was* this thing? Whatever the stuff was, it clearly wasn't supposed to be touched. He needed to get it back into place and quickly, before it did any lasting damage to his skin.

He reached up to press the putty back into the box, but the ball slipped from his grasp and fell. It landed in the toilet with a plop, and he felt the splash of cold water on the lower legs of his pants.

Danny cursed his luck. The ball sat in the belly of the toilet, taunting him from its berth underneath the water. He could fish it out and place it back in the box, but should he? After all, he had no idea what the thing did, and if it would even work now that it had gotten wet. The box seemed to be functioning just fine without the putty—the lights still blinked green, and he'd heard no intercom announcements about a downed network. Maybe he could just put the cover back on and forget about the gray lump.

Besides, he had no desire to touch the thing again. He glanced at his hand, and the red welts on his palm that throbbed in time with his heart. He shook his head at the sight and let out a sigh. He should have left the damn stuff on the floor and feigned ignorance about the whole incident. But instead he'd tried to fix things, as if he had any business messing with those boxes. He might as well put the cover back on, but he damn sure wasn't going to reach into the toilet and get his other hand burned for his troubles.

His mind made up, Danny popped the cover back into place and climbed down. He folded the ladder up and put it back on his cart. Then he flushed the toilet, sending that little gray ball of pain into the septic tanks of the ship, where it couldn't hurt anyone else.

He flipped on the tap and ran his hand under the cool water, sighing in relief as some of the stinging ache eased. Might as well use the soap, too—perhaps the gray stuff had been coated in a chemical of some kind, and that had resulted in the burn.

The paper towel felt rough against his sensitive skin, so he gingerly patted his palm dry. He stared at the red marks, shiny under the overhead lights of the bathroom. Should he go to sick bay? The ship's doctor could probably put some kind of ointment on the welts, and maybe give him something for the pain. But if he went to the clinic he'd have to disclose how he'd gotten the marks in the first place, and he'd rather not tell anyone about the box or the gray putty. Sure, the box seemed to be working okay now, but what if he'd just flushed away a key component that kept things running? Maybe it was only a matter of time before the network went down, and if he was on record as saying he'd broken this box, he'd get fired for sure.

It was a risk he simply couldn't take. George was in his senior year of college, and Luke was about to graduate high school. He couldn't lose his job now, not when there were still so many bills to pay.

He grabbed a clean rag from his cart and wrapped it around his hand, covering up the welts on his palm and providing a little bit of cushion so the raw skin didn't get further irritated by the wooden mop handle. Then he began wiping down the walls again, gritting his teeth as a fresh jolt of pain traveled up his arm.

The door swung open and Danny jumped, his stomach twisting into knots. It had to be someone from security—they knew what he'd done. Maybe the box had sent some kind of distress signal when he'd knocked the cover off, and now all his efforts were for nothing because they were here to fire him for tampering with the thing.

A split second later his friend Abel rounded the corner. "Hey, Danny, you got any more of the green stuff? I'm almost out and I don't want to have to walk all the way back to the supply room."

"Sure thing." The adrenaline left his system in a rush of breath, and Danny felt a little light-headed in the aftermath. He reached for the spray bottle of cleanser and handed it to his friend, his hand shaking slightly.

"You okay?" Abel frowned and nodded at the rag wrapped around Danny's hand. "You cut yourself or something?"

"No, nothing like that. Just a little blister on my palm. I'm fine."

"Maybe you should get it checked out," Abel pressed.

"I'm sure the doctor can give you something better than a rag to protect it."

"You're probably right," Danny said, wanting to appease his friend and end the conversation. "I'll go after my shift ends."

Abel nodded, apparently satisfied by this answer. He glanced around the room. "You done in here? It looks good."

Danny popped the mop into place on his cart and started for the door. "Thanks."

Abel stopped him as he walked past. "You sure you're okay, man? You look a little pale."

"Just tired," Danny said. "Not enough coffee this morning. I'm fine."

He pushed out the door and into the hall, headed for the next bathroom he was due to clean. As he walked, he flexed his fingers experimentally, pleased to find the movement helped ease the ache in his palm.

"It's all good now," he murmured, happy to be leaving the box and the mysterious gray putty in his wake.

Everest pushed open the door to the clinic with his shoulder, being careful to keep the cups he held in one hand steady so as not to spill them. The reception area was empty—that was a good sign. Hopefully the cases Mallory had seen this morning were isolated and not the start of a shipwide outbreak.

One of the nurses walked in, drawing up short when she saw him standing there. "Can I help you?" she asked.

"I'm here to see Dr. Watkins," he said. "Is she available?" He hadn't warned Mallory he was coming, but hopefully she could take a quick break and eat lunch with him.

"Let me check. Wait here, please," the woman said.

She disappeared into the main body of the clinic and returned a few seconds later. "She's in her office. Do you need any help?" She nodded at the sack of food he held tucked under his arm and the drinks he held in each hand.

"No, thanks. I can manage." He'd made it all the way from the dining hall—he could carry the food a few more feet.

He walked through the body of the clinic and paused at the doorway to Mallory's office. It was a small space, not unlike his own office. She had a porthole for a window, just like he did. But where his desk was neat and tidy, a holdover from his time in the army, Mallory's desk was strewn with papers and pens, with a few coffee mugs among the chaos. And was that—? He tilted his head to the side to get a better look. Yes, it was a box of needles sitting next to a handful of wrapped syringes. An interesting choice for a paperweight, but maybe it came in handy at times?

He cleared his throat, and she swiveled in her chair to face the door. She smiled when she saw him, and her undisguised pleasure at seeing him set off a warm tingle in his chest.

"Hello." She stood and gestured for him to come inside, then leaned over and grabbed her white coat off the seat of the spare chair in the corner. "What brings you to my corner of the world?"

"I heard through the grapevine there might be noro on board," he said, using the shorthand term for the common cruise ship illness. "I figured you'd be too busy to meet me for lunch, so I decided to come to you."

She winced. "I'm sorry. I meant to page you, but I got distracted." She gestured to her computer screen and the mess on her desk.

"It's no problem," he said. "Do you have a minute

now, or should I just drop off the food and leave you to your work?"

"No, please stay." She grabbed papers and began stacking them, clearing a small corner of her desk. "You can set the bag and drinks here. This is so thoughtful of you."

"I don't mind," he assured her. "I know what it's like to be so busy you can't stop to eat. Makes for long, miserable days."

"Yes, it does." She watched him while he opened the brown paper bag and retrieved their sandwiches. He offered her one, and she placed it in her lap while he continued to divide up the bags of chips and napkins.

He sat down again and began to unwrap his sandwich. Mallory followed suit, her movements just a few seconds behind his own. But while he took his first bite, she studied the food in her lap, staring at it as if she'd never seen a sandwich before.

Everest chewed and swallowed, wondering if he'd made a mistake. He'd guessed when it came to the lunch order—maybe she didn't like turkey. His heart rate spiked as another possibility occurred to him—was she a vegetarian? But no, he'd watched her eat a piece of bacon at breakfast. Why wasn't she eating? Was she not hungry?

"Everything okay?" he asked. "I wasn't sure what you liked, so I told them to put everything on it. I figured you could pick off the stuff you didn't want."

She smiled absently, and he got the impression she wasn't really listening. "No, it's fine. I appreciate it."

"If you're not hungry now, I can come back later." He started to refold the wrapper, ignoring the protests of his stomach. He couldn't very well sit in Mallory's office chowing down on lunch while she sat there quietly. A gentleman never ate in front of a lady when she herself wasn't eating. It was one of those old-fashioned Southern manners his *grand-mère* had instilled in him from a young age. If she saw him now, speaking through a mouthful of food while a woman sat without taking a bite, she would tan his hide.

"No, I'm good. I am hungry. I just needed a minute."

He paused, studying Mallory's expression for any sign of what she was thinking. She picked up her sandwich, took a deep breath and bit into the end.

Interesting. It was almost as if she'd had to gather her courage before she could take a bite. What was that about?

Everest searched for something to say, a neutral topic of conversation that wouldn't make her uncomfortable. He got the sense she wouldn't want to discuss anything too personal, and he didn't blame her. A small office in the middle of the clinic was no place for a heart-to-heart.

"Have you had any additional patients since this morning?"

Mallory shook her head. "No. Well, I did see one man who'd fallen in the shower, and a pretty bad case of sunburn. But no more GI issues, if that's what you're asking."

"That's good, right?" he asked, taking another bite. "Maybe it won't turn into a problem for this voyage."

"I hope so," Mallory replied. "I asked for a deep-clean of the ship this morning, and we have some surveillance set up to check on the passengers. Things look good so far. It's possible we may have dodged a bullet here."

"I'll keep my fingers crossed."

"What about you?" she asked. "Are things quiet from a security perspective?"

Her dark brown eyes were big and beautiful, reminding him of a doe. He could stare into them for hours, but he didn't think she'd appreciate that. "Just the usual stuff.

A passenger got drunk last night and tried to get into the wrong room. He didn't exactly appreciate our help, but we got him back in the correct cabin for the night. He's probably not feeling too great today, though," he said with a shrug.

"Maybe I'll see him later," Mallory said with a smile.

"Maybe so."

"How long have you been doing this?" She bit into a chip with a crunch, and Everest hid a smile behind his cup. Maybe she wasn't as skittish as he'd originally thought…

"A few years." He debated a second on how much to reveal, then decided to tell her most of the truth. "I started working for the company after I got out of the army."

She nodded, as if he had just confirmed a private suspicion. "Do your friends know you turned into a sailor?" There was a sly note in her voice he'd never heard before, and he realized being teased by a beautiful woman was sexy as hell.

He swallowed and assumed a serious expression. "They've forgiven me," he said soberly. "Mostly." In fact, they still ribbed him pretty hard about his career choice, but that was to be expected. The official language of their friendship was sarcasm, and thanks to their time in the service, they were all fluent in creative insults.

The thought of his buddies made him smile. Mallory's jibe made it clear she'd fit right in with his fellow vets— she had the wits to spar with them, although she seemed to lack their impressive command of profanity.

"So I take it you joined the company because you wanted to keep seeing the world?"

Everest huffed out a laugh. "Something like that. But trust me, these accommodations are much nicer than anything I experienced in the service."

"I imagine so. Were you ever stationed overseas?"

Now they were getting a bit too personal for his liking. He didn't want to talk about the explosion, or his leg. Not until he had a better idea of how Mallory would react to the news. She didn't seem like the type of woman to be turned off by his prosthesis, but he wasn't crazy about the thought of discussing his injury in her tiny office with the door open.

He shifted a bit in the chair, taking a sip of his drink to stall. She deserved an answer, and he wasn't going to lie. But he didn't have to tell the whole truth…

"I was stationed in Iraq," he said finally.

Mallory was quiet for a moment, digesting this news. Her brown eyes were full of kindness when she met his gaze. "I can't imagine what that must have been like. Thank you for your service."

Everest cleared his throat, a little uncomfortable with her expression of gratitude. He appreciated the sentiment, but he didn't feel like he was deserving of it. He'd simply been doing his job, nothing more. And he wasn't the one who had lost everything in the desert. The men who had died that day deserved the accolades and praise, not him.

But he didn't want to correct her. Mallory's words were sincere, and he didn't want to make her feel bad by rejecting her support.

So he simply said, "Thanks."

He gave her a minute to finish chewing, then asked, "What about you? How did you land the glamorous job of cruise ship doctor?"

Her laugh was a bright, lilting sound that bounced off the walls of the small room. "I don't know that I'd call it glamorous," she said.

"Oh, come on," he teased. "You travel to exotic locations, sailing the high seas. Your biggest worry is sea-sickness, right?"

She nodded with an enthusiasm that was obviously forced. "Absolutely. Just like all you have to worry about is people losing their room keys."

They both laughed, and Everest shook his head. "Seriously, though, what drew you to this line of work?" He was genuinely interested—cruise ship security hadn't been his first career choice, but he didn't regret it. Was it something Mallory had always wanted to do, or had she fallen into the job the way he had?

"To be honest, I hadn't really known this was an option until my final year of medical school." She lifted one shoulder in an elegant shrug. "I mean, I knew on some level that cruise ships need doctors, but it hadn't occurred to me I could actually be that person. I ran into one of my instructors at a coffee shop one day, and she mentioned it offhand—it was something she'd done for a few years before settling down and going into private practice. It sounded appealing, so I decided to look into it."

"Did you have to do a residency, or did you start fresh out of medical school?"

"Oh, no, I put in my time in residency. Can't really skip that step, no matter how much you might want to. But after I was done, I applied at the company and got the job. I've been doing this for three years now, and it's been good for me."

Interesting, he mused. She'd said it had been good for her, not that she liked the job or enjoyed the work. It was a small thing, but it renewed his curiosity about her past. Was she running from something? Or was he merely reading too much into the actions of the one woman who'd managed to catch his eye in recent memory?

"How much longer do you think you'll do this?" It was

a personal question, but he figured they were beyond superficial conversational niceties now.

She tilted her head to the side, considering the question. Everest caught himself leaning forward a bit, his breath trapped in his chest as he waited for her response. He forced himself to exhale. He was acting like something important hinged on her response, when really, her plans had no bearing on the rest of his life.

Pity, that.

The thought sent him running in the opposite direction, and he was so caught up in denial he almost missed her reply.

"Maybe a few more years. After that, I'd like to stay on land. Buy a house, put down some roots. Traveling all the time is nice, but it has its drawbacks, too, you know?"

He nodded automatically, still a little spooked by the tangent his traitorous brain had tried to explore.

"Your turn," she said with a smile. "Do you see yourself doing this forever?"

"No," he said, shaking his head. He absently fiddled with the straw in his cup, spinning it this way and that as he composed his thoughts. "I like the work, but at some point I want a home and a family. I know there are guys in this job who are married with kids, but when I was in the service, I saw what being gone all the time did to marriages. It's a lot to ask of someone, to take care of the kids and the house alone."

Mallory nodded her agreement. "Long-distance relationships are never easy."

"Besides," he continued, "if I'm lucky enough to have children, I want to be there to see them grow up."

Her eyes softened, and he realized she liked what he'd just said. He hadn't been trying to impress her—it was simply the truth. He'd been fortunate enough to have both his parents around while he was a kid, but some of his friends hadn't been so lucky. Now that he was an adult, he recognized the important role his father had played in his life, and he was determined to have that same connection with his own children.

"That's a nice sentim—" she began, but at that moment one of the nurses rapped on the door.

"Dr. Watkins? I'm sorry to interrupt. We need you in the clinic right away, please."

Mallory shot him an apologetic look. "Of course. What's going on?"

The nurse frowned, her lips pressing together in a thin line. "We have another case. It's bad."

Chapter 7

Mallory slid her arms into the sleeves of her white coat as she walked into the main body of the clinic. Everest kept pace with her for several steps, but instead of heading toward the gurneys he peeled off for the exit with a wave and a nod.

"See you later?" she asked. Lunch with him had been nice, and she'd enjoyed learning more about him. Maybe they could try for dinner, if both of their schedules allowed.

"Definitely," he said. "I'll page you."

He walked out of the clinic, and Mallory turned her attention to the business at hand. Her newest patient sat on a bed, clutching a pink plastic basin to his chest with a white-knuckled grip. He was pale with a greenish tinge to his skin, and his dark hair was damp with sweat.

Oh, no, she thought. *It's spreading.*

"Hello," she said, donning a pair of gloves before she

came to a stop next to him. The scent of stale vomit wafted off the man, and she fought to hide the instinctive revulsion that made her want to wrinkle her nose and take a step back. She had encountered a lot of unpleasant odors in her time as a doctor, but the only one that really got to her was the sour-tangy scent of stomach acid mixed with food. It was a challenge to hide her disgust every time, but she wouldn't let herself react while in view of a patient. It wasn't his fault, and she didn't want to embarrass him over something he couldn't control.

"My name is Dr. Watkins. What's your name?" He wore the khaki pants and orange polo uniform of housekeeping staff, but his badge was obscured by the basin he held.

His dark eyes were full of misery as he looked up at her. "Danny."

She began her physical exam, careful to keep her touch light as she asked him questions about his symptoms. He'd started throwing up about an hour ago, he said, and hadn't stopped since.

"Normally, I wouldn't come in for something like this," he said, sounding apologetic. "But it's not just the vomiting. My stomach really hurts, like someone is taking a razor blade to the inside. I've never felt this kind of pain before."

Mallory frowned and guided him onto his back. It wasn't uncommon for patients with norovirus to experience cramping, but sharp, acute pain was unusual. "I'm going to examine your abdomen." She placed her hands on his belly and began to gently palpate his organs, searching for any unusual swellings or bulges. "Tell me if anything hurts."

The words had barely left her mouth when Danny

let out a loud groan and gripped her wrists, stilling her hands. "Please stop."

"Okay," she said soothingly. "I'm almost done. I just need to check a couple more spots."

He stared up at her, doubt and despair on his face. She could tell he was afraid, and she tried to project a calm confidence so he would know things were under control. After a few seconds, his hands slipped off her wrists and he nodded slightly.

Mallory worked quickly, trying to be as considerate as possible as she wrapped up the exam. But despite her efforts, Danny was clearly still in pain. He sucked in a breath through clenched teeth, and fresh drops of sweat beaded on his forehead.

"All done," Mallory said. She hadn't found anything unusual, but it was clear Danny was suffering greatly. She placed her hand on his shoulder. "Would you like to sit back up, or are you more comfortable lying down?"

"I'm not sure," he admitted. "I think I need to sit up again, though, because—"

He began to retch, and Mallory quickly rolled him onto his side and brought the basin up to his mouth. She closed her eyes and tried to imagine she was some-where—*anywhere*—else while Danny heaved so hard his body curled into a C shape on the gurney.

After an endless moment, he relaxed again. He rolled onto his back and lifted his hand to wipe his mouth. There was a rag wrapped around his palm, a makeshift bandage of some kind.

Mallory handed the basin to a nurse and grabbed a clean towel and a small bottle of water from the mini-fridge in the corner. She handed both to him and nodded at his hand. "What happened there?"

"Huh?" He followed her gaze and frowned at his palm. "Oh, that. Uh, that's nothing."

Something about his denial didn't ring true. "Why don't you let me put a clean dressing on it?"

"No," he said quickly. "It's fine. I'm fine."

Mallory arched her brow but let the matter drop for the moment. She turned to the nurse and began issuing orders. "Please start an IV and administer a saline drip along with some Phenergan for the nausea."

"Thank you," Danny breathed, clearly finding some consolation in the promise of relief.

"You're welcome," she replied. "Now, I'd appreciate it if you'd let me take a look at that hand. I want to check for signs of infection."

He hesitated a moment, cradling the appendage close to his chest as if to protect it from her gaze. Mallory waited in silence; she couldn't force him to let her examine the injury, even if it was for his own good.

After a moment, he slowly extended his hand, silently granting permission. Mallory untied the knots in the rag, and the fabric fell away to reveal a series of raised red welts and large blisters strewn across his palm.

She winced in sympathy. "That looks like it hurts," she said.

Danny shrugged, but the way he pressed his lips together told her it bothered him.

"What happened?"

"Nothing."

Mallory unwrapped a square of alcohol-soaked gauze and gently ran it over the inflamed skin. He let out a little hiss that turned into a sigh as the alcohol evaporated, bringing cool relief. "Really?" she asked conversationally. "You just woke up like this?"

"No," he muttered. He paused, as if he was mentally

debating what he could say. Then he sighed. "Please don't tell anyone this, okay?"

Mallory leaned in and nodded. "Just between you and me."

He glanced around, as if to verify they were alone. "I was cleaning one of the bathrooms on A deck. We got a message to institute more stringent cleaning measures because of a sickness on board." He snorted. "Guess it's not doing that much good."

Mallory didn't say anything, but she hoped he was wrong on that point.

"Anyway, I was scrubbing the wall, and my mop hit one of those black boxes mounted high up by the ceiling. The cover fell off, and this wad of gray stuff dropped to the floor."

"Gray stuff?" she repeated, trying to make sense of his story.

"Yeah. I picked it up to put it back inside, and while I was holding it my skin began to tingle. Then it started to burn. I looked down and saw the red marks." He gestured to his palm with his free hand. "I tried to shove the stuff back into the box, but I accidentally dropped it into the toilet."

"I see. And then what happened?"

"Well, I wasn't about to fish it out of the toilet and burn my other hand. So I flushed it and put the cover back into place."

Mallory nodded. "Okay." She took a closer look at his hand. The damage to his skin *could* be due to a chemical burn of some kind, which fit the details of his story. But what kind of material had he touched? She knew the boxes were part of the ship's information network. It sounded strange that there would be anything but a tangle of wires inside each one. Surely the captain would have informed them if some kind of toxic substance was inside, as that presented a safety issue for both the passengers and crew.

"Have you seen this substance inside any other boxes?"

Danny shook his head. "No, and please don't tell anyone about what happened." His tone grew urgent. "If my boss finds out I broke one of the hubs, I could lose my job."

"I don't think you broke it," Mallory replied. "Things still seem to be working as they should. But if there is something dangerous in the boxes, I need to know so I can protect the people on board."

His eyes grew wide with panic. "You said you wouldn't talk about this." He struggled to sit up, and Mallory put her hand on his shoulder to restrain him.

"I'm not going to use your name," she said, holding his gaze so he could see she was serious. "No one will know I got this information from you. But I do have to investigate it."

Danny looked like he wanted to say something, but the nurse approached with the IV supplies and medication. Mallory gestured to his hand. "Please treat his palm with some Silvadene cream and apply a dressing."

The woman nodded, and Mallory took a step back to give her room to work. "I want you to rest now," she told Danny as she pulled off her gloves. "Try to relax, okay?"

He stared at her, doubt shining in his eyes. "It's going to be all right," she told him. She held his gaze, silently willing him to believe her. She couldn't explain why, but it was important that she earned his trust.

Finally, he nodded once and turned his head to stare up at the ceiling. Mallory quickly returned to her office and picked up the phone. She didn't know what to make of Danny's story, but she knew just who to call for a second opinion.

Everest.

"You want me to what?"

"Check the communication boxes mounted throughout the ship," Mallory replied promptly.

"Because you think there's some kind of dangerous substance inside," Everest finished.

She nodded, and he mentally sighed. "That's what I thought you'd said," he muttered. He rubbed his forehead with his hand, trying to stave off an incipient headache. Where had Mallory gotten this idea?

She gestured for him to sit down, and she did the same. Her small office still carried the scent of their lunch from a few hours ago, but he was here on business now.

"I have reason to believe the boxes might present a danger to the passengers and crew."

"What kind of danger?" he asked. There had to be hundreds of the boxes scattered throughout the ship. Checking them would be a major ordeal, and he didn't want to devote the time and manpower on a project that wasn't urgently necessary. Besides, if he asked his team to examine the boxes, they risked damaging them and impairing the ship's communication network.

"I think there's a toxic substance inside that will cause some pretty nasty chemical burns if people touch it." She sounded confident about this, but Everest still wasn't convinced.

"But as long as it's sealed in the boxes it's not a threat, right?"

Mallory frowned, apparently considering that for the first time. "I suppose. But until I get a look at the stuff

I can't be sure. It's possible the material could cause respiratory problems if inhaled."

Everest nodded. He knew a fair bit about chemicals thanks to his time in the army. He'd been part of the CBRN Reconnaissance Platoon, which meant he and his men had worked to detect chemical, biological, radiological and nuclear threats. He'd received extensive training in chemical recognition and detection. If he could get a look at this mysterious substance, it was possible he might recognize it and be able to identify it.

"Do you know what it looks like?"

"I'm told it's gray and feels like putty."

Everest frowned. That could describe any number of things. They'd have to run tests to determine the exact identity of the chemical, and he didn't have access to those kinds of supplies.

"How many patients do you think have been harmed by this stuff?"

Mallory shifted. "Well…" she hedged. "Just one. So far," she added quickly. "There might be more later, if additional passengers are exposed."

"It sounds like the problems result from direct contact with the substance," he said. "Which means as long as no one touches it, there won't be any more issues."

"I suppose that's true," Mallory said slowly. "Does this mean you're not going to check the boxes?" She sounded disappointed, and Everest found himself wanting to defend his decision so she would understand. He didn't want to let her down, but it just didn't seem practical for his team to go poking around looking for trouble.

"It sounds like an isolated problem to me," he said, leaning forward to place his elbows on his knees. "I'm sorry someone was injured, but as far as I can tell, the boxes and their contents are secure. If we disturb them, we risk interrupting the communication network and exposing more people to the material inside."

"But don't you think it's strange the boxes have this stuff inside?" she pressed.

Everest shrugged. "Maybe not. I'm not an electrician. For all you know, the putty is an adhesive designed to keep the wires in place, or the cover attached. Besides, lots of structures are safe on the surface, but if you were to dissect them you'd encounter something dangerous. Have you seen the rodent traps in the lower levels of the ship?" She nodded and he leaned back. "There you go. If you cracked one of those open it would be hazardous, but that doesn't mean we need to inspect every one of them."

"You have a point," she said begrudgingly.

Relief flashed through him—he was glad she wasn't angry over his refusal to act. He'd hate for this issue to interfere with getting to know her better.

"I'm sorry I bothered you." Mallory stood and he followed suit. It was clear this meeting was over.

"You didn't," Everest said simply. "I'm glad you paged me. Please don't hesitate to reach out to me whenever you have a question or concern."

Mallory nodded and walked with him to the door of the clinic. He noticed the privacy curtain was pulled around one of the beds. *That must be her patient.*

"Let me know if anything else comes up," he said, pausing at the door.

"I will." Her demeanor had changed in the last few minutes—her disappointment had been replaced with an air of resolve that made him think she might have something planned.

"Please don't do anything rash," he said.

Mallory blinked in surprise. "What makes you think I would?"

He tilted his head to the side as he studied her. "You seem determined, like you've made up your mind about something."

"Don't worry," she told him breezily. "I'll be careful."

Everest sighed, knowing there was nothing more he could say. Short of sticking by her side 24/7, there was no way to make sure she stayed out of trouble. "I know you're worried about the material in the boxes, but exposing yourself is not the way to protect the passengers and crew."

She waved away his concern. "I'm not going to bother the boxes," she told him. "Everything is fine."

He nodded skeptically. "Call me if you need anything."

"Okay."

Everest left the clinic, feeling a bit uncertain. He wanted to help Mallory, but it just didn't make sense to crack open all the communication boxes on the ship to identify a potentially dangerous substance that appeared to pose no threat in its current state. Better to keep whatever it was safely behind the plastic covers and minimize exposure.

But why did he get the feeling Mallory didn't agree with him? And just what did she have planned?

Chapter 8

Mallory leaned against the reception desk at the front of the clinic, mentally weighing her options. She could take a page from Everest's book and forget about the mysterious substance Danny insisted he'd encountered. Or she could do a little digging on her own.

It would be safer to drop the issue. Everest did have a point; if she went poking about in the boxes, she would only expose herself to the material and risk getting injured. But since she knew ahead of time it was caustic, she could take precautions before examining it...

She glanced into the body of the clinic, and her gaze caught on the curtain that provided a measure of privacy for Danny. He was resting quietly now, but she couldn't get the image of his damaged palm out of her mind. It had to be causing him pain, and yet he'd intended to suffer through it because he was worried about his job. It simply wasn't right, and if Mallory could find out more about the material that had caused him such trouble, she might be able to better treat the wound.

Her mind made up, she walked into the clinic and marched over to the corner, staring up at the innocuous-looking black box mounted high on the wall. Maybe she could simply lift the cover and take a good look at the mysterious gray substance Danny had described. At the very least, she could confirm his story and issue a warning to the rest of the crew—she didn't want anyone else mishandling the material if they happened to encounter it.

Mallory dragged a chair over to the corner, then donned a pair of gloves and grabbed a tongue depressor. She glanced around quickly to make sure no one was watching her and climbed onto the seat of the chair.

She only had to stretch a little to reach the black box. Working carefully, she inserted the flat wooden spatula into the seam between the body of the box and the lid. She applied a little pressure, and the lid popped off and sailed through the air, landing on the floor with a clatter.

"Whoops," she murmured. Hopefully it didn't break when it hit the ground...

She turned back to the box and frowned. The black plastic framed a panel of some kind that was mounted to the wall, with a collection of colorful wires and cables running in and out of various ports. It looked like the kind of thing that would be found inside a computer terminal, at least to her untrained eye. But she was most interested in what was missing.

There was no gray putty.

She peered closely at the guts of the box, going so far as to reach up and feel around in the corners and under jumbles of wires. Nothing.

"Maybe it's on the lid?" she mused. It was possible the putty had stuck to the interior wall of the lid and been pulled free when she'd sent it flying. Mallory hopped down and retrieved the object in question, but when she flipped it over she saw nothing but a smooth expanse of plastic.

"What is going on?" she muttered. If Everest was right, and the gray putty was an important part of the communication hubs, then the stuff should be found in every box on the ship. But this one was empty. And she was willing to bet if she popped the lid off the box in the hall, that one would come up empty, as well.

That meant whatever Danny had encountered, it wasn't supposed to be part of the boxes. So what was it? And how had it gotten there?

More important, were any other boxes affected?

Her stomach dropped as her imagination took flight. What if the putty was distributed in some of the passenger cabins? If the material were to escape the confines of the box, any unsuspecting person who came across it could be injured. Danny had sustained his injuries in a matter of moments, which was impressive, considering his skin was toughened, thanks to regular exposure to cleaning solutions and chemicals. The average passenger would probably suffer from more extensive burns, which made this substance a liability.

She popped the cover back into place and stepped off the chair, her mind whirring. If she wanted to make the argument that passengers were in danger, she had to prove the gray putty was present in the boxes found in the cabins. But she couldn't very well waltz into someone's room and start fiddling with the communication hub.

Or could she?

There was one cabin she knew without a doubt was unoccupied. Now that Jeff and his friend had been turned over to the Jacksonville police, their room was empty. She could slip inside Jeff's former cabin, examine the box and have an answer once and for all. If that box was devoid of the gray putty, she would chalk up Danny's exposure as a random occurrence and stop worrying. But if she did find the stuff, she'd have evidence to take to the captain.

And Everest.

But how could she get inside? She didn't have a master key for the passenger cabins, which presented a bit of a challenge. Everest would have access, but she didn't want to bother him. He hadn't been too enthusiastic about the prospect of searching the boxes, and she didn't think he'd be interested in helping her now, especially when her little expedition might turn out to be a waste of time. She'd rather investigate this alone, to spare herself potential embarrassment if she turned out to be wrong.

"Doc? Is that you?"

Danny's voice was weighted with fatigue, and she frowned. He should be feeling better by now, but it sounded like he was getting worse. She strode over to his bed and pulled back the privacy curtain, dismayed to find his color had not improved since the last time she'd seen him. He was still pale, and the pinched set of his mouth revealed his discomfort.

"How are you?" she asked.

He winced. "My head is killing me. Do you think I could have something to take the edge off?"

She nodded and turned to the laptop mounted on the wall by his bed so she could type in an order for pain medication. A glint of light caught her eye, and she glanced back at the bed, searching for the source of the distraction. Her gaze zeroed in on the ring of keys and access cards clipped to Danny's belt.

Oh, perfect, she thought, hardly daring to believe her luck.

"Danny," she said, trying to sound casual while she typed her orders. "Do you happen to have a master key to the cabins on your ring?"

"Yeah," he said. "Why?"

"I locked myself out of my room this morning," she said. "Would you mind letting me borrow your key card so I can get back inside? I left mine on the dresser, and it will only take a minute for me to grab it."

He hesitated a moment, and she tried not to let her eagerness show. "It's fine if you'd rather not," she said. "I can always call security and have them send someone to meet me there at the end of my shift. I was just kind of hoping to take care of it now while I had a moment."

"Okay," he said with a little sigh. "Technically I'm not supposed to let the keys out of my sight, but if I can't trust you, who can I trust, right?" He laughed weakly, and Mallory tried to smile. Guilt nipped at her thoughts as he unclipped the ring from his belt and flipped through it. He'd taken her at her word, but she had lied. She felt terrible about it, almost bad enough to tell him not to bother. But she had misled him for a reason, she reminded herself. She had to make sure the passengers were safe.

He held up the ring, one card gripped between his thumb and forefinger. "It's this one," he said, passing it over to her.

"Thank you," she said, accepting it from him with a smile that she didn't have to force. "I really appreciate it."

"No problem," he replied. "Just be quick about it, yeah? I'd hate for my boss to drop by and see my keys are missing."

"Don't worry," she assured him. "This will only take me a minute. I'll be back before anyone notices I'm gone."

* * *

Mallory's stomach churned as she walked along the corridor to Jeff's old room. She forced herself to act naturally, nodding to passengers and other crew members as she passed by them. She wasn't doing anything wrong, per se, but snooping around in a passenger's cabin wasn't exactly in her job description, even if the passenger in question was no longer on board and she was only trying to protect others.

She glanced down at her hand, double-checking the room number she'd scribbled onto her palm after checking Jeff's chart. She was getting close... There it was.

Mallory stopped in front of the door and took a deep breath, resisting the temptation to look around to make sure no one was watching her. It was hard to appear normal when her nerves were clanging, but she knew if she showed any hint of worry it would only draw attention to herself and what she was doing.

"In and out," she muttered, inserting the key card into the electronic lock. Just a few minutes, and she'd have her answer. One way or another.

She slipped inside the room and let the door swing shut behind her. The room was cast in shadows, thanks to the shades being drawn over the windows on the far wall. She flipped on the lights and glanced around, a little surprised to find the room was spotless. Everest and his team had gathered up the men's belongings and sent them with the Jacksonville police, and it seemed the housekeeping staff had wasted no time in flipping the room after the occupants had left.

The network hub sat perched in the corner, and Mallory dragged the desk chair over so she'd have something to stand on. She donned a fresh pair of gloves, and within a minute, she had the cover off and was peering inside.

The now-familiar jumble of wires and blinking lights greeted her, but her gaze immediately caught on the lump of gray material pressed to the inside wall of the box.

"Bingo," she breathed.

Excitement made her fingers tingle as she studied the foreign material. Part of her felt vindicated at her discovery, but her satisfaction at being right was quickly replaced by a growing sense of worry.

The gray putty didn't look like anything she'd seen before, but that didn't mean much. She wasn't exactly an expert in the workings of communication networks, and she didn't know what kind of materials were required to make them function properly.

"But this isn't required," she said, thinking aloud. If the material was a necessity, it should be found in every box. But the hub in the clinic had been empty, and it seemed to work just fine. That meant this stuff, whatever it was, didn't need to be here.

"So what's it doing?" And was it in the other passenger cabins, as well?

All of a sudden, her mind flashed to her first patients of the day. The woman she'd examined had had a sunburn on her neck and the side of her face, as if she'd dozed off while lying on one of the lounge chairs.

I haven't been in the sun that much, the woman had said. *I've mostly stayed inside, shopping and watching the shows.*

At the time, Mallory had just assumed the woman had underestimated her sun exposure. But after seeing the burns on Danny's palms, now she wasn't so sure...

If this material was in the woman's cabin and in other places throughout the ship, perhaps it had caused the woman's sunburn-like rash. Mallory closed her eyes, picturing the markings on her patient's skin and seeing them in a new light. Maybe she hadn't been sunburned after all; maybe her skin was showing signs of irritation due to chemical exposure.

But what kind of chemical could induce such an obvious response without direct contact? Mallory racked her brain, but came up empty. There was another possibility, though, one that filled her with a heavy sense of dread.

Radiation.

She'd seen the effects of radiation treatment on cancer patients during medical school and her residency. People who received radiation to shrink their tumors often displayed red, sunburn-like rashes on the areas of their body that had been exposed. And the other common side effects of the treatment? Nausea and vomiting.

"Oh, my God," she whispered. Was it really possible? The pieces seemed to fit, but it strained credulity to think radioactive material was scattered throughout the ship.

Mallory looked again at the putty, suddenly very aware of how close she was to the box. Her stomach twisted, and she quickly popped the cover back onto the box and climbed down, needing to move so she could think things through.

She paced the confines of the room, searching for a more plausible explanation for her observations. But none of the alternatives she came up with seemed to fit in quite the same way.

Implausible as it sounded, Mallory was forced to admit the idea that the gray putty was radioactive was worth investigating further. But she couldn't do it alone.

It was time to call Everest and tell him what she was thinking.

She walked over to one of the beds and sat on the edge, then reached for the phone on the bedside table. She dialed his pager number and typed in a quick message, asking him to meet her here. He'd want to see the evidence firsthand, and then they could formulate a plan.

Mallory let her gaze wander around as she waited. The box could be seen from every part of the room, which meant whoever was inside would be continually exposed. Not good.

Jeff's words echoed in her head. *There's a body in the walls.*

"I don't think so, buddy," she murmured. Everything looked normal on that front, as far as she could tell. The closet door was cracked open, and she stood and walked over to look inside. It gave her something to do while she waited for Everest to call back.

She noticed the damage right away—a piece of cardboard had been tacked to a spot on the wall, probably to conceal a hole or some other flaw. It was hanging precariously by one corner, the other having pulled free from the pin holding it in place.

Mallory knelt and pried the pins from the wall, intending to straighten the cardboard and put it back in place. Just as she'd thought, there was a hole behind the makeshift barrier, likely the result of Jeff or his friend kicking through the drywall while high.

She leaned forward to put the cardboard over the gap, and the light from the overhead bulbs glinted off something inside. "That's odd," she muttered. As far as she knew, there shouldn't be anything shiny inside the walls...

She bent over so her face was directly in line with the hole. At first, she couldn't tell what she was looking at. Then realization struck, and she gasped.

The light she'd seen had reflected off a thick sheet of plastic, the kind of tarp found on construction sites. And it was wrapped around what looked like a human foot.

Mallory jerked back, falling onto her bottom with an involuntary shout. She scrambled to her feet, her heart in her throat and her mind racing.

Jeff hadn't been hallucinating. There really *was* a body in the wall of his room.

Her panicked brain latched on to one thought: Everest. She had to find Everest, and now. She couldn't sit here and wait for him to arrive any longer—she had to go track him down. She was way out of her depth and needed help.

The door shushed over the carpet as it opened behind her, and she felt a wave of relief.

"Thank God you're here—"

The blow was unexpected and came without warning. One second, she was turning to greet Everest. The next, she was on the floor, her vision blurring as spots of light danced across her eyes. The back of her head felt like it was on fire, and she tried to lift her hand to touch the spot. But a wave of dizziness swamped her, and she closed her eyes, sinking into the inky-black depths of unconsciousness.

Chapter 9

Everest rounded the corner and walked swiftly down the corridor, headed for Jeff's room. He was filled with a mixture of curiosity and exasperation; he'd known as soon as he left Mallory standing in the clinic that she was going to do something, and sure enough, she had conducted her own little investigation.

Part of him was interested in seeing what she'd found, but a larger part wished she had left this kind of thing up to him and the members of his staff. She was a doctor who had no training in security issues, and if there really was some strange toxic substance on board, she may have put herself in danger by charging off on her own.

The door to the room was open, and he pushed inside to find Wesley, his right-hand man, kneeling on the floor next to a body.

No, not a body. Mallory.

Everest's heart jumped into his throat, and he quickly moved forward. "What the hell is going on here?"

Wesley's head jerked around, his wide eyes relaxing when he recognized Everest. "I'm not sure. I was down at the end of the hall when I heard a shriek, and then a man came bursting out of the room and took off. I started to follow him, but I saw her on the floor as I went by." He turned back to Mallory. "I couldn't just leave her here like this."

Everest lowered himself to the floor by her head, worry gnawing at his stomach. "Mallory," he said loudly. "Mallory, wake up." What had happened? Had she been stabbed? Beaten? It was impossible to tell from this angle—she was lying on her stomach, and while he saw no sign of injuries on her back, he couldn't see the front side of her body.

His battlefield instincts kicked in and he ran his hands over her body, starting at her ankles and moving up her legs, over her hips, across her back and shoulders and down her arms, searching for any signs of injury. He couldn't feel anything through her clothes, but perhaps he was just missing something…

Mallory moaned and began to stir. Everest carefully helped her roll onto her back and leaned over her face, calling her name. She winced and moved her hand to her head, rubbing her temple with her fingers.

"Are you okay? What happened?"

She squinted up at him. "Everest? Is that you?"

Her question made his blood freeze. Could she not see him?

She blinked up at him, and he realized the overhead lights were probably blinding her. "It's me, Mallory. Do you want to try to sit up?"

"Yes." Her hand gripped his arm, and she held on tight while he eased her into a sitting position. He settled down next to her, keeping one arm around her shoulders to make sure she didn't fall back again.

"Can you tell me what happened?"

"I'm not sure," she said. She shook her head, then winced at the movement. "I was waiting for you, and I thought I heard you come inside. But when I went to turn, something hit me on the back of the head."

"Not something," he said grimly. "Someone. Wesley said he saw a man run out of the room and take off down the hall."

Mallory glanced over, apparently noticing Wesley for the first time. "Did you get a good look at him?"

Wesley shook his head. "I'm afraid not. I just saw the back of him as he ran away."

"Why don't you see if you can track him down," Everest said. "I know it's a long shot, but maybe you'll see him again."

"Maybe," Wesley said, sounding doubtful. He rose to his feet, his expression skeptical. "Are you sure you'll both be okay here?"

Everest glanced at Mallory, who nodded subtly. "Yes. I'll escort Dr. Watkins back to the clinic and then find you so we can discuss what you saw and review the security tapes. Hopefully the cameras caught a good view of his face so we can track him down."

Wesley nodded. "Good point. I'll see what I can find in the meantime." He glanced at Mallory. "I hope you're okay, ma'am."

She offered him a small smile. "I will be. Thanks for coming to my rescue."

"Just part of the job," he replied. He turned and left the room, and Mallory relaxed into Everest's side.

It was nice holding her, feeling the warm softness of her body pressed against his own. He would have preferred to embrace her under different circumstances, but he'd take what pleasure he could from this moment. If nothing else, his time in the service had taught him that life could change in an instant, and he needed to enjoy what he could, while he could.

Mallory let out a sigh. "I'm so glad you're here," she said softly.

Everest tightened his arm around her shoulder and turned his head, resting his nose in her hair. She smelled fresh, like melons and honey, and he took a deep breath, drawing the scent of her into his chest.

"What were you doing here?" he said softly, trying to keep his frustration out of his voice. He'd been afraid Mallory would hurt herself if she went off on her own, and he didn't enjoy being proved right. More than that, though, he was worried. He'd assumed any danger she faced would be due to the mysterious substance she thought was in the communication hubs. But now there was an unknown assailant loose on the ship, and he'd already demonstrated his willingness to employ violence against an unarmed woman.

Everest had to wonder—had Mallory been targeted specifically, or had she simply been in the wrong place at the wrong time? More important, was she still in danger?

"I came here to check the hub," she said, her tone sheepish. "I realized I had seen patients earlier in the day who had sunburn-like rashes. I thought they might be due to exposure to the same stuff Danny touched."

"Danny?" Everest seized on the new name, realizing it must be the patient who claimed to have found this mystery material in the first place.

A guilty look flashed across Mallory's face. "Dammit," she muttered. "I told him I wouldn't reveal his name. Please forget I said anything."

Everest nodded, but he filed the name away in case he needed the information later. "Did you find anything?"

A light shudder ran through her body. "More than I bargained for," she said cryptically.

Before he could ask what she meant, she began to push herself up. He maneuvered to help her stand, keeping his hand on her waist for support.

She stood in place for a second, swaying slightly. Then she shook her head and glanced up at him, her eyes full of dread. "It's over here."

"What?" he asked, his stomach sinking. Mallory was clearly upset by something she'd discovered, and Everest got the feeling he wasn't going to like it.

She led him to the closet and stopped in front of the door, which was half-open. "Do you remember Jeff's rantings last night? About finding a body in the wall of his room?"

"Of course," Everest said. "I sent Wesley to check things out, just to make sure everything was fine."

"And what did Wesley say?"

"That there was nothing to the story. He didn't find anything."

Mallory nodded. "Maybe he didn't look hard enough."

A tingle shot down Everest's spine. "What are you saying?"

Mallory opened the closet door and pointed inside. "See for yourself."

Everest walked forward, his gaze immediately drawn to the hole in the drywall about twelve inches off the floor. He knelt to get a closer look and blinked in disbelief at the sight that greeted him. "Is that... Is that a foot?" he said incredulously.

"I think so," Mallory confirmed grimly. "It seems Jeff was right. There really is a body in the wall."

Everest inserted his finger along the edge of the hole and pulled, ripping another chunk of drywall free so he could get a better look. Maybe his eyes were playing tricks on him, and this was simply trash that had been left inside the wall during the ship's construction.

But as the hole enlarged, he realized with a growing sense of horror that this was no overlooked piece of debris that had been accidentally sealed up. A leg emerged, the outline of the bones clearly visible under faded blue pants.

"Holy hell," he murmured. He rocked back on his heels, trying to collect his thoughts as his mind whirred with questions.

Who was this? How long had the body been here? And how did it get here in the first place?

First things first: he had to seal the room. Dead bodies didn't just spontaneously appear in the walls of a ship. Someone had put this here deliberately, which meant a crime had taken place. He had to do what he could to preserve whatever evidence remained until a forensic team could examine the scene. Then he needed to notify the captain and call the authorities. They were due to make port in Charleston in the morning—the police could hopefully meet them as soon as they docked to take possession of the body and start collecting evidence.

At least he knew this crime hadn't taken place on his watch. Whoever it was in the wall, they'd been put there during the construction of the ship; that much was clear.

He rose to his feet and turned to Mallory. She was staring at the newly enlarged opening in the wall, her expression a mix of pity and sadness. "I didn't imagine it," she said softly.

Everest walked to her and gathered her into his arms, pulling her close so his body blocked her view of the macabre scene. She initially stiffened at the contact but quickly relaxed against him. "No, you didn't imagine it," he said.

Her breath was warm against his chest, and she wrapped her arms around his waist. "Who do you think that is?"

"I don't know," he replied. "It could be someone who helped build the ship. Or maybe it's someone who had no connection to the boat at all—it's possible a local criminal used the construction site as a way to get rid of a problem. Whoever it is, hopefully the police will be able to make an identification soon."

She sighed and rested her forehead against his shoulder. "I hope so, too. I can't imagine how worried the family must be."

If there is any family, Everest thought darkly. He hated to be so cynical, but he suspected whoever was in the wall hadn't been missed.

But he didn't say that to Mallory. She was already upset, and he didn't want to add to her distress.

He pulled back and looked down into her face. Her expression was somber, but she was calm. "I need to report this to the captain and call the authorities in Charleston." He shook his head. "This is the second time in twenty-four hours I've had to call the police. My boss is going to think I'm not doing my job properly."

"It's not your fault," she said, squeezing his arm.

"I know," he said, appreciating her support. "But I still feel responsible because it's my boat." He guided her to the door. "Let's get you back to the clinic. I'm concerned about your injuries, and I want someone to check you over."

Mallory lifted her hand to rub the back of her head. "I'm fine," she said, her tone dismissive. "Just a little bump."

"You lost consciousness," Everest pointed out. "That's not fine in my book."

"You don't need to worry about me," she said. "And we can't leave yet—there's something else I need to show you." She stopped walking, forcing him to stop as well so he didn't shove her forward.

"I've had about all the bad news I can handle right now," he warned her, only half joking.

"Well, brace yourself, because I have more." She gestured to the communication box mounted on the wall. "I know you think I'm freaking out over nothing, but after you left, I decided to check the box in the clinic so I could at least see for myself what my patient had encountered."

Everest shook his head, his suspicions confirmed. "I should have known," he muttered.

If Mallory heard his comment, she didn't acknowledge it. "I popped open the lid, but there was no putty-like material inside. The box was empty except for wires and ports, the kind of stuff you'd expect to see involved in a communication network."

"So why check this room?" he asked, frustration flaring in his chest. Why had she continued to dig when there was no reason to? It didn't make sense.

"Like I told you earlier," she said evenly, "I saw some patients this morning who had a rash. I initially thought it was sunburn, but the woman claimed to have spent most of her time indoors. I started to wonder if the material that caused such painful blistering upon contact would irritate skin if a person were exposed from a few feet away. And it got me thinking—what if the mystery material is in the hubs located inside cabins? That would explain the sunburn-like rash. If she's been spending all her time indoors, she'll be exposed to the stuff most of the day."

Everest nodded. "I see your point. But I was in the

Chemical Corps in the army, and I had extensive training with chemical and biological weapons. I haven't heard of anything that behaves in the way you've described. Generally there are respiratory symptoms involved following such an exposure."

Mallory was quiet a moment. "This is going to sound crazy, but do you think the material might be…radioactive?" She glanced up through her lashes, appearing suddenly shy, almost as if she was embarrassed to even ask the question.

Her words hit him like a fist to the gut, and Everest sucked in a breath. That was a pretty serious charge she was making. What were the odds that radioactive materials were spread throughout the ship? His first instinct was to deny the possibility. It certainly seemed far-fetched, at least on the face of it. But her question forced him to look at the information at hand in a new light, and the more he thought about it, the more plausible the idea became.

Besides, after finding a body in the wall, could he really afford to dismiss any hypothesis out of hand?

"Walk me through your reasoning," he said. "I'm not saying I agree with you, but I want to know how you reached that conclusion."

Gratitude flashed in her eyes as she apparently recognized he wasn't going to laugh off her suggestion. "The patients I've treated today have displayed symptoms consistent with exposure to radiation. The rash, the nausea and vomiting and other GI issues—they're all possible consequences of a low-level exposure."

"They're also consistent with patients who have the cruise ship gastro bug, if I'm not mistaken." Everest wasn't trying to pick a fight with her, but it seemed much more likely they were dealing with a viral outbreak rather than radiation exposure.

Mallory nodded. "True. But the burns experienced

by the man who touched the material look like those of a person who has been burned by radiation."

Everest thought back to the time he'd spent at CBRN school, where the army had taught him all sorts of useful information about chemical, biological, radiological and nuclear weapons. They'd spent a lot of time looking at the aftermath of radiation exposure on the human body, and he recalled all too well the graphic photos of patients with charred, damaged skin.

"You said you were in the Chemical Corps," Mallory said softly. "Did you learn anything about radioactive materials?"

He nodded automatically. "Yes. We were trained to safely interact with them. They sent us to Iraq so we could accompany infantry units on the search for WMDs. They wanted us there so we could identify and contain any chemical, biological or nuclear hazards."

Mallory nodded, as if he'd confirmed one of her suspicions. "Will you look at the material in the box? Maybe you can tell what it is by sight alone."

Everest frowned. "I doubt it." Her face fell, and he quickly rushed to explain. "There isn't one characteristic appearance for a radioactive material. It can be made to look like pretty much anything. But I'll take a peek."

The chair was already in the corner of the room, likely from Mallory's earlier explorations. He climbed up and popped off the cover to the black box. Sure enough, a lump of gray material adhered to the side of the casing.

He studied it for a moment, committing its features to memory. It didn't *look* dangerous, but he knew from experience sometimes the most deadly substances had the most benign appearances.

Thinking quickly, he pulled his cell phone from his pocket and snapped a few pictures from different angles, hoping to capture a good representation of what he was seeing. He still had a few friends in the Chemical Corps. He'd send them the pictures and ask what they thought. If this truly was radioactive material, maybe they would recognize it.

Everest snapped the cover back into place and climbed down. He turned to find Mallory watching him, her expression both hopeful and hesitant. "Well?" she asked, taking a step toward him.

"I saw the material," he said, running a hand through his hair. "But I don't recognize it."

"So we're back to square one," she said, disappointment weighing her words.

"Not necessarily." He punched a few keys on his phone, typing out a quick email. "I'm sending some pictures to a few friends of mine who are still in the service. They might recognize this stuff."

"Good idea," she said. "I hope someone can identify it soon."

Everest shoved his phone back into his pocket and took Mallory's arm, guiding her to the door once more. "In the meantime, I have to inform the captain about these developments and call the Charleston police. Please tell me you'll take it easy and stay in the clinic. No more running around the ship by yourself, especially since we don't know who attacked you."

Mallory's eyes widened. "Don't you think that was just a one-time thing? That he hit me because I was in the wrong place at the wrong time?"

Everest bit his lip, uncertain how to respond. He wanted her to take the potential threat to her safety seriously, but he didn't want to scare her needlessly. It was a tough needle to thread, but he had to give it a shot. "I don't know," he said honestly. "I don't know if you were targeted because of your search for this mystery material, or because you stumbled across the body. Or maybe it's as simple as an attempted burglary gone wrong. The guy who hit you may have seen the door was open a crack, assumed the room was empty and walked in to do a quick snatch-and-grab." He lifted one shoulder in a shrug. "The point is, until I know more, I want you to be careful."

It bothered him to know the man who had attacked Mallory was still on the loose, especially since he wasn't sure if she was in some kind of danger. He didn't like the idea of leaving her unguarded, but he simply couldn't stay by her side all the time. Especially now that he had this crisis to handle. He was just going to have to trust that Mallory would take his warning seriously and either remain in the clinic or stay near her friends until he had some answers.

"You don't have to worry about me," she said, slipping her hand into the crook of his elbow. "I'm coming with you."

"Is that right?" Her assertion surprised him—he'd assumed she'd want to go back to the clinic and monitor the man with the burns on his hands. He wasn't going to complain, though. If she stayed with him, he wouldn't have to worry about her safety. One less concern to occupy his thoughts...

She nodded. "We might not know exactly what this putty is yet, but I do know it's a health and safety issue for the people on board. It's my recommendation that we end the cruise when we dock in Charleston in the morning."

"We'll have to cut things short anyway, thanks to this discovery." He gestured to the wall and its macabre contents, hidden no longer. "The police are going to need to tear this room apart looking for evidence. That's going to take time, which means we'll be docked for a while."

He shrugged. "I don't see how we'll be able to continue under those circumstances."

"I hope the captain agrees with us."

"He won't have a choice," Everest said. "It's a legal matter now. The decision is out of our hands."

"We have a problem."

There was a pause, and Wesley mentally winced at his poor choice of words. The men he worked for didn't like hearing about difficulties. They only wanted results.

"Elaborate."

"A body was found behind the wall of one of the passenger cabins."

"Hmm." Despite the noncommittal sound, Wesley knew he had the man's full attention.

"We dock in Charleston in the morning. I'm sure the police will be waiting, and they'll have to search the room for evidence. Our trip will be cut short."

"That is unacceptable." The man's words held a slight edge, and Wesley's anxiety spiked a notch.

"It's out of my control," he replied. Panic nipped at the edges of his mind, threatening to drown out logical thought. He did not want to be held responsible for this development. Wesley didn't know all the details of the plan, as his contact only updated him with the bits and pieces of information he needed to know. Still, it was clear the Organization required the *Abigail Adams* to dock in New York City on the Fourth of July, and any delay would not be tolerated.

"I can't influence things once the police get involved," he said. "They'll want to conduct an investigation, and if I try to obstruct their activities, it will only raise suspicions."

"That's fine," the man said. "We will take care of things."

It was on the tip of Wesley's tongue to ask how, but he caught himself just in time. He swallowed, wishing he could hang up now, on this semipositive note. But there was another matter he had to report.

"There's more."

"Oh?"

"The ship's doctor thinks there's some kind of toxic material in the communication hubs mounted throughout the ship." The idea was so far-fetched he felt a little foolish even suggesting it, but if the woman turned out to be a problem, he didn't want to be accused of concealing information from his contact.

"What?" The man's voice sharpened with interest, and Wesley realized the idea maybe wasn't so silly after all.

"What does she know?"

"I'm not sure," Wesley replied. "I was only able to hear bits and pieces of their conversation, but from what I gathered, she thinks the communication hubs contain some kind of dangerous substance. I think I heard the word *radioactive*, but I'm not confident about that."

The man cursed softly, and a chill slid down Wesley's spine. Was the doctor actually right?

"This woman sounds like a problem. Can you handle her?"

There was only one acceptable response. "Yes." He paused, then decided to throw caution to the wind. "I take it her speculations have merit?"

His contact laughed softly, the sound surprisingly sinister. "Do you really want to know?"

"I do." Wesley was tired of operating in the dark. He was risking a lot, both personally and professionally. He had a right to know exactly what was going on.

"Very well. Yes, the doctor is correct. The ship was modified during construction. Small parcels of semi-enriched uranium were distributed throughout the vessel."

"Ah," Wesley said, the pieces clicking into place as the man spoke. "So after I distribute the explosive charges, the ship will be a floating dirty bomb."

"Indeed," the man confirmed. "And when the ship docks in New York Harbor to receive her distinguished guests…" He trailed off, and Wesley filled in the blanks.

"It will be the most memorable Fourth of July in history." A thrill shot through him, burning away his fears of discovery and energizing him for the task ahead.

"Do you see now why you were chosen for this mission?"

"I do." It was perfect, and he felt a bit humbled by the opportunity they had given him. "Thank you."

"You can show your gratitude by doing your job," the man replied. "I trust you will do your part to ensure things go off without a hitch?"

"Oh, yes," Wesley said, nodding even though the man couldn't see him. "I will."

He hung up and tucked the phone into his pocket, unable to keep the smile off his face. The Organization's plan was perfect, beyond his wildest imaginings. Justice was finally going to be served, and he was going to be a part of it.

He'd been fifteen when the planes had hit the Twin Towers of the World Trade Center. A bout of flu had kept him home from school, and he'd been stretched out on the sofa, eyes glued to the television. At the time, he'd thought he was experiencing some kind of fever dream. The events were simply too terrifying to actually be real. But then his mother had called, her voice thick with tears.

"I just want to check on you," she'd said. "I love you very much."

"Love you, too," he'd replied automatically. "Is this really happening?"

"I'm afraid so. I'm going to pick up your brother from school and come home. Your father should be on his way there now."

And so the family had gathered, huddling together to watch history unfold. Ryan hadn't even complained about being forced to leave his car at school overnight. In fact, his older brother had been uncharacteristically quiet throughout the day and the remainder of the week. At first, Wesley had thought Ryan was simply trying to come to terms with what had happened. They hadn't known anyone who lived in New York or Washington, DC, but Ryan's class had gone on a school trip to New York City the year before, and he'd loved it so much he'd decided he wanted to go to college there.

Wesley had tried to talk to his brother, but Ryan had rebuffed his attempts at conversation. It was clear Ryan was planning something, but he kept telling Wesley to wait. "I'm going to tell everyone at once," he'd said.

And two weeks later, on his eighteenth birthday, Ryan did.

They had just finished singing "Happy Birthday," everyone seated around the table to watch Ryan blow out the candles on his cake. "I joined the Marines," he said, without preamble. He leaned forward with an impatient huff, and the tiny flames snuffed out, sending slender pillars of smoke rising into the air.

A shock had rippled through Wesley, followed quickly by an intense burst of jealousy. He'd tuned out his parents' stunned objections and begun to daydream about ways he could join his brother. It would be so cool to fight side by side—they could watch each other's backs, and they could keep each other from getting too homesick. He'd be sixteen in a few weeks, and if he could figure out a way to take the GED test soon, he might be able to ship out to basic training with Ryan.

Provided his parents approved.

"I want to join, too," he'd said.

"Absolutely not," his father had said.

"No." His mother's voice had been tight with fear. "You're going to finish high school."

"I can get a GED," he began, but his father had cut him off.

"No. This isn't up for discussion. Go to your room, please."

"But—"

"Now."

Ryan had caught his eye as he'd left, and Wesley knew they'd talk later. So he'd retreated to his room and spent the rest of the evening online, researching his options. Maybe he could get a fake ID, or try to get emancipated from his parents...

It was almost two hours before Ryan came upstairs and knocked softly on his door. "Are they gonna let you go?" Wesley had asked.

"They don't have a choice," Ryan responded. He sounded tired, and there were lines around his eyes that hadn't been there before. Wesley studied his brother's face, noting with surprise that Ryan looked much older than his eighteen years.

"I'm an adult," he continued. "And I'm graduating high school in May. Legally, Mom and Dad can't stop my enlistment. That's why I waited until today to sign the papers."

"I'm coming with you." Wesley had expected Ryan

would be happy about his determination to join him, but his brother shook his head.

"No. You need to stay and finish school. Wait until you're eighteen and join up then."

"But I want to go with you now."

Ryan smiled at him, and in that moment he looked more like their father than his brother. "I need you to stay here and take care of Mom. She's taking this pretty hard."

Wesley couldn't argue with that. But he hated the idea of being stuck at home while Ryan was off in some foreign land, defending their country.

"Those two years will go by faster than you think, and then you'll be able to join me," Ryan had said. "Just please do me this favor now."

Wesley had agreed, knowing he didn't have much of a choice. Ryan had shipped off to basic training just a few days after his graduation, and Wesley had begun to count the days until he'd be able to join his brother.

A little over a year later, Ryan had been sent to Iraq. Six weeks into his tour, he was dead.

At first, the military had provided very little information regarding the circumstances surrounding Ryan's death. His mother had been nearly catatonic with grief, but his father had grown angry and refused to accept the paltry facts thrown their way. He'd started digging, writing letters to senators and congressmen, anyone he thought could help. After several months, it was finally revealed Ryan had been killed by friendly fire.

The news had broken Wesley, shattering his illusions. He'd dreamed about following in Ryan's footsteps and serving alongside him. But he couldn't stomach the thought of putting his life on the line for a country that had failed his brother in such spectacular fashion and then tried to cover it up in an attempt to save face. It was a transgression he could neither forgive nor forget.

As his mother shrank into herself, Wesley's bitterness grew, threatening to overtake him. Until one day three years ago when he'd been contacted by a man who said he could help.

And now here he was, on the verge of finally avenging his brother.

For the first time since Ryan's death, Wesley felt hopeful. He wanted to call his parents and share the news, to let them know that even though he couldn't bring Ryan back, he was going to make this country pay for the way it had betrayed them all. But he knew better than to reveal any hint of what was to come. Soon enough, his family would hear the news. And then he could reveal his part in the operation, so they would know that he had never stopped fighting for justice for Ryan.

"I've still got your back, Ryan," he whispered. "I will make this right."

Chapter 10

It seemed to take forever to find the captain.

Mallory and Everest went straight to the bridge, but he wasn't there. "He received a personal call," said one of the officers on duty. "He's in his cabin right now."

"Damn," muttered Everest.

"Should we go wait outside his door?" Mallory asked, only half joking. With everything going on right now, they needed to talk to him right away. Every minute that ticked by resulted in passengers being further exposed to the material in the communication hubs...

Everest shook his head. "No. At least not yet. He's bound to come back here once he finishes his call. If we head for his cabin we might miss him, and then we'd waste too much time tracking him down. Better to wait here."

Mallory sighed, but she knew he was right. It was hard to tamp down her impatience, though, especially now that she and Everest had come up with the beginnings of a plan to address the problems on board.

If the captain agreed, the ship would dock in Charleston as scheduled. The police would come on board and begin their investigation concerning the body, and the passengers would be taken off the ship. Once that occurred, Everest could coordinate a hazmat team to collect and identify the mysterious substance while Mallory conducted exit screenings to determine if any of the passengers were experiencing symptoms that might be due to exposure to the material.

It wasn't a perfect plan, and it would take a lot of effort and participation from the staff to pull it off. But it was a good start, and Mallory knew she'd feel better once she started doing something concrete to address the problem.

But as the minutes ticked by with no sign of the captain, her nerves began to fray. She glanced over at Everest, who was staring intently at the doorway, as if he could cause the captain to appear by sheer force of will alone.

"Still think we should wait here?" she murmured.

His jaw clenched and he glanced at her. "Maybe we should go check on him." He turned and took a step, his lower right leg hitting the bottom edge of a desk as he moved.

A loud metallic clang rang out, and Everest froze. He closed his eyes, and Mallory got the distinct impression he was silently wishing the ground would swallow him whole. Then he swallowed and looked at her. "Ready?"

Mallory nodded. Whatever had just happened here, it was clear Everest didn't want to talk about it. Unless she missed her guess, he was wearing some kind of leg prosthesis, which would explain the subtle hitch she'd noticed in his gait.

He probably lost his leg in the war, she thought. Which explained the hesitation he'd displayed when she'd asked him about his service during lunch. He'd answered her questions, but she had gotten the impression he wasn't being entirely forthcoming with his responses. Not that she blamed him. She had her own secrets, and while she was growing to trust Everest more and more, she wasn't excited by the prospect of telling him about the assault she'd suffered in college.

They set off down the hallway, walking side by side. Mallory could practically feel the waves of discomfort emanating off Everest, and she wished there was something she could say to let him know that she didn't want to pry into his personal life or force him to talk about things he didn't want to share. She respected him too much for that. She was curious to know more, of course, but if she did find out the details of his situation, she wanted it to be because he'd felt comfortable enough to tell her, not because she'd pried the information out of him.

"Do you think the captain will accept our recommendations?" She was genuinely curious to know his thoughts on the matter, but she also hoped he'd view the question for what it was: a conversational olive branch, a sign she was willing to ignore the strange moment that had just happened on the bridge until he was ready to talk about it on his own terms.

Everest nodded. "I don't know him that well, but he seems like a reasonable man. I made a few recommendations before we got under way, and he was receptive to my suggestions. I'm hoping he'll do the same now."

"He didn't hesitate to start decontamination procedures when I told him about the suspected norovirus patients," Mallory said. "It seems like he has the safety of the passengers and crew as a priority. Maybe that will make it easier to convince him to cut the cruise short." She made a mental note to check on Avery and Olivia and warn them of the potential danger in their cabins. There

FREE Merchandise is 'in the Cards' for you!

Dear Reader,

We're giving away FREE MERCHANDISE!

Seriously, we'd like to reward you for reading this novel by giving you **FREE MERCHANDISE** worth over **$20** retail. And no purchase is necessary!

You see the Jack of Hearts sticker above? Paste that sticker in the box on the Free Merchandise Voucher inside. Return the Voucher today... and we'll send you Free Merchandise!

Thanks again for reading one of our novels—and enjoy your Free Merchandise with our compliments!

Pam Powers

Pam Powers

P.S. Look inside to see what Free Merchandise is **"in the cards"** for you!

We'd like to send you two free books like the one you are enjoying now. Your two books have a combined cover price of over $10 retail, but they are yours to keep absolutely FREE! We'll even send you 2 wonderful surprise gifts. You can't lose!

REMEMBER: Your Free Merchandise, consisting of **2 Free Books** and **2 Free Gifts**, is worth over $20 retail! No purchase is necessary, so please send for your Free Merchandise today.

YOUR FREE MERCHANDISE INCLUDES...

2 FREE Books **AND** 2 FREE Mystery Gifts

FREE MERCHANDISE VOUCHER

2 FREE
BOOKS
and
2 FREE
GIFTS

Please send my Free Merchandise, consisting of
2 Free Books and **2 Free Mystery Gifts**.
I understand that I am under no obligation to buy
anything, as explained on the back of this card.

240/340 HDL GLTJ

Please Print

FIRST NAME

LAST NAME

ADDRESS

APT.#   CITY

STATE/PROV.   ZIP/POSTAL CODE

Offer limited to one per household and not applicable to series that subscriber is currently receiving.
Your Privacy—The Reader Service is committed to protecting your privacy. Our Privacy Policy is available
online at www.ReaderService.com or upon request from the Reader Service. We make a portion of our mailing
list available to reputable third parties that offer products we believe may interest you. If you prefer that we not
exchange your name with third parties, or if you wish to clarify or modify your communication preferences, please
visit us at www.ReaderService.com/consumerchoice or write to us at Reader Service Preference Service, P.O. Box
9062, Buffalo, NY 14240-9062. Include your complete name and address.

NO PURCHASE NECESSARY!

RS-517-FM17

▼ Detach card and mail today. No stamp needed. ▼

® and ™ are trademarks owned and used by the trademark owner and/or its licensee.
© 2016 HARLEQUIN ENTERPRISES LIMITED. Printed in the U.S.A.

wasn't another place for her friends to sleep tonight, but perhaps they could put some kind of makeshift shield over the boxes on the wall to limit their exposure to the toxic material inside.

"Let's hope you're right," Everest said, letting out a small sigh. He shook his head. "I just can't get over how badly things have gone on this voyage. I've never had so many problems all at once."

"Me neither," Mallory said. "I once worked on a boat that had a huge outbreak of norovirus. It swept through everyone—even the captain fell ill. It was terrible, but at least I knew what I was dealing with and how to handle it." She bit her lip. "I wish I could say the same right now."

Everest placed his hand on her shoulder. His touch was warm and reassuring, and her anxieties dimmed a bit at the reminder that she wasn't alone. "We'll get some answers soon," he said. "As soon as my friends respond to my message, I'll ask them to compare the photos I sent to a database of images of known materials. That will tell us something in a few hours at the latest."

"That's encouraging," Mallory replied. They stopped in front of the captain's door, and Everest lifted his hand to knock. But Mallory stopped him with a hand on his arm.

He turned to look at her quizzically, and she took a deep breath. There was something she wanted to do, and she needed to gather her courage. "I want to thank you," she said softly.

"For what?" His bright blue eyes were kind as he tilted his head to the side.

"For listening to me. For actually taking my crazy idea seriously and not laughing me off the ship. For lunch today. For all your help last night." She shrugged and smiled. "Take your pick."

Everest stepped toward her, until he was standing only inches away. Mallory braced herself for the familiar jolt of panic that came whenever she got too close to a man, but it didn't happen. Instead, a frisson of excitement tingled down her spine, making the fine hairs on the back of her neck stand on end. This close, she could see the darker blue rings rimming Everest's pupils, and the small freckle on the lower right side of his neck, just above the collar of his shirt. He smelled of soap and sunscreen, and Mallory found herself leaning toward him, her body drawn to him with a yearning that surprised her.

Everest lifted his hand and brushed a strand of loose hair behind her ear. "It's my pleasure," he said, his voice husky. "I'd say I was just doing my job, but, well…" He ducked his head, seeming suddenly shy. Then he met her eyes, a hint of vulnerability in his gaze. "I like you," he said simply.

A thrill shot through her at his words, followed quickly by a hint of sadness. "I like you, too," she replied.

"Don't sound so happy about it," Everest joked.

She smiled sadly at him. "It's not you. It's me." She shook her head. "I know that sounds like a cliché, but I have a lot of trouble trusting men."

"Bad breakup?"

If you only knew. A shudder ran through her at the reminder of the assault. "Something like that."

Everest was quiet a moment, studying her. "We all have our secrets," he said gently. "And I'm not going to pressure you to talk to me. But if you want to, I'm here."

Gratitude welled in her chest. Seized by impulse, Mallory rose onto her toes and pressed a kiss to Everest's cheek. "Thank you," she said. "Same goes for you."

A look of shock crossed his face, followed by a flare of heat in his eyes. He lowered his head, and for a thrilling second, Mallory thought he was going to kiss her.

His breath was warm against her lips and smelled faintly of mint. She leaned toward him, a subtle pull drawing her closer until she could feel the heat from his body. Her breath caught in her throat, and for a second, the time seemed to stop as the moment stretched between them.

A noise from inside the captain's cabin startled them both. Mallory jumped and Everest jerked his head back, his eyes growing wide. They stared at each other for a second, and Mallory was suddenly very aware of their surroundings. She had almost kissed him while standing in the hall, in full view of any staff who happened to wander by. They were here to talk to the captain about a serious matter, and yet their intentions had very nearly been derailed by temptation.

Everest smiled sheepishly and rubbed the back of his neck with his hand. "Um, maybe we should knock."

"Yes," she said, nodding vigorously. She swallowed, trying to push down the unfamiliar feelings and urges Everest had stirred up inside her. "Let's get back on track here."

Everest rapped smartly on the door, and she held her breath while they waited for the captain to answer.

She glanced over at Everest, taking in his tall, strong frame standing patiently next to her. What was it about this man that cut through years of fear and worry, that made her want to test the waters and maybe risk her heart again?

But the timing couldn't be worse.

When this is over, she thought, turning her focus back to the job at hand. *I can figure this out later.*

* * *

Everest stared at the captain's door, fighting hard to keep his eyes off Mallory. He knew if he so much as looked at her he would kiss her, and he couldn't afford to indulge in his attraction to her at the moment. There was too much at stake right now.

Never in his life had he allowed himself to get distracted from his mission to such an extent. He'd practically kissed her in the damn hallway, for crying out loud! Would have, too, if not for the interruption. It wasn't like him to notice a woman, much less to notice her to such a degree that all other thoughts flew out of his mind. But Mallory was different. He found himself thinking about her when they were apart, and when he was around her he felt hyperaware of her presence, his eyes drawn to her no matter what else was going on in the room. She was an intriguing combination of strong and vulnerable, and he found her fascinating.

But now is not the time. His attraction to Mallory might be the silver lining in this troubled voyage, but right now, he had to focus on his job. And that meant breaking the bad news to the captain.

If the man ever opened his door...

Everest raised his hand to knock again, and a few seconds later the door swung open. The captain glared at him, clearly upset by the interruption. He held a phone pressed to his ear and held up one finger in the universal gesture to wait. Everest nodded, and the captain closed the door again, leaving him alone with Mallory once more.

"That was odd," she said softly. "I wonder what's going on."

Everest shrugged. "Who knows? But I can tell you his day isn't going to get much better."

"Let's hope he doesn't take it out on us."

"He won't," Everest said. In truth, he didn't know how the captain would respond to their news, but he did know he wasn't going to let the man vent his anger toward Mallory, or any of the other staff, for that matter. Events on the ship were unprecedented, but no one could have predicted any of it. The important thing was to wrap the trip up as quickly and safely as possible. They could worry about assigning blame later.

The door flung open and the captain nodded at him, then glanced at Mallory. "What can I do for you?" His tone was businesslike and his expression neutral; whatever his conversation had been about, he'd appeared to put it behind him.

"We'd like a word, please," Everest said. "Can we come inside for a minute?"

The captain stepped back and gestured them in. "Make it quick. I need to get back to the bridge."

Mallory glanced at Everest, and he nodded. "We found a body behind the wall of one of the guest rooms."

The captain blinked. Under any other circumstances, his expression of disbelief would have been comical. But Everest wasn't laughing.

"I'm sorry, what did you say?"

Everest repeated himself, forgiving the man for his disbelief. He could hardly believe he was saying the words himself.

The captain shook his head. "That's what I thought you said," he murmured. "Do you know who it is and how they got there?"

"No. But I'm going to notify the Charleston police. They'll come on board when we dock in the morning and take possession of the scene."

The captain nodded. "That's fine. We'll be in port all

day tomorrow. That gives them about eight hours to collect evidence."

"Sir," Everest began, trying to sound diplomatic, "it's unlikely that will be enough time. The police will want to retain control of the room until they are certain they've gathered all the evidence. They'll likely need us to remain in port for several days, at least."

The captain shook his head. "That's unacceptable. We can't afford that kind of delay."

"With respect, sir," Everest said, "it's not up to us. We cannot refuse to cooperate with law enforcement."

The captain straightened his shoulders and lifted one brow. "I will talk to the officer in charge of the investigation. I'm sure accommodations can be made."

Everest shook his head, knowing it wasn't worth the effort to argue with the man. He slid a glance to Mallory and shrugged slightly, yielding the floor to her.

"There's more," she said, taking a half step forward.

"Has the outbreak spread?"

"I'm not sure," she admitted. "But there's another issue of concern. There's some kind of strange material in the communication hubs mounted throughout the ship. I think it's making people sick."

"I see." But the man's tone made it clear he didn't really believe what she was saying.

Mallory bit her lip, and Everest could tell she was trying to remain patient. "It's my recommendation we end this trip in Charleston and evacuate the ship. We need to find out what this mystery substance is, and we can't afford to risk the safety of our passengers while we try to identify it."

"Dr. Watkins." The captain spoke slowly, his cheeks turning a dull red. "What you are suggesting is not only implausible but impossible. We cannot terminate our voyage in Charleston. It is simply not an option."

"But we have to get people off the ship and away from—"

The captain lifted his hand, cutting her off. "Do you know for certain this material is responsible for any illnesses on board?"

Mallory's shoulders sagged slightly. "Not conclusively, no. But I do have a patient—"

The captain raised his voice, talking over her. "Then I will not sanction the evacuation of this ship. Honestly, you two." The man looked from Mallory to Everest, clearly disappointed. "I had heard such good things about you both. I was told you were the best of the best. But now here you are in my cabin, presenting far-fetched tales of passengers in danger and sharing bad news with no viable suggestions to address the problem." He shook his head. "I have to get back to the bridge. I don't have time for this nonsense." He shooed them out of the room and shut the door behind them with a thud.

Mallory turned to Everest and saw her confusion mirrored on his own face. "What just happened?"

Everest shook his head and placed his hand on her arm, coaxing her into a walk alongside him. He waited until they were several feet away from the captain's door before answering her. "I'm… I'm not exactly sure."

"That is not the same man I spoke to this morning," she said. "Just a few hours ago he was very concerned about the possibility of a norovirus outbreak on the ship. I don't understand why he's had such an about-face now."

"I don't understand it either," he said. "It seems very out of character. But as I told him, once the police get involved we won't have much of a choice."

"What can we do?"

Everest was silent a moment, considering her question. "Start planning. Brief your staff. If we wait for the captain to accept the reality of the situation, we'll be caught flat-footed when it's time to act."

"You sound like you've done something like this before," she observed. "Were you in charge of a lot of operations while you were in the army?"

"Enough to know that sometimes it's better to ask forgiveness than permission," he said drily.

They came to the stairwell at the end of the hall and stopped. "Want me to walk you back to the clinic?"

She hesitated for a second, then shook her head. He squashed the flare of disappointment. He had his own work to do, and while it would be nice to stay near her, they couldn't afford to waste any time.

"I appreciate the offer, but we should both probably get started." Her pager beeped insistently, and she pulled it off her belt and glanced at the display.

"Everything okay?"

She frowned as she read the message, and he caught a glimpse of the display over her shoulder: Need help ASAP.

"I'm not sure," she said. Dozens of possibilities flitted through Everest's mind, none of them good. A jolt of adrenaline hit his system, and his heart beat hard against his breastbone. What was going on in the clinic? Had more patients presented with GI symptoms? Had any of the passengers touched the material in the black boxes? Whatever was happening, it was clear she needed to get back there quickly.

"I'll let you know later," she said, already starting down the stairs. "Sorry to run."

"Good luck," Everest called after her. "Keep me posted."

She waved absently, and he fought the urge to follow. She was a professional and could handle anything that might be going on in the clinic. Besides, if she really needed help, Everest was only a page away.

The thought made him feel a little bit better as he watched her hurry down the hall.

Chapter 11

Everest sat at his desk and logged into the computer. He needed to call the Charleston police and alert them to the situation on board, but there was something else he wanted to do first.

He found the contact information for the Norfolk, Virginia, Police Department and punched the number into his phone. He knew the *Abigail Adams* had been built at a Norfolk shipyard, and it stood to reason the body in the wall had been placed there while the boat was still under construction. Maybe the Norfolk PD had a missing persons case open that could shed light on the identity of this victim.

A few minutes later, he had an answer.

"Yeah, we've got a cold case open for a missing dockworker. Guy never showed up for work after a holiday weekend. His boss seemed to think he'd just quit without giving notice, but one of his coworkers was adamant that wasn't the guy's style. So we opened a file. Never really went anywhere. The man was a loner, and we didn't have much to go on."

"I might have found him for you," Everest said grimly.

"That would be nice. It'd be good to get this case closed up."

"We make port in Charleston in the morning," Everest said. "I'm going to call their police department after I hang up with you. I'll tell them to contact you."

"Appreciate it," the officer said. "It's a hell of a lucky break for us. Not so much for him, though."

"I wouldn't be too happy if I were you," Everest said. "Instead of a missing person, you now have a murder case to investigate."

"True," the officer said. "But that's a different department." He laughed at his own joke, then said goodbye and hung up.

Everest shook his head and looked up the number for the Charleston Police Department. It didn't take long to update them, and they assured him they'd be waiting at the pier when the ship docked in the morning.

"In the meantime, seal the room as best you can."

"Already done," Everest said. "We're keeping everyone out until you can take possession of the scene." He told the detective about his conversation with the officer in Norfolk.

"Thanks," the man said. "Sounds like we'll be able to pass this one off fairly easily."

That job done, Everest turned his attention to the matter of Mallory's assailant. Maybe Wesley had discovered something while he'd been dealing with the captain. He paged his second-in-command, then pulled up the video surveillance files of that corridor. Perhaps the security cameras had caught a good look at the man's face...

Wesley tapped on his door a few minutes later. "Come in," Everest said, gesturing for him to take the chair across from his desk.

The young man sank into the seat, an air of suppressed energy radiating off him. He looked as if he'd made some kind of discovery, and Everest felt a flare of hope. Maybe there was some good news to be found in this crapshoot of a day.

"You look like you've got something for me," Everest said.

Wesley smiled a little. "Maybe," he said. "I'm still trying to track down the guy who hit Dr. Watkins, but I might have a lead."

"Oh?" That was good news—if they could find and detain the man, it would be one less thing for him to worry about.

"The guy had a good head start on me, but I spoke to several passengers who saw him run past. I have a pretty decent description, and I'm cross-referencing his approximate age with the passenger manifesto. Once I get that information, I can go cabin by cabin until I find him."

Everest nodded. "Good work. I'm checking the security footage now, hoping to get a clear picture of the guy's face. But so far, I haven't found anything." Everest turned back to his computer, and Wesley came to stand next to him. They watched the monitor together for a few seconds, but then the crystal-clear footage dissolved into a blizzard of black-and-white snow.

"What the hell?" Everest muttered. He turned to Wesley. "Have we had reports of camera issues?"

Wesley frowned. "Not that I've heard. But I have noticed a bit of static on the feed here and there. I don't know what's causing it, though."

Everest's stomach sank as he watched a potential lead

slip through his fingers. Based on the time stamp on the footage, the camera had crapped out during Mallory's visit to the cabin. It flickered back to life a few minutes later, but by that time, the deed had been done. He had a nice view of Wesley's legs as the man ran down the hall in pursuit of the mystery assailant, but there was nothing that could help them identify the man.

He cursed softly.

"Don't worry," Wesley assured him. "I'll find the guy."

Everest nodded in thanks. "That's not all I'm worried about," he said.

Wesley returned to the chair and leaned forward. "What else is going on?"

"I've notified the Charleston police about our…situation."

"I'm sorry about that," Wesley said. His cheeks flushed, and he looked down at his lap. "I still can't believe I missed something so obvious when I checked the room."

"It's fine," Everest said. "If you didn't specifically inspect the closet, there's no way you would have found him."

"I didn't," Wesley admitted sheepishly. "I just glanced around the room itself. It was a crazy story, and I didn't expect it to be true."

"That makes two of us," Everest said. "Anyway, the Charleston police will come on board in the morning to recover the body and begin their investigation."

Wesley nodded. "Sounds good. Do we want to block off that hall so passengers aren't in the way?"

"Yes, but to be honest, I'm expecting our voyage to terminate tomorrow. The police are going to need to collect evidence, and I can't imagine they'll be willing to release the scene after only a few hours."

"Yeah, but it's a pretty cold case, isn't it?" Wesley

pointed out. "Do you really think there's that much evidence remaining? We've had people in and out of that cabin since the ship was built. Construction workers, cleaning staff, guests. There can't be much forensic information left."

"True, but it's possible there's some kind of clue that was sealed in the wall with the body." Everest waved his hand, brushing aside the topic. "My point is that we don't know how extensive their activities are going to be. But I'm going to operate on the assumption they'll want time."

"Fair enough." Wesley stood. "I'd better get back to looking for this guy. If we really are terminating the trip tomorrow morning, I don't have long to find him."

"One more thing," Everest said, holding up one hand to stall Wesley. "Dr. Watkins is concerned the communication hubs spread throughout the ship contain a toxic material that might be responsible for some patient issues. So if you see any damage to the boxes or notice any with the cover off, let us know."

"A toxic material?" Wesley echoed doubtfully. "Is this something we need to announce to everyone?"

Everest shook his head. "No, not yet. I'm not fully convinced there's an issue, and a shipwide announcement would only cause alarm. Still, it never hurts to be cautious, so just try to keep an eye out for anything unusual."

"Sure thing," Wesley said. "I'll let you know if I find something."

"Keep me posted on the search for the attacker," Everest said. "I'll ask Dr. Watkins if she's interested in pressing charges against him. If so, we can turn him over to the police in the morning."

"Yes, sir."

Everest turned back to his computer and watched the

security footage again, squinting at the fuzzy picture in the hopes of making out some kind of detail. But it was no use. For whatever reason, the camera had stopped working at the exact time of Mallory's assault. He made a note to send one of his staff to check on it, then clicked over to his email, hoping to find a message from his friend still in the Chemical Corps. But his inbox was disappointingly empty.

He pulled out his phone and began to go through the pictures he'd taken of the mystery substance. It didn't look like anything he'd seen before, but that didn't mean much. Contrary to popular belief, radioactive materials didn't glow in the dark, and they didn't always come with a warning label. And that was the problem. A motivated bad guy could potentially put radioactive material into anything, or place it just about anywhere without attracting too much attention.

But they had to get their hands on it first. And fortunately, radioactive substances that could do real harm didn't just grow on trees.

Which was why he was having such a hard time accepting Mallory's theory. He didn't discount her experience with her patient, or her assertion that the mystery stuff was dangerous in some way. But that didn't mean it was radioactive.

He knew better than most the type of panic triggered by the threat of radiation. People lost all rational thought when faced with an invisible danger, particularly one they'd been taught to fear since childhood. And even if Mallory's presumption turned out to be correct, and the gray substance in the boxes was radioactive, he still thought people would be safer if they didn't know. It would be better to have an orderly procession off the ship rather than a stampede.

Briefly, he wondered how things were going in the clinic. He reached for the phone, then hesitated. Mallory probably wouldn't appreciate the interruption... But if she was truly too busy to talk, one of the nurses would let him know.

It took a minute to get her on the phone, but when she answered, she sounded fine. Everest relaxed a bit— surely if things were going badly, he'd be able to hear it in her voice.

"I wanted to check in and see how things are going. Any updates?"

Mallory sighed, and he imagined her leaning against the wall as she held the phone to her ear. Was her hair still contained in a ponytail, or had some of the strands slipped free to frame her face?

"I've had five more patients present with gastrointestinal issues."

His stomach dropped. "That sounds like a lot."

She laughed softly. "It is when they all come in at the same time, that's for sure."

He winced, imagining the scene all too easily. "Do any of them have sunburns?"

"Oh, yes," she said. "But they've all admitted to spending a lot of time outside, so that doesn't necessarily tell us anything."

"That's the problem, isn't it? All of these symptoms could be due to norovirus, right? There's no clinical smoking gun that points to, er, a different cause." He'd almost said "radiation" but caught himself just in time. He didn't want to bandy that word about casually, and he'd hate for someone walking past his office to overhear and get the wrong impression.

"That's correct." He could hear the frustration in Mallory's voice. "And I really hope this is all just due to the virus. But there's no way for me to know for sure. I'll feel much better once everyone is off the ship."

"Not much longer now," he said. "We're still working on finding the man who attacked you. Wesley is narrowing in on him, and he should have a name soon."

"That's good," she said. "Please thank him for me."

"I will. When we do find him, do you want to press charges?"

Mallory was silent a moment, apparently taken aback by the question. "Uh, no," she said. There was a strange note in her voice, and Everest got the feeling he'd inadvertently touched on a sensitive subject.

"Are you sure? Don't you want this man to pay for what he did to you?"

She laughed, but there was no humor in it. "Of course. But I have some experience with this. Let's just say what I want and what actually happens are two different things."

"Mallory—"

"What's the point?" she interrupted. "It'll be my word against his. He said, she said cases never end well. Trust me."

A cold chill skittered down his spine. "Mallory, what happened to you?"

"It doesn't matter." Her voice was flat, and for the first time since he'd met her, she sounded defeated. "I have to go."

She hung up before he could say another word. Everest slowly replaced the phone in its cradle, puzzling over her response. Mallory wasn't a cynical person. It was clear something had happened in her past to make her think there was no point in pursuing a case against her assailant.

I have a lot of trouble trusting men. Her words echoed in his mind, and he considered them in a new light.

At first, he'd thought she was burned out from a bad breakup. But given her reaction just now, he had to wonder if something more serious had happened.

Had she been assaulted before? That might explain some of the behavior he'd noticed, like the way she shied away from touching men. She'd found an excuse not to shake hands with Wesley or Taylor last night. And she always had a watchful air about her, like she was constantly assessing the situation. It was one of the first things he'd noticed about her when he'd seen her in the fitness room. He'd thought she was just sensitive, but now he wondered if she was on guard, trying to protect herself against something.

Anger surged in his chest, and he clenched his fists, pounding lightly on his desk. He wanted to pull Mallory out of the clinic and convince her to tell him what had happened to make her so cynical. Then he wanted to find whoever had hurt her and make him pay.

The intensity of his feelings stunned him. Mallory was a grown woman, capable of taking care of herself. Yet his protective instincts insisted on viewing her as a damsel in distress, as someone he needed to protect.

He wasn't going to tell her that, though. How could he explain that his desire to protect her was not because he thought she was helpless, but because he cared about her? Would she even listen? Or would she shy away once he started talking about something so personal?

She'd said he could talk to her, but he had a feeling she'd meant about his leg. If he started prying into her past, she might close up and shut him out before he'd had a chance to really get to know her. And while he was curious to find out what made Mallory tick, he didn't want to push her too far, too fast and risk her walking away.

Be patient, he told himself. It rankled him to have to

go slow when he wanted to charge in and fix things, but from what he knew of Mallory thus far, she was a woman worth waiting for.

"Dr. Watkins? You have some visitors."

Mallory smiled absently at the nurse. "I'll be right there," she said. The woman nodded and left, and Mallory took one last look at her computer screen. She'd been scouring the internet for insights as to the identity of the mystery substance, but so far, she'd come up empty. Hopefully Everest's friends would have better luck…

She stood and smoothed the wrinkles out of her white coat. Maybe Everest had sent some of his staff to update her on the evacuation plans. That young man from last night was nice enough, and although she wouldn't mind dealing with him again, she wasn't crazy about Wesley. She couldn't put her finger on it, but there was something about Everest's second-in-command that rubbed her the wrong way.

Maybe she'd get lucky and Everest himself had come to talk to her about his plans. Even though it had been only a few hours since they'd talked to the captain—or tried to talk to him, she mentally corrected—she was looking forward to seeing him again. It was strange, this pull she felt toward him. They'd spent so much time together since the voyage started she was surprised to find she wasn't tired of him yet. In fact, it was quite the opposite. And after that incident on the bridge this morning, she was eager to know more about him.

For starters, how had he lost his leg? And how extensive were his injuries? He was obviously a proud man who didn't want people to know about his prosthesis. But maybe she could earn his trust and learn more about his past.

She entered the clinic, anticipation thrumming through her. She glanced around, searching for Everest. But he wasn't there.

"Mallory!" Avery waved at her from the entrance to the clinic, a big grin on her face. Olivia stood next to her, smiling brightly.

A sense of disappointment settled in her stomach, feeling like a small stone. On its heels came a jolt of shock. Never before had she felt bummed about seeing her friends. What was happening to her?

Mallory swallowed and pasted on a smile, hoping they wouldn't detect her momentary dip in mood.

No such luck.

"What's wrong?" Olivia asked as soon as Mallory got close enough to talk. "You look upset."

Mallory shook her head, trying to cast off her mood. "Just feeling a little overwhelmed," she said.

"Is this a bad time?" asked Avery. "We can come back later."

"No, it's fine," Mallory assured her. "There's kind of a lull now, so I can hang out with you guys for a few minutes at least. What brings you to my neck of the woods?"

Olivia held up a small bag Mallory hadn't noticed she was carrying. "It's dinnertime. And we figured if the mountain won't go to Muhammad…"

"We'd come to you," Avery finished.

Mallory smiled with genuine appreciation. "Thanks, ladies. Taking care of me, as always." She gestured for them to follow her back into her office, snagging an extra chair as she walked. "Come on in," she said, dragging the chair into place. "It's small, but we can all fit."

Avery and Olivia settled into the chairs, and Olivia passed Mallory the bag. She opened it, smiling at the contents: a tuna sandwich, an apple and a bottle of water. It was the same food she'd practically lived on in medical school, and she felt a flash of gratitude that Avery and Olivia had remembered.

"Still a fan?" Olivia asked, watching Mallory's face as she perused her dinner.

"Oh, yeah," Mallory said. "Thanks a lot. I didn't think I was going to get to eat for a while." She unwrapped the sandwich and took a healthy bite, her stomach suddenly feeling like an empty pit. "Where are the guys?" she asked around a mouthful of food.

"They're playing pool in one of the game rooms," Olivia said. "We thought it would be a good time for us to check on you."

"Sounds like you're staying busy," Avery said, glancing around the small office. "How many cases of norovirus have you seen?"

"About eight so far," Mallory said. She took another bite, mulling over how much to tell her friends. On one hand, she probably shouldn't share information about the ship's problems with people who weren't on staff. But these were her best friends, and she valued their opinions. Not to mention, Avery and Olivia were the smartest women she knew. It would be nice to get a second opinion on her theory. Everest had listened dutifully to her concerns, but she could tell he didn't really buy into her idea. Avery and Olivia would tell her if she was on to something or simply being paranoid.

She took a swig of water to clear her throat. "Can I ask you guys something?"

"Of course!" Olivia said. Avery leaned forward, a gleam in her eye. "Is it about that hot security guard?"

"Avery," chided Olivia.

Mallory laughed. "What happened to Grant?" she teased.

Avery shrugged. "Grant has nothing to worry about. He knows I love him. But I'm not blind. You have to admit, Everest is a handsome man."

Olivia nodded, her smile turning a bit sheepish. "He is quite nice-looking."

Yes, he is, Mallory thought. But she waved away Avery's question. "It's about my patients."

"Oh," Avery said, a hint of disappointment in her voice. She leaned back in her chair. "That's probably a question for Olivia, or even Grant. But if you need help tracking the source of the outbreak, I'm your girl."

"I want both your opinions," Mallory said. She described her observations and concerns, starting with Jeff and his friends and ending with her worries about the material in the black boxes. It felt good to talk to her friends, even if the topic of conversation was somewhat dire.

"So what do you think?" she asked, glancing from Avery to Olivia as she finished.

Both women sat still for a moment, clearly processing what Mallory had told them.

Olivia spoke first. "I had no idea you were dealing with something like this."

"Why didn't you come to us earlier?" Avery chimed in.

Mallory shrugged. "You guys are on vacation. Besides, I probably shouldn't be telling you now."

"Are you okay?" Olivia rose and reached for Mallory's head. "Let me check your injury."

Mallory submitted to her friend's attentions, knowing if she didn't, Olivia would only fuss. "I'm fine," she said. "Really."

"You lost consciousness," Avery pointed out, sounding so much like Everest that Mallory wanted to laugh. "That's not normal."

"She's right," Olivia said. She conducted a basic neurological exam, which Mallory passed.

"Happy now?" Mallory asked, smiling up at her friend.

"Hardly," Olivia said. "But I feel a little better." She sat back down and studied Mallory, her expression one of concern.

"So you really think there's radioactive material on board?" Avery said. She shook her head. "That's a scary thought."

"I know, but it would explain everything I've seen."

"I don't mean to be a naysayer," Olivia said, "but your patients' symptoms are consistent with norovirus. Why search for another explanation, especially one that seems rather implausible?"

It was the same question Mallory had been asking herself for the past several hours. "I know it sounds crazy," she said. "But norovirus doesn't explain the welts and burns on that man's hands. They look like the kind of thing I saw during med school when I did that oncology rotation."

Olivia and Avery were silent for a moment. "And you say he has GI symptoms, as well?" Avery asked.

Mallory nodded. "But they didn't start until after he had contact with the material."

"That is a bit unusual," Olivia said thoughtfully.

"How many people are on board this ship?" Avery asked.

"About five hundred passengers, and maybe one hundred staff," Mallory replied. "Why?"

Avery cocked her head to the side. "So eight out of six hundred people have presented with symptoms that are consistent with either norovirus or radiation exposure. That's just barely over one percent of the population on board." She closed her eyes for a second. "One point three five percent, to be more precise."

Mallory and Olivia exchanged a smile. It seemed Avery had donned her disease investigator hat. Mallory always enjoyed hearing about her friend's assignments, but she'd never considered the possibility she would need Avery's expertise herself.

"Correct me if I'm wrong," Avery continued, "but if this material is spread throughout the ship, wouldn't you expect a larger portion of the population to be affected?"

"She has a point," Olivia said.

"I don't think it's in every box," Mallory said. "It's not in the hub in the clinic. I know for certain it was in one of the men's bathrooms on A deck and in a passenger cabin on C deck. I haven't been able to check any other locations, though."

"Maybe it's not as bad as you think," Olivia said.

"Or maybe it's worse," Avery said. They both turned to look at her, and she shrugged. "I'm just playing devil's advocate here. She hasn't seen that many cases yet, but it's possible people are sick but not coming to the clinic. Is there a way to check the sales of anti-nausea medication from the ship's general store? If there's been a spike in demand, it's likely more people are affected but are trying to self-medicate before they come to the clinic."

"That's a good point," Mallory said, grateful for her friend's insight. "I can ask around. It shouldn't be too hard to find that information."

"It would be nice to know exactly which boxes have the mystery material," Avery said. "We could map out locations and triangulate passenger exposure, to see if there's a correlation between their distance from a box and symptom intensity."

Mallory grinned, appreciating Avery's suggestions.

"It's a good thought," she said. "But we might not have the time to do all that. Everest thinks we're going to have to cut the voyage short in Charleston, so the police can retrieve the body and collect evidence."

"That's a bummer," Olivia said. "I understand why it's necessary, but I was really enjoying the cruise so far."

"What does Everest think of your theory?" Avery said. "Or have you not told him?"

Mallory poked at the water bottle cap with her fingertip, sending it scooting across the desk. "I told him. I think he's skeptical, but he seems to be keeping an open mind."

"That's good," Olivia murmured.

"He took pictures of the material in the cabin and sent them to a few friends. He used to be in the Chemical Corps in the army, so he's hoping his friends who are still enlisted might be able to recognize the stuff."

"Wow," Olivia said. "The Chemical Corps? That's pretty intense."

Mallory nodded, a sense of pride budding in her chest. It was a little silly for her to feel that way, but she liked Everest and she was happy to hear her friends seemed to like him, as well.

"Was he ever deployed?" Avery asked.

Mallory nodded. "Iraq," she confirmed. It was on the tip of her tongue to tell them about his injury, but she stopped herself just in time. Everest was a proud man, and it was clear he didn't talk about his war wounds with just anyone. In point of fact, he hadn't talked about it with her yet either. She'd happened to guess, thanks to the incident on the bridge. And while she knew Avery and Olivia would never say anything to him about it, the fact remained he hadn't trusted her with this part of his story yet, and she had no business sharing her accidental knowledge with anyone else.

"So..." Avery stretched out the word, and based on her oh-so-casual tone, Mallory knew exactly what was coming next.

Her friend didn't disappoint. "Breakfast was nice, huh?" She smiled brightly, and Mallory resisted the urge to laugh at Avery's transparent attempt to circle around to the topic she was really interested in.

She decided to play dumb. "I'm glad you enjoyed it," she said sweetly.

Avery lifted one eyebrow, dropping the subtle approach. "It seemed you and Everest had a bit of a spark," she said.

"Think so?" Mallory asked.

Olivia nodded. "Yes. And since this is the first time we've seen you interested in anyone, we just wanted to make sure you're okay."

Mallory felt a flash of gratitude, touched by their concern. Her friends knew her so well, and even though they were here on vacation with their men, they still worried about her. It was enough to make her tear up, and she blinked hard to clear the stinging wetness from her eyes.

"I'm fine," she said.

Avery tilted her head to the side but said nothing. "Really, I am," Mallory assured her. "I do feel a pull toward Everest, which is something I haven't experienced in years. It's strange, but also a little exciting."

"Well, for what it's worth, I think he's interested in you, as well," said Olivia.

"I kind of figured that out," Mallory admitted.

Avery leaned forward, a grin tugging at her mouth. "Does that mean you guys have had a moment? You have, haven't you? Did you kiss him?"

Mallory laughed and shook her head. "No—"

"Did he kiss you, then?"

"No," Mallory said, a bit more firmly this time. "There has been no kissing." *Except for the one I planted on his cheek*, she thought, but that hardly counted.

"Bummer," Avery said, her shoulders slumping a bit. "I had my fingers crossed for you."

Mallory squirmed a bit in her chair. "To be honest, I'm not sure if I'm ready for that kind of physical contact. I know that sounds crazy, but—"

"No, it doesn't," Avery said, interrupting her. She reached out and grabbed Mallory's hand, her touch supportive. "Don't do anything you're not comfortable with. If Everest is as good a guy as he seems, he won't push you. And if he does..." She trailed off, but her meaning was clear.

Mallory smiled, feeling a little foolish. "I can't help but think I should be ready by now. I mean, it's been eight years since I was assaulted! Shouldn't I be over it?"

"Not necessarily," Olivia said, her voice kind. "You were raped. That's not the kind of thing you just shrug off."

"I know," Mallory said. "This is the first time I've felt any kind of interest in a man since the attack. It's a bit overwhelming, because I don't know how to act. I feel torn—I want to get to know him better and maybe try to date him, but I'm also scared of what might happen. What if we start to get physical and I can't handle it? What if I tell him about the rape and he decides he doesn't want to get involved with me and my baggage?" She glanced from Avery to Mallory, searching their faces for answers. "I don't know what to do."

Olivia's eyes were full of sympathy. "We can't tell

you what the right choice is here. But I think the fact that you're attracted to Everest is a good sign."

"I agree," Avery said. "Look, I'm not going to pretend that the issues Grant and I faced were anything like what you're dealing with. But I can tell you that the fear of the unknown, of rejection... It's there in the beginning of every relationship. At some point, you have to decide if you want to take the chance and risk your emotions, or play it safe and maintain the status quo."

Mallory nodded, knowing she was right.

"What is your gut telling you?" Olivia asked. "I know you're worried about how Everest will react to the news of your attack, but how do you feel when you think about telling him?"

Mallory closed her eyes, trying to picture the conversation. Her stomach tingled with nerves, but as she imagined herself speaking the words, a great sense of relief swept over her.

"I feel relieved," she said, her eyes popping open in surprise.

Olivia and Avery exchanged a smile. "I'd say that's a good sign," Olivia said encouragingly.

"But don't you think that's a pretty weighty piece of information to drop on someone?" Mallory asked. "I mean, I can't guarantee I'm not going to pull away from him at some point, if it all gets to be too much. Is it really fair for me to ask him to put up with that?"

"Hell, yes," Avery said, her tone indignant. "First of all, you are an amazing person and you deserve a supportive partner. If he can't be there for you while you navigate these uncharted waters, he's not worthy of you. Second of all, you're not asking him to 'put up with' anything." She scrunched her fingers into air quotes as she spoke, the movement of her hands matching the intensity of her words. "You're communicating your needs, and if he's a grown man, he'll respect and understand that." She sounded so protective that Mallory half expected Avery to storm out of the office in search of Everest so she could light into him for these hypothetical crimes.

"I appreciate the sentiment," Mallory said. "I'd just hate to find out the hard way he's not the right guy for me."

"I can understand that," Olivia said. "Believe me, I know how scary it is to take that leap."

Mallory studied her friends' faces, wishing they had some magic insight that would tell her what to do. "How did you get over your fears?"

Olivia smiled. "I didn't," she said simply. "But I decided I'd rather live with the pain of rejection than miss out on the opportunity to be with Logan."

"Same here," Avery said quietly. "I don't want to dismiss your concerns, but at the end of the day, that's really the only question that matters."

"You're not going to tell me what to do here, are you?"

"Nope," Avery said with a smile.

"Definitely not," added Olivia. "That's for you to decide. But whatever you choose, we'll be here for you."

"I'm counting on that," Mallory said. "I'll need you both, now more than ever."

"You don't have to make a decision right away," Avery said. "Are you feeling rushed for some reason?"

Mallory shook her head. "Not especially. But…I'm tired of feeling scared. I'm at the point where I'm tempted to take a chance just because it means a change. Even if things don't work out between us, at least I'll have tried something new."

"From what I've seen, and from what you've told us, I think Everest is a good prospect," Olivia said. "And if it makes you feel any better, Logan's a pretty good judge of character, and he likes him."

"So does Grant," Avery said.

"That does help," Mallory admitted. "It's nice to know what other guys think."

"Speaking of guys," Olivia said, pushing out of the chair, "we should probably let you get back to work and go find them before they get into too much trouble."

Mallory rose as well and reached out to hug Olivia. "I'm glad they get along so well," she said.

"Like peas in a pod," said Avery. "Sometimes I think Grant would rather hang out with Logan than with me."

Mallory laughed and hugged Avery. "I'm sure that's not true."

"I'm not," quipped Olivia, her brown eyes flashing with humor. "I feel the same way about Logan."

The three of them left the office and walked through the clinic, coming to a stop before the entrance.

"Thanks for dinner," Mallory said. "And for listening."

"Of course," Olivia replied. "We're always here for you, you know that."

"I do." Mallory nodded. "But it's nice to hear you say it."

"I guess we'd better start packing," Avery said. "Let us know if you need any help with your other worries. Grant can pitch in if you need a hand with patients, and I'm happy to map out exposure patterns."

"I appreciate it," Mallory said. "I hope it won't be necessary, though."

"Hang in there," Avery said.

"I will," Mallory promised. "Tell Grant and Logan I said hello."

"We'll come see you in the morning," Olivia said.

With a final hug, her friends left the clinic and Mallory

returned to her office. It seemed paradoxically smaller now that she was alone. The walls closed in, making her feel claustrophobic. She tried to focus on her computer, but sitting at her desk left her feeling restless and unsettled. She needed to move so she could think.

Things were quiet in the clinic. There hadn't been any new patients in over an hour, and the nurse practitioner was also on duty right now. It was the perfect time for her to slip away to the gym.

The promise of a workout put a spring in her step, and it didn't take long for Mallory to find the nurse practitioner and let her know she would be gone for a bit. Then she headed for her cabin to change clothes.

Talking with Avery and Mallory had given her a lot to think about, and their unconditional support made her realize that no matter what she chose, her friends would be there for her. It was a comforting point of stability in her life, one that she didn't take for granted.

Especially since this voyage was shaping up to be so unusual.

Chapter 12

The morning sky was a vibrant blue as the *Abigail Adams* docked in Charleston. Everest stood at the railing, enjoying the cool breeze on his face as the ship completed the delicate maneuvers required to snug up to the dock. He never got tired of watching this process; it was amazing how the officers on the bridge could coax such a large ship with a little nudge here or a thrust there.

Probably a lesson to be learned in that, he mused. But he wasn't in a philosophical mood at the moment. Now that they had docked, he had an hour to get the police on board before the passengers lined up to disembark. He hoped they would take their time gathering evidence. It would create a PR headache if the vacationers saw the police wheeling a sheet-covered body through the halls. Maybe he could convince them to wait to do that until after everyone was off the ship. It was a cold case, after all, so a few more hours wouldn't make much of a difference.

A small cluster of people stood on the dock next to a gurney. Light glinted off the lenses of their sunglasses as they stared up at the ship. They all wore navy wind-breakers with the word *Police* printed on the back in bright yellow, but Everest would have recognized them without the identifier. It was the way they stood—feet braced, arms folded, their bodies relaxed but wary. It was the default body language of cops and soldiers the world over. Even now, years after getting out of the ser-vice, Everest caught himself assuming a modified pa-rade rest stance whenever he stood. It was habit, a pose so ingrained into his muscle memory that he did it with-out conscious thought.

The group gave him a friendly nod as he approached. "Morning," said one of the men.

"Hello," said Everest. He introduced himself, shak-ing hands and filing away names. "Thanks for coming out this morning."

"No problem," said Will, the officer who seemed to be the leader of the small group. "We're happy to help with all your body disposal needs."

Everest chuckled, appreciating the gallows humor. "I don't think you'll have any trouble," he said, leading them up the gangway. "We figured you would need a lot of time to collect evidence, so we're going to terminate the voyage here and evacuate the ship."

"That won't be necessary," Will said. "Our orders are simply to retrieve the body and take it to the morgue."

Everest stopped walking and turned to stare at the man. "Are you serious? You're not worried about evi-dence collection?"

Will shook his head. "Norfolk PD has already reached out to us. They feel the scene has been too compromised to yield anything usable, so they just want the body."

Everest had a hard time believing that, but elected to keep his mouth shut. He wasn't a cop. He didn't know all the policies and procedures they had to follow when confronted with a murder victim. It did seem strange that they appeared so indifferent to the prospect of actually investigating the area, though.

"Is that the normal course of action?" he asked, resuming his progress onto the ship. "Leaving the scene untouched, I mean."

Will shrugged. "It's a little unusual, but this comes straight from the top."

"I see."

"Between you and me," Will said, his voice taking on a confessional quality, "I think the boss doesn't want us to open up any kind of case here. It would mess with our stats, and we don't need that kind of publicity right now. Better for us to pass things along to Norfolk and let them deal with the fallout."

It made sense, but Everest didn't like it. It felt wrong somehow for the police to simply collect the body and leave. He'd hoped they would find justice for this man, whoever he was. But how could they do that when they weren't going to try to obtain any kind of forensic evidence that might point to his killer?

Maybe I'm wrong, he thought as he led them through the ship. Maybe there was enough evidence on the body itself to solve the crime. He hoped so, for the unknown victim's sake.

He nodded at Taylor Higgins, the young man he'd asked to watch the room overnight. Since the motivation for the attack on Mallory was still unknown, he hadn't wanted to take any chances by leaving the room unsecured. He wanted to believe the man who had hit her had simply been looking to rob the room, but this voyage was shaping up to be so strange anything was possible.

Everest unlocked the room and held the door open for the officers and their gurney. Once they were inside, he closed the door and led them to the closet. "The body's in here," he said, pointing to the wall.

Will knelt and pulled his phone off the clip on his belt. He flipped on a spotlight and aimed it inside the shadowy gap, leaning in close to see. "Yep," he said, standing up and reholstering his phone. "You've got a body."

He gestured to the other men on the team, and they stepped forward with a black bag that Everest quickly learned was full of tools. It took a matter of minutes for the police to cut the panel of drywall free, exposing the sad scene beneath.

Everest forced himself to look, to register what he was seeing. Based on Will's earlier words, he didn't have a lot of confidence this murder would be solved. The least he could do was pay respect to the victim, before he was taken away and passed from one police department to another.

It was a depressing sight. The body was wrapped in a thick plastic tarp, which obscured the man's features. Everest could see snippets of fabric pressed against the wrap, along with fine granules of what looked like rock salt. *That would explain the lack of smell,* he thought. No wonder no one had noticed this addition during the construction of the ship.

A pang of sadness hit Everest as he watched the police arrange the body on the gurney. If this really was the missing employee, that meant he'd been hidden away in the very place he'd worked. How many times had his friends walked past this spot, oblivious to his presence on the other side of the thin wall?

It didn't take long for the team to place the remains in a thick, black body bag and secure it to the gurney. One of the men drew a white sheet over the bag, a small gesture that somehow softened the horror of the moment.

They opened the door and wheeled their burden into the hall. Everest glanced at the damage to the wall, then turned to Will. "You guys sure you don't want to take a look around?"

Will shook his head. "Not necessary. We got what we came for."

"Okay." Everest knew it would be pointless for him to argue further. Will wasn't going to contradict any orders he'd been given simply to make Everest feel better about the poor man who'd been trapped in this room.

Everest escorted the team off the ship. "Let me know if you need anything," he said.

Will stuck out his hand, and Everest shook it. "Appreciate it," Will said. "I don't think I'll need to call you, but I've got your number just in case."

Everest watched the team load the gurney into the back of a white van, feeling at a loss. He'd spent about an hour last night working on a response plan to investigate the communication hubs after the passengers had disembarked. Even though he didn't know what the mysterious gray substance was, he wanted to act as though it truly was radioactive to ensure the safety of his team and anyone else who came into contact with it. But now that the passengers weren't going to leave the ship, it might not be safe to go forward. It might be better to leave the material undisturbed, so as not to increase the risk of exposure to those on board.

Mallory wouldn't be happy, he mused. And he couldn't blame her. She'd outlined her concerns to the captain, but he hadn't seemed to take her seriously. Still, she didn't seem like the type of person to simply roll over and accept this turn of events, and he could only imagine what her response would be.

The thought of her brown eyes sparking with temper was enough to make him smile for the first time that morning. He admired her spirit and liked the way she carried herself, especially in response to the unexpected. She was strong and sure of herself, and she would have made one hell of an army officer.

He needed to inform her of this turn of events. She deserved to hear it from him, and the sooner the better. Then he'd seek out the captain. Even though the police didn't need the *Abigail Adams* to stay in port, Everest still felt the journey should end here. The presence of the mystery material made him uneasy, and he couldn't shake the unnerving sensation that he was missing something. He'd learned in Iraq to trust his instincts, and he couldn't start ignoring them now.

One man had already died, but there were hundreds of other lives at stake. And while he hadn't known about the first victim, he was determined to do everything in his power to ensure there weren't any more.

"You have got to be kidding me." Mallory stared up at Everest, unwilling to believe the news he'd just told her.

His lips pressed together in a thin line. To his credit, he didn't look any happier than she felt, but it was cold comfort right now. "I'm afraid so. The police said they don't need to collect any evidence, so there's no reason to remove the passengers and delay the voyage."

"I can give you a reason," she muttered. "In fact, I can give you several reasons. Where should I start?"

Everest held up his hands in a "don't shoot" gesture.

"You're preaching to the choir here. Have you had any more patients?"

"A few," she said. "It's been a slow trickle, which to be honest isn't that unusual for a ship of this size."

"But that's good, right? No massive influx of people with sunburns or stomach troubles must mean things aren't as bad as you thought."

Mallory nodded reluctantly. "I suppose you're right. But I still think that stuff—whatever it is—is bad news."

"It's strange, I'll grant you that. I think we're stuck with it, though, at least until this trip ends. Since you're not seeing a huge uptick in the number of patients, I doubt the captain will entertain the idea of cutting the trip short. You saw the way he reacted to that suggestion yesterday, and that was when I thought the police would want to force us to stay in port."

A surge of disappointment threatened to overwhelm her, but Mallory knew Everest was right. Aside from a handful of patients whose symptoms could be explained by the cruise ship virus, she didn't have any concrete evidence that the mystery material posed a hazard to the rest of the passengers. Her hunch simply wasn't going to cut it.

"Have you heard from your friends yet?" It was a long shot, but maybe if a member of the Chemical Corps recognized the stuff as dangerous, the captain would be forced to listen. The company officials might not like the idea of cutting the inaugural voyage of their new flagship short, but if they continued to cruise knowing people were in danger, it would open them up to all sorts of lawsuits and bad press. Businessmen listened to dollar signs, if nothing else. It was possible the liability they'd face would convince them to do the right thing, even if her medical opinion didn't.

Everest shook his head, and her heart dropped. "Not yet. I'll give them a few more hours and then try to call."

"Hopefully no news is good news," she said. "If it was something they'd recognized on sight, surely they would have called you immediately."

"Probably so," he said. "Provided they've read the message. They might be doing a field training exercise, which limits their access to email."

A heavy stone of worry settled in her stomach. Mallory hadn't even considered the possibility his communication hadn't been seen yet. When Everest had contacted his friends, she'd felt a surge of relief at the fact they were *doing* something to identify the gray material. But maybe that hadn't been the case after all.

"Do you think we'll have an answer before we dock in New York City?" There were three days left in the trip before the ship would dock in New York Harbor in time for the Fourth of July festivities.

"I hope so," Everest said somberly.

A dark thought floated to the surface of her mind, and Mallory shook her head as a sense of dejection settled over her like a cloak. "Is it even worth pursuing at this point? There's not much time left, and most of the passengers spend their days exploring the city in shore excursions, which limits their exposure to the material in the boxes. Maybe I should just drop it."

Everest studied her face a moment, his blue eyes kind but piercing. "Is that really what you think? You don't strike me as the type to quit when things don't go your way."

Her cheeks warmed at his compliment, but she tried to play it cool. "I don't want to stop investigating. But I don't think we'll find anything conclusive in the time we have left." And given the captain's reaction to her warning yesterday, she might very well be risking her career if she kept pushing the issue.

"Maybe we won't. But we have to try."

"We?" she asked. A flare of hope cut through her disappointment like a glimmer of sun on a cloudy day. "Does that mean you believe me?"

Everest lifted one shoulder. "I honestly don't know if this material is radioactive. But something about the situation seems off to me. I don't feel comfortable ignoring your observations, especially when we don't know anything about the putty."

The weight of her worry lifted a bit, and she felt a surge of gratitude as she stared up at Everest. It meant a lot to know that he supported her, even though she didn't quite believe in herself.

"So where do we go from here?"

Everest ran a hand through his hair. "I'm of two minds right now. We need to search the ship and determine exactly which boxes contain the putty so we have an idea of the scope of the problem. It would be nice to have my team help with this, but if the material really is radioactive or otherwise dangerous, I don't want them exposed to it."

Mallory nodded. "I agree. The fewer people who come into contact with this stuff, the better."

"I figured you'd say as much. Which leaves the two of us to search the entire ship." A half smile flitted across his face, and he smoothed his hand down the flat expanse of his stomach. "I've let myself go a bit after getting discharged from the army, but I think we can make progress. If you'll have me, that is."

Mallory laughed, ignoring the way her stomach flip-flopped in response to his question. It was oh-so-tempting to read too much into his words, especially in light of her recent conversation with Avery and Olivia. But she pushed aside the distraction and focused on the issue at hand. "Of course I will."

His blue eyes were warm as he regarded her. "Shall we get started?"

Mallory felt optimistic for the first time since finding the material in Jeff's room.

"Ready when you are."

Chapter 13

The box was surprisingly light, and for a second, Wesley feared he'd picked up the wrong one. He double-checked the label to be sure; it still read Camera Supplies, which he'd been told was the code that identified the material he needed to complete this phase of the plan.

He wanted to check out the contents right away, but he forced himself to walk calmly back to his cabin so as not to draw attention to himself. It was difficult, though— even though the box was unadorned, he felt like a kid on Christmas morning carrying his gift from Santa.

Once he was safely inside with the door locked behind him, Wesley put the box on the bed and pulled out his pocketknife. He made quick work of the tape sealing the box and stood there for a second with the flaps closed, enjoying the sense of anticipation fizzing through his system. He hadn't been a part of placing the radioactive material throughout the ship, and he'd been looking forward to taking a more active role in the plot.

This was his chance.

Wesley took a deep breath and pulled open the flaps, peering at the contents inside. Twelve wrapped bundles stared up at him, each about the size of a cell phone. He picked one up, gingerly turning it over in his hands. It weighed about as much as a cup of coffee, and the bands of tape wrapped around it made it smooth to the touch. Two thin wires, one green, one red, protruded from a small digital display panel mounted to the top of the device, and there was a bump under the tape that covered the spot where the wires attached to the material within.

It was hard to believe that such a small, unassuming object would be the agent of massive destruction. Wesley brushed aside a vague sense of disappointment and returned the package to the box, nestling it among its fellows. He'd been expecting something bigger, a flashier device. But this was probably better. Thanks to the small size, he'd be able to anchor each package to the lid of the communication hubs spread throughout the ship. And although they didn't look like much, he had it on good authority the small bundles packed a big punch. Once he had them dispersed throughout the ship, the *Abigail Adams* would be a floating time bomb.

This was the first box of charges; he'd get the second when the ship sailed up the river and docked in Philadelphia, and a third when she stopped in Boston. Thirty-six explosive bundles in all, and he was responsible for placing them before they made port in New York Harbor. It would be difficult, but not impossible.

He slipped his hand into his pocket and ran his finger along the small electronic jammer he carried with him at all times. It was a useful little thing that emitted an electromagnetic pulse whenever he activated it, interfering with any electronic devices located within a twelve-foot radius. Everest thought there was an issue with the security cameras on board, but in truth they were fine. Wesley had been using the jammer to move around the ship undetected, which had allowed him to sneak up on Dr. Watkins without any video record of his movements.

He hadn't actually meant to hurt her. But when he'd seen her entering Jeff's former cabin, he'd panicked. No good could come of her poking around in the room, and he had to keep her from finding the body. So he'd crept up behind her and clipped her on the back of the head with the empty ice bucket.

She'd dropped to the floor with a thud, presenting him with another issue. He'd been so worried about keeping her from finding the body he hadn't thought what to do with her once she was incapacitated.

In any event, it hadn't mattered. His heart had nearly stopped when Everest had entered the room a moment later, but fortunately Wesley had been able to convince him another man had hurt the doctor. Now he just had to keep stringing his boss along with updates from his "investigation."

But first, he needed to update his contact.

"Yes?"

"I've received the first shipment," Wesley said. "Everything is on track here."

"Excellent. Has the doctor created any trouble?"

"Nothing I can't handle," he replied.

"Good. We have another agent on board, should you require assistance."

"Really?" Wesley couldn't keep the surprise out of his voice. He'd thought he was the only one. It was strangely comforting to know someone else was working toward the same goal.

"Your captain will be happy to help, if the need arises."

That was a shock. Of all the people on board, Wesley would never have guessed the captain was involved. It was delightfully ironic that the man charged with keeping the ship and her passengers safe was plotting to destroy it all.

"I had no idea," Wesley said. "That's good to know."

"Only use him in an emergency," the man cautioned. "The captain does not know the full extent of the plan, and he is not a true believer like yourself. He is a tool, not a leader."

"I understand," Wesley said. He didn't anticipate needing any help, but if Everest and the doctor kept poking around, he might need the captain to step in. The two of them would be forced to obey a direct order from the man or else risk getting fired and removed from the ship. Which might not be such a bad thing. With Everest gone, Wesley would be in charge. And there would be no one to police his actions...

"Keep me updated," the man said, interrupting Wesley's thoughts. "Don't do anything to draw undue attention to the ship. We're so close to the end—nothing must interfere with the execution of our plans."

"Of course." So much for his idea to have Everest escorted off the ship. If the *Abigail Adams* lost her head of security and her doctor, the news would ripple throughout the company and shine a spotlight on their voyage. Both Everest and Dr. Watkins would talk, and even though their story of radioactive material on the ship was fanciful, people would listen.

Both the president and vice president would be in New York City for the holiday. They were scheduled to watch the Fourth of July fireworks from the harbor, close to where the ship would dock. If the Secret Service got wind of Everest and the doctor's fears, they'd cancel the event.

Wesley would still be able to blow up the ship, scattering radioactive debris over a good portion of the city. But the event would be much more spectacular if he took out the country's leadership at the same time.

There was no help for it. Wesley was simply going to have to figure out a way to keep Everest and the doctor distracted so they didn't cause trouble. There were only three days left in the voyage. Three days before he avenged Ryan's death. This was his best chance to make things right for his brother and his family.

He couldn't fail now.

Everest braced his hands on the arms of the chair and sighed quietly. He and Mallory had been taking turns climbing onto furniture to reach the black boxes mounted high on the walls of the ship, and it was now his job to hold the chair steady while Mallory checked out the communication hub. It wasn't a difficult task, but their positions put her curvy bottom right at his eye level. The first couple of stops he'd been able to ignore the sight, but he was quickly running out of self-control.

She rose on her tiptoes, the muscles of her legs and bottom flexing under the fabric of her pants. Everest closed his eyes, digging deep for discipline. Mallory had suggested they take turns examining the boxes so one person didn't receive all the exposure to the material. It had seemed like a good idea at the time, but now he was having second thoughts.

"I can't quite get the cover off," Mallory muttered. She stretched and flexed, clearly wrestling with the plastic as she tried to pry the lid free. Her movements caused her to bounce a bit, and a flush of heat suffused Everest's body as he gave up trying to ignore the temptation right in front of him.

"Do you need any help?" The question sounded a bit strangled, so he cleared his throat and tried again. He forced his gaze away from her body and tried to see the box she was fighting with.

"No." She grunted and her muscles tensed. A popping sound punctuated her reply, and she let out a satisfied sigh. "I got it."

"Good," he said quietly. That meant this torture would be over soon. Forget taking turns—he was going to examine the rest of the boxes. Anything to keep his mind on the task at hand and off Mallory's body. If he allowed himself to be distracted much longer, he was going to embarrass himself.

"This one has it," she said, sounding grim. She replaced the cover and climbed down, and Everest stepped back to give her room. He expected her to head for the door, but she turned around to look at him. She was so close her breasts grazed his chest as she moved, and he sucked in a breath at the accidental contact.

"That's the third box so far." Her eyebrows drew together in a frown. "I know it's a little early to draw conclusions, but it doesn't seem like the material has been randomly placed to me. What do you think?"

Everest ignored his physical reaction to Mallory's proximity and focused on the observations they'd made so far. They'd looked at five boxes, and the three that had contained the gray material were all located in passenger cabins. The two that had lacked the material were in a supply closet and a hallway. It was a limited sample set, but he had to admit there did appear to be a pattern.

"I agree," he said. "It looks like the material is in spots where people spend a lot of time."

Mallory's brown eyes shone with concern. "I don't like it."

A kernel of worry formed in his stomach, an unpleasant gnawing sensation that overshadowed the tingling warmth triggered by Mallory's nearness. "It doesn't look good so far," he said. "But let's not panic yet. We've got a lot of rooms left to check."

She nodded and bit her bottom lip. "You're right." After a few seconds, her expression cleared and she smiled up at him. "Thanks again for helping me with this. Having you with me makes me feel like things are going to be okay."

"I'm glad I could help." He didn't know what they were going to do with the information they'd gathered so far, but Mallory's confidence in him made him feel ten feet tall. It was a sensation he hadn't experienced in a while, and he had to admit it was nice. For the first time in a long time, he felt whole again.

Did she move closer? Or was he suddenly more aware of her? Either way, something shifted between them, and the air grew heavy with possibility. Mallory's eyes widened, a flare of heat sparking in the depths of her gaze. Her lips parted and she drew in a quick little breath. The soft, intimate sound pulled him in, and he leaned forward, his eyes on her mouth.

Her tongue darted out to swipe across her lips, leaving them shiny and ready for his kiss. Need surged in Everest's chest, and he fought the urge to grab Mallory and pull her close. He wanted to feel her curves flatten against his body and fill his nose with her scent. But he knew if he moved too fast she'd pull away. He forced himself to go slow, to give her every opportunity to step back as he lowered his head.

But she didn't.

Everest brushed his mouth against hers, their lips

barely touching. Mallory stiffened and he stilled, freezing in place. She reminded him of a spooked deer, ready to bolt at the slightest provocation.

So he waited, giving her time to change her mind.

The moment stretched between them, but he didn't dare move. He wanted Mallory with an intensity sharper than any he'd felt in years. But more important, he wanted her to want him. He was eager to explore this connection between them, but if she didn't match his excitement, he was prepared to walk away. He knew from experience it was better to be alone than to have a partner whose heart really wasn't in it.

After an eternity of heartbeats, Mallory let out a gentle sigh. She stepped into his arms, her muscles relaxing as she snugged up against his chest. Her hands found the back of his neck and slid into his hair.

His heart beat hard against his ribs, and Everest was certain Mallory could feel it as he held her close. But if she noticed, she didn't say a word. Instead, she linked her fingers behind his head and pulled him down, silently asking for another kiss.

Everest was only too happy to grant her request.

His mouth found hers again, but this was no tentative inquiry. Mallory had responded to his earlier question, and now that he knew how she felt, he no longer had to go slowly.

He loosened the leash on his self-control, allowing some of his hunger for Mallory to rise to the surface. She tasted faintly of chocolate and bread, likely a testament to her breakfast. He inhaled deeply, drawing in the honey and melon scent of her skin. He didn't know what kind of bath gel she used, but he was never going to look at a cantaloupe the same way again.

Her hands trailed across his body, her touch growing bolder as he continued to explore her mouth. Goose bumps rose on his skin as she skimmed her fingertips down his side, her hand pausing at his belt to grip the loose material of his shirt in her fist. The fabric pulled on his shoulders and across his chest, sending a jolt of heat through him. He'd love nothing more than to shed the interfering garment and give Mallory free access to his body, but this wasn't the time or the place to let his libido overrule his sense of professionalism.

Besides, once their clothes started coming off, he'd have to show her his leg. Or rather, what was left of it. And while he got the impression that a doctor like Mallory wouldn't blink at the sight of his injury, it wasn't exactly a romantic sight.

He eased back, reluctant to stop kissing her. But it was important to get back to the business at hand, before he forgot what it was they were doing in the first place.

Mallory stared up at him, her lips slightly parted as she frowned slightly. Emotions swirled in the depths of her brown eyes, and Everest was able to detect confusion, arousal and what looked like a flash of relief before her expression cleared and she straightened her shoulders, putting a bit more space between them.

"Well," she said, after a few seconds of silence. Her voice had a husky note that made him think of satin sheets and champagne, and his imagination kicked into overdrive, picturing Mallory wearing nothing more than a scrap of red lace. It was an enticing sight, even if it wasn't real.

At least, not yet.

Everest took a deep breath, tightening his grip on his self-control before his desires got the best of him. He was suddenly very aware of the two double beds in the room, and he shifted to put them at his back. They needed to leave the privacy of this cabin and return to the more public areas of the ship. Short of a cold shower, it was the only way Everest was going to be able to reset his brain.

"Well," he echoed. He ran a hand through his hair and felt his face heat. Mallory had to think he was some kind of skirt-chasing oaf, the way he'd kissed her in the middle of an empty cabin while they were busy searching for this mystery material. *Way to pick a moment*, he thought wryly. He cleared his throat. They needed to keep searching, but he wanted to give Mallory an out in case she no longer wanted to be alone with him. "Shall we continue, or would you rather stop?"

Her response was immediate. "Let's keep going." She lifted her hand and rubbed a finger across her lips, then gave him a shy smile. "Maybe we can focus on one thing at a time, though?"

"Of course," he said quickly. "I'm sorry about that. I didn't mean to—"

"You don't have to apologize," she interrupted. "I'm not upset. I rather enjoyed it, actually." She sounded almost surprised, as if she hadn't thought that was possible. "But let's wait until we're someplace private to do it again."

Everest lifted one eyebrow. "I'm not disagreeing with you, but this cabin seems pretty private to me."

Mallory laughed softly. "Fair enough. But I'm sure we can find a location where we're not in danger of being discovered at any moment."

Her words knocked the last of his fantasies right out of his head, and he realized with a small shock that she was right. He'd been so caught up in kissing her he hadn't stopped to think about what would happen if a passenger walked in and found them pawing at each other in the middle of the cabin. Would the captain have fired him immediately, or waited until the voyage was over before handing him a pink slip?

Fortunately, he wasn't going to find out. "Let's get back to it," he said. The sooner they completed their investigation of the ship's communication hubs, the sooner they could find a quiet spot to talk. It wasn't the noblest motivation, but it would get the job done.

Mallory nodded and started for the door. He moved to follow her, and his view of her reminded him of an important point. "Just one thing," he said, as she reached for the doorknob.

She paused and glanced back at him, one eyebrow raised in inquiry. "What's that?"

"I'm going to take care of the rest of the climbing."

It didn't take long for Mallory and Everest to fall back into a working rhythm as they moved from room to room, checking the boxes and taking notes. Their earlier observations still held true; the boxes in passenger cabins all contained the gray putty, while the hubs in hallways or other less-trafficked areas were empty. There had to be an explanation for the unequal distribution of the material, and Mallory had a sinking feeling her concern about the situation wasn't misplaced paranoia after all...

She glanced at Everest, trying to read his expression for some clue as to his thoughts. But he'd been strangely quiet after their kiss, and she hadn't really felt like talking either. She still felt unsettled, and she didn't trust herself to speak coherently right now.

The kiss had been a revelation, answering questions she hadn't known she had, and stirring up feelings she'd never thought she'd experience again. Her first instinct had been to pull away, to break the connection and literally run down the hall, putting as much distance as possible between herself and Everest. But she was done letting fear rule her life. If she was going to move forward, she had to take a chance.

Everest had been so careful, so thoughtful. He'd given her every opportunity to change her mind or turn him down, and his calm, patient presence was a big part of why she'd been able to finally relax and take what he'd offered.

She hadn't really known what to expect. It had been ages since she'd let a man get close enough to kiss her. For several years after the rape, she hadn't been interested in any kind of sexual contact. Later, she'd been too scared to try anything.

As Everest had dipped his head to close the distance between them, Mallory had half expected to feel nothing, to find that her ability to respond to a man's touch had disappeared thanks to a lack of use.

She couldn't have been more wrong.

Everest's kiss had triggered a chain reaction of sensations in her body that had threatened to overwhelm her. It had been almost intoxicating, the way her body had responded without any input from her brain. Her stomach had fluttered like a butterfly wing, her skin had tingled, and a flush of warmth had spread through her chest and down her limbs. Her head had spun, leaving her no choice but to grab his shoulders or risk falling down. His muscles had been warm and solid under her hands, heightening the physical differences between them and reminding her of his strength.

The loss of control should have scared her, but it had actually left her feeling energized and eager for more.

She studied him now, sneaking glances as they moved from room to room. He didn't seem to be affected by any lingering aftershocks from their kiss, and she had to wonder if it had been as earth-shattering for him as it was for her.

Probably not, she mused. He'd likely had a normal dating life, and she hadn't given him any reason to suspect her experiences had been any different. She'd warned him about her trouble trusting men, but that was hardly uncommon.

How would he respond when she told him about her rape? Would he pull away and decide a relationship with her wasn't worth the trouble? She'd been pleasantly surprised by her body's reaction to his kiss, but what would happen when things started to heat up between them? She couldn't promise she wouldn't panic when they ventured into more intimate territory.

She could imagine it all too well. Everest touching her, moving over her. Terror clawing up her throat, trapping her breath in her chest until spots of color danced in her vision. *Nothing sexier than a panic attack at such a crucial moment*, she thought wryly.

Maybe it wouldn't be like that, though. After all, she was attracted to Everest, and she wanted to explore this connection she felt with him. Surely that would be enough to keep the hysteria at bay.

But what if it isn't? whispered her inner voice of doubt. What if no matter how much her brain insisted she was ready to take this step, her body couldn't handle it?

She was going to have to talk to Everest. There was simply no way she could keep him in the dark about her past, not when there was a very real chance he would be affected by her present responses. He deserved to know what he was getting into and to have a choice in the matter. He might not be willing to stick around, and she had to emotionally prepare herself for rejection. But there was an equal possibility he would stay, and she felt a little thrill at the prospect.

"Everything okay?" Everest's voice cut through her thoughts, dragging her out of the land of what-ifs and returning her focus to their current situation.

"Just worried," she said. It was easy to pass off her distractedness as concern over their findings, and it wasn't really a lie. She was troubled by the way things were shaping up, but she didn't know what they could do about it. They had to talk to the captain, and hopefully he would listen now that they had more evidence on their side.

"Me, too," he admitted. "I was hoping we wouldn't find any more of this stuff, but it seems to be everywhere."

"You still haven't heard from your friend?"

He frowned. "No. Which is unusual—he's usually a lot more responsive." He unclipped his phone and looked at the display, then swore softly. "I've got no signal," he said. "No wonder I haven't gotten a reply."

"This must be a dead zone on the ship," Mallory said. It wasn't uncommon to have cell phone issues thanks to the architecture of the vessel, with all its metal and compartments.

"I'm going to run to the railing and see if I can get a few bars of signal," he said.

"I'll head to the next room," Mallory said. "Meet me there when you're done?"

"Yeah," he said, a bit absently. He started to walk away, head bent as he focused on his phone.

Mallory watched him go for a second, allowing herself to be distracted by the play of muscles in his back. The slight hitch in his gait was no longer so noticeable to her; she'd grown used to his unique walking rhythm.

He seemed to have overcome his embarrassment from

the moment on the bridge, when his prosthetic leg had hit the desk and revealed his secret. She hoped he would tell her about it, and the circumstances surrounding his injury. Given his military service, it didn't take a rocket scientist to guess he'd likely been injured while on deployment. But she'd like to hear his story in his own words.

She moved to the next cabin and knocked on the door, letting out a small sigh of relief when no one answered. Most of the passengers were in the city, enjoying one of the many shore excursions the company offered. That made it a lot easier to search the ship.

She unlocked the door and opened it slowly, calling out as she entered in case the occupants were asleep or in the bathroom. "Hello?"

When there was no response, she walked fully into the room and propped open the door so Everest could get inside. Then she grabbed the desk chair and rolled it over to the corner, under the communication hub. She put one leg up on the seat and prepared to stand when a hand snaked around her waist and jerked her back hard.

Her back hit something solid, knocking the breath out of her chest. She grabbed at the arm holding her, trying to push away. If this was Everest's idea of a joke, it wasn't funny.

"Stop it," she said. She'd meant to scream the words, but they came out as more of a whisper. A hand clapped over her mouth, and an instant later, a sticky-sweet scent filled her nose and made the room spin.

Panic slammed into her and she thrashed about, kicking out with her legs in an attempt to dislodge her attacker. She couldn't be at the mercy of a man. Not again.

But her wild struggling only made him tighten his grip. The fight drained out of her as weakness stole over her body, her muscles going numb to her commands. She sagged in the man's arms, helpless against the encroaching darkness.

Chapter 14

Everest stepped to the railing and frowned, tamping down his impatience as his phone registered a signal and began to download emails. How long had he been without service?

Normally, the lack of reliable cell phone service wasn't an issue, as the portable radios and pagers used by the staff ensured he was plugged in to what was going on with the ship. But these were unusual circumstances, and he hoped his friends had good news for him.

After what seemed like an eternity, the emails finished downloading. He scanned them quickly, dismissing one after another until he finally saw the reply he'd been waiting for. He clicked it open, and his heart dropped when he saw the simple message: CALL ME NOW!

Everest cursed quietly and wasted no time punching in the number. Peter MacKenzie was an expert in the CBRN—chemical, biological, radiological and nuclear—

field, well versed in the myriad of threats that existed in the darker corners of the world. He was also rather unflappable. The exclamation point on his message might as well have been a scream, which only heightened Everest's anxiety.

"What the hell took you so long?" Peter snapped. "I've been trying to call you—why haven't you answered?"

"Bad service," Everest replied shortly. "Talk to me about this stuff. What is it?"

"I can't be sure just from the pictures," Peter said. "But it looks an awful lot like enriched uranium."

Everest tightened his grip on the phone as his guts turned to water. "But that's not possible," he said weakly. "It's not the right consistency. According to the guy who touched it, this stuff is pliable, like kids' clay. Enriched uranium is more cake-like."

"Normally, that's true," Peter said. "But it's not hard to break that stuff up into tiny pieces or even a powder that can then be added to pretty much anything."

"That's a big leap, don't you think?" Everest said. "Why go to all the trouble of modifying the uranium like that? Seems more dangerous than it's worth, if you ask me." He didn't doubt the possibility, but it was a rather complicated explanation. In his experience, things were rarely so convoluted.

Peter paused, and in the heavy silence that followed, Everest got the impression his friend was debating on telling him something. "You didn't hear this from me," Peter said, his voice dropping as he spoke, "but we made a pretty alarming finding in Afghanistan last month. One of the local warlords had been bragging about his 'new weapon.' The chatter was that he'd acquired some uranium and was building dirty bombs. The CIA felt the intelligence was credible enough, so they used a drone strike to take him out. Our team was sent in to examine the aftermath."

"And?" A band of worry tightened around Everest's chest, making it hard to breathe. He had a feeling he wasn't going to like what came next.

"We found stuff," Peter confirmed. "Not much, but enough to be troubling. From what we could piece together, they were pulverizing what material they had and adding it to suicide vests. Intel revealed they were going to target Islamabad first, and depending on how that run went, they'd aim for Western targets."

"My God," Everest whispered.

"I know," Peter said. "We stopped this guy, but how many more are out there?"

"Where did they get the uranium? That's not the kind of thing you can just pick up at the corner store."

"That's probably the worst part," Peter replied. "We traced it back to a facility in the States."

"What?" Everest couldn't keep the shock out of his voice. "How in the hell—?"

"We're still looking into it," Peter said grimly.

"But that means…"

"Yeah," Peter said. "If there's a leak, it's possible your material may have come from the same source."

Everest was stunned speechless. The idea that the material in the boxes was radioactive had gone from implausible to all too possible, and his stomach felt queasy as the ramifications began to sink in. The putty was scattered throughout the ship. If it really was sprinkled with enriched uranium, the ship was essentially a floating nuclear waste dump.

"You've got to cut the trip short," Peter said. "At least until we confirm if the mystery material is radioactive."

Everest knew his friend was right, but he didn't think

the captain would agree. "I don't know if that's possible," he said.

Peter made an exasperated sound in his throat. "You don't have another choice here," he said. "Look, I've got some time off coming to me. Where's your next stop? I can meet you there and come aboard and do a quick scan with a Geiger counter. If the results are negative, you guys can be on your merry way. But if I find something…" Peter trailed off, letting Everest fill in the blanks.

"It's not that I don't agree with you," Everest said. "But we tried to get the captain to terminate the voyage in Charleston due to some other circumstances. He refused."

"Did you tell him about the stuff in the boxes?" Peter challenged.

"We did," Everest confirmed. "We didn't have any proof the material is dangerous, aside from the symptoms of people exposed to it."

"What kind of symptoms?" Peter's voice sharpened with interest.

"Mostly stomach upset," Everest said. "One man actually touched the stuff, and his skin broke out in welts and sores."

Peter hummed thoughtfully. "That's consistent with radiation exposure."

"I know," Everest said. "But the gastrointestinal symptoms are also consistent with norovirus, which is what the ship's doctor initially suspected."

"What does he think now?"

"He is actually a she," Everest said. "And she's the one who suspected the substance was radioactive in the first place."

"That's quite a catch," Peter said.

The compliment made Everest smile, despite the circumstances. Even though Mallory deserved all the credit, he felt a small surge of pride in her abilities and intelligence. No one else would have put things together the way she had, and even if the material wasn't spiked with enriched uranium, she still deserved praise for being so conscientious about her job.

"So where are you docking next?" Peter pressed.

"Philadelphia," Everest responded. "But you can't be the one to come on board and do the test. You know that breaks all kinds of regulations about military operations in the US."

"It'll be fine," Peter said. Everest imagined his friend waving his hand as he dismissed the concern. "I won't be operating in an official capacity. Just meeting a friend for lunch, that's all."

"You're really worried about this, aren't you?" Peter's insistence on testing the material himself made Everest realize just how seriously he viewed the situation. A chill skittered down his spine, and he was suddenly acutely aware of the fact he and Mallory had been close to the stuff all morning long. He hadn't been that concerned before, when the possibility that the putty was radioactive had seemed so remote. But after talking to Peter, he wasn't so sure. What kind of damage had they done to themselves as they'd searched the ship?

"I'll sleep better knowing for sure," Peter said. "Email me your location. I'll meet you in Philly tomorrow."

"I will," Everest said.

"And quit searching for the stuff," his friend continued. "Until we know if the material is hot, try to minimize any exposure."

"Yeah," Everest said, his stomach heavy with worry. He *felt* fine, but paranoia made his skin prickle as he recalled everything he'd ever learned about the damages caused by radiation exposure. Images of charred skin flashed through his mind, each more unsettling than the last.

"I'm sure you're fine," Peter said, apparently reading his thoughts. "I'll see you tomorrow."

Everest ended the call and quickly typed out an email detailing their docking location in Philadelphia. It would be good to see Peter tomorrow, though he wished the circumstances were different.

He slipped his phone into his pocket and headed back down the hall in search of Mallory. She'd likely be happy to know they would get some solid answers tomorrow, one way or another.

The door to one of the cabins was propped open, and he gave a perfunctory rap on the door as he entered. "Good news," he began. He drew up short and scanned the room, frowning. Mallory wasn't there.

A cloying scent hung in the air, and he sniffed experimentally as he moved around the room. Chloroform. He was certain of it.

The realization made his heart drop, and Mallory's disappearance took on a new, sinister edge. She wasn't taking a bathroom break and she hadn't been called back to the clinic. Someone had taken her.

The blood froze in his veins, and he hit the door at a run. He didn't know who had taken Mallory, or why they wanted her. But he had to find her.

Before it was too late.

Mallory woke up suddenly, her head pounding and her throat dry. She sat up, fists at the ready, then slumped back as a wave of nausea threatened to overwhelm her.

It took her a second to register her surroundings. She was in a passenger cabin, if the furniture was anything to go by. The room was dim, except for a thin strip of light on the floor by the edge of the door.

One of the shadows at the end of the bed shifted, and she realized with a start that she wasn't alone. She tried to scream, but her throat was too tight for any sound to escape.

There was a soft "snick," and the room flooded with light. She winced, blinking against the sudden brightness. A man stood at the edge of the bed, his features obscured by a black ski mask that left only his eyes visible. He wore a dark robe and gloves, and she got the impression he was trying to hide his appearance from her. Was that so she couldn't identify him later, or so she wouldn't recognize him now?

"Who are you?" Her voice was shaky, betraying her fear. "Why are you doing this to me?"

He didn't answer, but she hadn't really expected him to. He stepped closer and she scooted back, trying to put as much distance between them as possible.

It had to be the same man who had attacked her earlier. But why was she a target in the first place? She didn't have any enemies, not that she knew of at least.

"What do you want?"

Still no response. But there was something about the way he moved as he walked around the bed that struck her as familiar. If only she could figure out why...

Enough was enough. She wasn't going to simply sit here at the mercy of this silent stranger. She lunged for the bedside table lamp, but her brain still felt fuzzy and her movements were uncoordinated.

The man grabbed her arm and yanked it back, sending a searing bolt of pain through her shoulder. "Help!" she cried. Her scream was hoarse, so she tried again. "Someone help me!"

The blow came from out of nowhere, striking her across the chin and causing her head to snap back. Her body went limp, and she was dimly aware of being rolled onto her stomach.

"No," she mumbled weakly. She tried to struggle, but her synapses were still firing with random aftershocks of pain and she couldn't get her muscles to respond.

There was a sharp sting in the muscle of her thigh, followed by a warm rush. Her limbs grew heavy and she felt herself sinking into the bed. The light cut out, returning the room to darkness.

She heard the sound of a door opening and the murmur of noise from the hallway. Words rose in her throat, but her eyelids dropped down and she floated into an uneasy oblivion.

Everest stormed into his office and flung himself into his chair, hands already reaching for the keyboard. The security cameras. There had to be footage of the hallway, something that would tell him who had taken Mallory and give him some idea of where they had gone.

Assuming she was still on the boat. There was always the possibility her assailant had tossed her overboard to get rid of her quickly, before she woke up. The idea made his stomach cramp, but he had to believe that hadn't happened. If someone had truly wanted to kill her, why bother to drug her first? Whoever had attacked her could have simply bashed her on the head and tossed her over the balcony rail of the room she was in. Why go to the trouble of incapacitating her first?

No, whoever had taken her must want to keep her alive. That meant she was still here, that he could find her. He clung tightly to the hope as he typed, his hands shaking so much he could barely pull up the video recordings. He clicked on the camera that surveyed the hallway where they'd just been, then ran the footage back so he could see what had happened while he'd stepped away to talk to Peter.

It started out fine, the picture clear and sharp. But a moment after he left the room, the signal faded and the image grew fuzzy, until a blizzard of pixels filled the screen.

Everest swore and pounded the desk with his fist. Of all the times for the camera to malfunction!

As he watched, the image began to return. Details emerged until once again, the picture was clear. Just in time for him to watch his own progress back to the empty room.

He leaned forward, the hairs on the back of his neck rising as his instincts prickled with awareness. Something was off about the security footage...

The cameras had been acting strangely since the voyage began, but while he'd originally thought the bursts of static were random occurrences, now he wasn't so sure. This wasn't the first time they had just so happened to malfunction where Mallory was concerned. Unless he missed his guess, someone was tampering with the cameras in a deliberate attempt to evade detection.

And maybe he could use that to his advantage.

Whoever had used chloroform on Mallory had wanted to remain undetected. Surely that desire for secrecy extended to the person's actions after she was unconscious, as well. He doubted the assailant wanted to be caught on camera carrying her limp body throughout the ship. So if he could find a pattern to the camera malfunctions, perhaps he could narrow down her current location...

It took him more time than he liked, but by carefully examining each camera's footage and piecing together the timing of the outages, he was able to parse the likely route Mallory's attacker had taken. The last outage affected a camera monitoring a hallway of passenger cabins, about twelve in all. It shouldn't take long to search them, especially with his anxiety about Mallory's condition driving him. He took a closer look at the doors, and a bolt of recognition struck him. He wasn't going to have to search all twelve cabins after all.

Just one.

Jeff's former stateroom.

Chapter 15

The vibrations reached her first, jarring her loose from the cold stasis of sleep. Something had taken hold of her shoulders in a tight grip, and she was being shaken insistently.

"Mallory!" The sound of her name cut through the fog in her brain. The voice was distorted, as if she was hearing it while underwater. But there was something familiar about the sound, some element that tugged insistently at her memory.

She felt herself being lifted, her body floating through the air. Her mind fought to come back online, but she kept losing her grip on consciousness. Warmth spread down one side as she was moved, then something solid and cold pressed against her back. Her muscles twitched, and she was dimly aware that she was shivering.

"Oh, God. Please be okay."

Whom was he talking to? It was a him, that much she

knew. She tried to respond, but it was too much work. Fatigue pulled at her, and she surrendered her tenuous grip on consciousness, sinking back into the dark depths.

Everest pushed the desk chair into the clinic, careful to keep his hand on Mallory's shoulder so she didn't fall out as he wheeled her into the room.

"I need help!" he yelled.

Two nurses approached, their eyes widening when they saw Mallory in the chair.

"What happened?" one of the women asked.

Everest shook his head. "I'm not sure. I found her like this about five minutes ago. She hasn't woken up, and I don't know what to do." Panic tinged his words, but he didn't care about showing his fear. He brought her over to one of the beds and helped the nurses lift her out of the chair. She looked so pale and fragile lying against the white sheets. He wanted to gather her in his arms and hold her close, but he forced himself to step back so the nurses could examine her.

The woman moved quickly but carefully, inserting an IV and hooking Mallory up to all sorts of machines. A steady beep filled the air, and Everest realized it was the sound of Mallory's heart. He focused on the noise and stared at the green tracing as it moved across the screen of the monitor. As long as he heard that sound, he could convince himself that she would be okay.

"How long has she been like this?"

"I don't know." Helplessness welled up in his chest along with a feeling of despair. He didn't know what had happened to Mallory. He didn't know anything that could help the nurses take care of her. He was useless.

"I never should have left her," he muttered. He'd gotten so wrapped up in their search and the possibility of answers from Peter, he'd forgotten that Mallory's assailant was still unaccounted for. Wesley had stopped by his office earlier in the morning to report he was still looking for the man, and Everest had foolishly assumed it was only a matter of time before he was in custody. But he'd been wrong, and now Mallory was paying the price.

"What do we do now?" one of the nurses said. The other woman shook her head, her expression grave. "I don't know."

"What do you mean, you don't know?" Everest said harshly. He didn't mean to take his fears out on these women, but he refused to believe there was nothing more to do for Mallory. There had to be something they could give her to make her wake up. He wasn't going to be able to relax until he heard her voice again.

The nurses both looked at him, and he saw his helplessness mirrored in their eyes. Mallory's heart beat steadily now, but would it continue to do so? Whatever drug she'd been given might even now be doing untold damage to her system. She might wake up in the next five minutes, or she might slip into a coma and die—either outcome was a possibility. And the uncertainty of it was killing him.

The door to the clinic opened, and he turned to find Avery and Olivia standing in the entry. The smiles slipped off their faces as they saw the group clustered around the bed.

"Sorry," Avery said. "We were hoping to catch Mallory."

"We'll come back later," Olivia said. The pair started for the door, but Everest couldn't let them leave. They were both doctors—they had to know something that could help Mallory.

"Wait!" he called out. His voice boomed in the small

room, and the two women flinched. He hurried over to them. "You've got to help me. Mallory's unconscious."

"Mallory?" Olivia's disbelief was plain, but she and Avery turned back to the bed. One of the nurses moved away, revealing Mallory's face. Avery let out a gasp, and Olivia practically ran to her friend's side.

Olivia wasted no time starting an exam, firing a series of questions at the nurses as she moved. "Go get Grant," she instructed Avery.

Her words drove a spike of fear into Everest's heart. "Why do you need him?" he asked. "Is Mallory too sick for you to handle on your own?"

Olivia spared him a glance. "I'm not sure what's she's been dosed with," she said. "My specialty is plastic surgery. Grant's is emergency medicine. He's a lot more familiar with drug and overdose patients than I am, so I want him in here."

"Overdose?" Everest whispered, fear tightening his throat to the point he could barely breathe. He grabbed Mallory's hand, her skin disturbingly cold. Someone had wanted her out of the way, that much was clear. It was possible whoever had attacked her had given her too much sedative, either accidentally or intentionally. Once again, he cursed his mistake. *I should have made her come with me.* If they'd gone together, she wouldn't have been vulnerable to a second attack.

Someone brushed past him, and Everest realized Grant had arrived. He took charge, assessing Mallory and asking many of the same questions as Olivia. The nurses didn't seem to mind the repetition, though, and Grant rattled off a list of medications to administer.

When there was a lull in the activity, Everest decided to risk a question. "Is she going to be okay?"

Grant glanced at him, his gaze sympathetic. "I think

so. Her vital signs are strong, which is a good sign. If we can just keep her supported, she should wake up eventually."

"There's nothing you can administer to speed up the process?"

The other man shook his head. "Not without knowing what she was given to begin with. I've ordered the standard medications, but there's a lot of stuff out there that can't be counteracted. We might simply have to wait this out."

Everest nodded, but inside he was screaming. "I see. Should we evacuate her to a hospital on shore?" They were currently under way to Philadelphia, their next port. But he could arrange for an emergency medical transfer, if that was what was needed to help Mallory.

Grant tilted his head to the side, considering the question. "She's stable right now, and I don't see that changing. We're doing everything a hospital would in a case like this. But if she doesn't regain consciousness in a few hours, then yes. We'll move her when we get to Philadelphia."

His words made Everest feel a little better, and he exhaled slowly. The selfish part of him was happy to know Grant didn't think she should be moved; he wanted to keep her close, and if they transferred her to a hospital on shore, he'd have to leave her there and stay on board the ship as she continued her journey.

"Do you know how this happened?"

Everest turned to find Logan standing off to the side, his expression serious. He hadn't seen the other man come in, but then again, he hadn't been paying attention to anything other than Mallory.

He sighed, mentally debating how much to reveal. He couldn't talk about their search for the material in the boxes, or his conversation with Peter. It might all be for nothing, and he didn't want to alarm Mallory's friends or the clinic nurses unnecessarily. So he settled for a version of the truth.

"We were in one of the passenger cabins, investigating an issue reported by one of the guests. I stepped out to take a phone call, and when I returned, she was gone." He told them about the stench of chloroform in the air, and her earlier assault in Jeff's cabin. They all listened intently, but Avery and Olivia didn't seem too surprised. *Mallory must have spoken to them about it*, he realized. What else had she told her friends?

"You said you have a lead on this guy?" Logan asked.

Everest nodded. "Wesley, my second-in-command, tells me he's getting close to identifying the man who attacked her. He thought the guy had gone ashore for the day, but that doesn't seem to be the case."

"Do you have security tape footage we can look at?"

Everest felt a flash of gratitude at Logan's use of *we*, but in truth, there wasn't much the other man could do. He was a guest, not staff, and if Everest were to call upon him to help in an official capacity, it would spell the end of his career. "That's how I found her," he said, nodding at the bed where Mallory lay, looking peaceful under the bright lights of the room.

Logan opened his mouth, and Everest shook his head subtly, glancing at the nurses. He didn't want to talk about the security camera outages in front of an audience. In fact, he didn't want to discuss them at all. If his suspicions were true, and someone was using a jammer to interfere with the signal, the timing of the outages suggested the culprit knew the ship very well. How else to explain the loss of the video feed just before something bad happened? Whoever was doing this was familiar with the placement of each camera and the areas under surveillance. That ruled out any of the passengers.

It pained him to admit it, but only the staff members would have the know-how to move throughout the ship undetected. And until he had a better idea of who might be skulking about, he didn't want to share his thoughts. The only advantage he had at the moment was his hunch. If he tipped his hand it would be even more difficult to discover what was really going on.

A chill slithered down his spine as another, more sinister thought occurred to him. What if Mallory's assailant wasn't a passenger after all? What if he was a member of the crew?

Everest's heart sank as he followed the idea to its logical conclusion. Wesley had supposedly been tracking the man. But if the attacker was a member of the staff and not a passenger, his second-in-command was on the wrong track. Was he deliberately trying to hinder the investigation, or was it an honest mistake?

Questions swirled in his mind, each more disturbing than the last. He wanted to trust the men on his team, but he couldn't risk Mallory's safety. She'd already been targeted twice, and the severity of the attacks was escalating. If he made another mistake, she might not survive a third assault.

"Since you don't know who is hurting Mallory, I think one of us should stay with her at all times." Avery pulled a chair over to the side of Mallory's bed and sat, her expression determined.

"I agree," Everest said. He considered telling Avery and Olivia that he'd stay with Mallory until she woke up, but he knew her friends would want to stay close. "We can take shifts, if you like."

Olivia nodded. "We'll sit with her now. I'm sure you have things to do."

He did, but he hated to leave Mallory. Logically, he knew there was nothing he could do for her right now, but he was loath to let her out of his sight again. Still, he needed to try to identify her attacker while the evidence was fresh. The longer he stayed here, the more time her assailant had to cover his tracks.

"I'll be back as soon as I can," he said. "Please page me if anything changes." He nodded at the nurses. "They have my number."

"We'll take care of her," Grant said.

"Go find the bastard who did this." Avery's voice was calm, but her eyes were bright with emotion.

"I will."

Everest took one last look at Mallory. He didn't know if she could hear what was being said around her, but he wanted her to know he wasn't leaving her for long. He leaned over and pressed a kiss to her cheek. "I'll be back soon," he whispered near her ear. "I have a lot to tell you."

He straightened and headed for the clinic door. Logan fell into step next to him. "I want to help. Unofficially, of course," he said, smiling wryly. "I don't want to cause any more headaches for you."

"I appreciate that," Everest said. They paused at the door. "Do me a favor and stay close to Mallory. I'm beginning to think this is some kind of an inside job, and I don't trust anyone right now."

Logan nodded somberly. "I can do that. Keep us updated when you're able."

"Will do." Everest left the clinic. He felt a little better knowing her friends were there. Avery and Olivia would keep a close eye on her, and having Grant and Logan nearby eased the band of worry in his chest. Three doctors and a DEA agent—he couldn't ask for better guardians while Mallory recovered.

Now he just had to figure out his next move. The captain hadn't wanted to delay the trip for a murder investigation, so the chances of him taking action in the wake of Mallory's assault were slim. Still, Everest needed to update him on the situation. Part of him wanted to see the man's face when he learned the ship's doctor had been attacked. There was something strange about the captain's recent behavior, and Everest was going to report him once the trip was over. The higher-ups in the company needed to know about the captain's erratic responses to the events on board, and Everest hoped they would seriously reconsider putting him at the helm of another ship.

But that would have to wait. Right now, he needed to go back and study the security footage in the hopes of finding some clue that would reveal who was running around the ship.

He might not be able to help Mallory, but he could at least do a better job of protecting her from here on out.

Chapter 16

She was gone.

Wesley stared at the bed, unwilling to believe his eyes. He'd injected the doctor with enough tranquilizer to fell an elephant. How in the hell had she disappeared?

He checked the bathroom, hoping to find her there but knowing it was unlikely. Sure enough, the small room was empty.

Where was she? More important, who had found her? He'd placed her in Jeff's old cabin precisely because no one was using it, and the housekeeping staff had been instructed not to service the room. No one could have accidentally stumbled upon her in here, and he simply couldn't believe she had been able to call out for help.

"I should have gagged her," he muttered. But hindsight was always twenty-twenty...

His heart began to pound as the gravity of the situation sank in. Dr. Watkins had proved herself to be a liability to his mission, and he could no longer tolerate her interference. He'd initially intended to temporarily incapacitate her, but upon further reflection, he'd decided a more permanent solution was in order. So he'd returned to the cabin to collect her, and he'd planned to throw her overboard now that they were under way. Once she was out of the picture, Everest would be so busy trying to find her he'd forget all about the mystery material, and Wesley would be free to plant the explosives without fear of discovery.

It was the perfect distraction. But she was nowhere to be found. And since a drugged woman couldn't walk off by herself, there was only one explanation.

Someone had found her and moved her.

It had to be Everest. If anyone else was responsible, he'd have heard about it by now. Word traveled fast on the ship, and news like that wouldn't stay secret for long.

The pager on his hip buzzed to life, and his gut cramped when he saw the display: Everest was summoning him to his office.

He doesn't know it was me, Wesley told himself as he clipped the pager back into place. He *couldn't* know. There was no way the doctor had seen his face—he'd worn a mask and he'd concealed his body and clothes with a robe and gloves. He hadn't spoken either, afraid of giving the woman any kind of information that might allow her to identify him.

"He probably wants to tell me about what happened to the doctor." Everest would want to launch an investigation, and Wesley could pretend to help. It would give him the perfect excuse to roam about the ship, and he'd be able to plant the explosives while he worked. If anyone questioned his presence, he could simply say he was searching for the doctor's assailant.

Feeling much better, Wesley ran a hand through his hair and took a deep breath. He had to appear calm and composed, or Everest would suspect something was going on. After a quick glance in the bathroom mirror, Wesley set out for Everest's office.

The walk took only a few minutes, and Wesley rapped on the door. "Come in," Everest said, his voice slightly muffled through the wood.

Wesley stepped into the small office. "Take a seat," Everest said, gesturing to the chair in front of his desk.

Wesley did as he was asked, and took a second to study his boss. Everest wore a serious expression and his eyes were tired. But there was no accusation in his gaze, and the knot of anxiety in Wesley's chest eased a bit.

"What's on your mind?" Wesley asked.

"I'd like an update on your investigation into Dr. Watkins's assault," Everest said. "Now that the passengers are all back on board from the day's shore excursions, have you been able to find the man who attacked her in Jeff's cabin?"

"I'm still questioning some of the guests," Wesley replied. Then inspiration struck, and he fought to keep a smile off his face. "I'm a little worried the man may have stayed behind in Charleston."

Everest frowned. "What makes you say that?"

Wesley adopted a concerned expression. "There's one man I haven't been able to track down—a Brad Hastings. He hasn't been in his cabin, and I'm not sure where he is."

Everest nodded thoughtfully. "He might know you're looking for him. Have you checked the casino rooms? He could be hiding there."

"That's a good idea," Wesley said, pretending to consider it. "I'll check as soon as we're done here."

"People don't just vanish," Everest said. "I'm sure you'll find him."

Wesley's stomach did a little flip, and he watched Everest carefully, searching his face for any sign of a hidden meaning. But there was no hint of sarcasm or glimmer of awareness in his eyes. He appeared to simply be making conversation.

"Keep me in the loop," Everest said. He turned back to the computer monitor, and Wesley stood, recognizing the gesture as a dismissal.

"Did you need anything else?"

"No."

The answer surprised him. Wesley had figured Everest would tell him about Dr. Watkins. Either he hadn't been the one to find her, or he wasn't willing to talk about it. But why would he keep news like that so close to the vest?

Is he trying to protect her? he wondered. But if that was the case, why not tell the security team about it and post guards?

Something strange was going on, that was certain. But Wesley couldn't afford to be complacent. He was so close to realizing his goal. He wasn't going to let the mystery of the missing doctor ruin things now.

One way or another, he would have justice for Ryan.

Everest watched Wesley walk away, anger and disappointment swirling in his chest. He'd thought he could trust Wesley. The two of them had worked together on several cruises, and he'd found the younger man to be thoughtful and responsible, someone he could rely on. Even now, Everest didn't want to believe his second-in-command was capable of such deception, but he couldn't ignore the evidence.

Everest had pulled up the security camera feeds on his computer, the dual monitors displaying a patchwork of tiny square movies. He'd meant to check the cameras in search of any irregularities that might yield useful information as to the identity of Mallory's attacker. He'd also paged Wesley, wanting to see the man's face when he asked about the hunt for her unknown assailant.

Right after he sent the page, the feed for the camera monitoring the hallway outside Jeff's cabin had fuzzed out, disintegrating into a sea of black-and-white snow. Everest had immediately glanced to the one monitoring the neighboring hall, curious to see if it would go down next.

But it didn't.

Everest had watched in fascination as Wesley had rounded the corner and strode into view, his hand in his pocket as he walked. Perhaps it was simply a coincidence Wesley had been walking down the hallway at the exact same moment the security camera experienced an outage. But Everest didn't believe in coincidences. Unless he missed his guess, Wesley had been in Jeff's old room when he'd received the page. He hadn't wanted anyone to see him leaving, so he'd jammed the signal on the camera when he left.

There was no good reason for Wesley to be in that cabin. The only possible explanation was that he had returned to check on Mallory.

And the only way he'd need to do that was if he'd been the one to drug her and put her there in the first place.

It had taken every ounce of Everest's self-control to remain seated when Wesley had walked into his office. Rage had surged in his chest, and he'd wanted to spring forward and grab Wesley by his shoulders to shake some answers out of him. Why was he targeting Mallory? She hadn't done anything to him. Moreover, it seemed completely out of character for Wesley to do something like that. In their time working together, Wesley had never displayed any hint of violence. What had made him snap now?

"If it's really him," Everest muttered to himself. The evidence he had against Wesley was circumstantial at best, and he needed to keep an open mind. His second-in-command was acting a bit strange, but until Everest had solid proof, he couldn't afford to get so fixated on Wesley that he ignored any signs that might point to someone else.

He glanced at the monitors, watching Wesley as he made his way through the ship. He didn't seem to be headed in the direction of the casino rooms, but Everest hadn't really expected him to check them out. But where *was* he going?

Disbelief and dismay warred for dominance as Everest watched Wesley's progress. The man was going to the clinic—he was sure of it.

His actions cemented his guilt in Everest's mind. Wesley had no business going to the clinic. He was likely only headed there now because he hadn't found Mallory in Jeff's cabin. He had to be feeling nervous and wondering where she was, and Everest was glad Logan and the rest of Mallory's friends were at her side. Wesley wouldn't dare try to harm Mallory in front of so many witnesses.

Everest wanted to rush to the clinic and confront Wesley, but he forced himself to stay put. He still didn't have any hard proof of wrongdoing on Wesley's part, and if he went after the man now, it might provoke him into doing something rash. Better to wait and watch in the hopes of catching him in the act.

Everest knew he'd made the right decision, but he still

held his breath as he watched Wesley walk into the clinic. Minutes ticked by, each one slower than the last. What was going on in there? If he stayed any longer, Everest was going to head there himself, patience be damned.

Just as he pushed to his feet, the door to the clinic opened and Wesley stepped out. Everest sank back into his chair with a sigh of relief and leaned forward to get a better look at the man's face. Wesley wore a sour expression, as if he'd just bitten into a lemon. It certainly wasn't the look of a man who was happy to discover his coworker was recovering from an attack.

Wesley glanced back at the door to the clinic, then down at his watch. He nodded to himself, and even from this remote distance, Everest could practically see the wheels turning in the man's mind.

"I don't think so," he murmured. Wesley likely figured he'd return to the clinic later, when Mallory's friends were gone for the night. What he didn't realize was that Everest had no intention of leaving Mallory unguarded, especially when she was unconscious and vulnerable.

"You're not getting near her again," he said grimly. He had let himself get distracted once, and Mallory was paying the price. He wasn't going to repeat that mistake.

Mallory came awake slowly, feeling her way back into her body. She felt…good. A little foggy, but her mind was clearing rapidly. The masked man. The room.

She shot up, her heart in her throat. Her stomach protested the sudden change in position, and she put a fist to her mouth and swallowed hard.

She was hooked up to an IV. When had that happened? She glanced around the room, but it was too dark to make out many details.

A hand landed on her shoulder, and she realized with a jolt that she wasn't alone in the bed.

Mallory reacted on instinct, swinging wide with her fist clenched. She made contact with something hard, and heard a satisfying "oof." The grip on her shoulder loosened, and she rolled to the side. A painful pinch told her the IV lines were dangerously strained, but she had to get away. Someone was in the bed, someone she hadn't invited in or known about. What the hell had happened while she was passed out?

Her heart sank and she fought for breath. Had she been raped again? She began a mental inventory of her body, searching for any intimate pain that would indicate if she'd been violated while she was unconscious.

"Mallory."

She dimly heard her name over the rush of blood pounding in her ears. It sounded like—

"Mallory."

She stilled, trying to gather her thoughts. Her brain felt like it was coming apart at the seams, but she had to make sense of what was happening.

"Everest?" The name came to her suddenly, a lightning strike of realization that burned away some of her fears. If he was truly here, maybe she was okay after all...

"It's me." His voice was deep and calm, and she relaxed enough to take a deep breath. The back of her head ached, and her arm hurt a bit at the IV insertion point, but other than that she felt fine.

Relief washed over her, flushing most of the anxiety out of her system. She hadn't been assaulted. Not this time.

The air moved behind her, and suddenly the lights flicked on. Mallory blinked, blinded by the sudden flood of brightness. She glanced around as her eyes adjusted, frowning as she realized she was in her…office?

"What…?" The question died in her throat as she tried to process this unexpected development.

Everest stepped in front of her, his blue eyes warm as he watched her face. "We moved you here so you'd have a bit more privacy," he explained.

She looked around, surprised they'd been able to make space for the bed. The desk had been pushed up against the wall, leaving just enough room for the bed and the IV pole. It must have taken quite a bit of jostling to get the gurney rolled into the room. How had she managed to sleep through that?

A sudden wave of fatigue hit her, and she sank down on the edge of the bed. "How long was I out?"

"Almost eight hours," Everest replied. "I found you around noon. We had no idea what you'd been given, but Grant has been monitoring your condition. He was pretty confident you just needed to sleep it off." The corner of his mouth lifted in a sheepish smile. "I'm glad he turned out to be right."

"Me, too." She rubbed her eyes, the movement reminding her she was still tethered to the IV pole. Fortunately, her sudden bid for escape had only pulled away some of the tape holding the cannula in place. She smoothed the edges back down, glad she hadn't accidentally ripped the thing out of her arm in her panic.

The mattress shifted as Everest sat beside her. He was quiet for a moment, giving her time to adjust to being awake. Then he spoke, asking the question she knew had to be at the top of his mind. "Want to tell me what happened?"

"I'm not sure," she said, deliberately misunderstanding his meaning. "I went into the next cabin while you left to check your email. Someone grabbed me from behind and put a rag over my mouth—I think it was soaked with chloroform. I woke up on a bed, and there was a man in the room wearing a mask and a robe to cover his body. He injected me with something, and I passed out again."

Everest nodded. "That's good to know." He waited a second, then tried again. "But I was asking about your reaction just now. Do you always wake up swinging?"

She'd known this question was coming, but it still made her stomach quiver to hear him speak it. She had talked about the rape before, to her therapist and to Olivia and Avery. But she'd never shared that part of her past with a man she was interested in.

On an intellectual level, she understood he needed to know it had happened. It was a part of her life, and she was still dealing with the repercussions of the event. But that didn't mean she actually wanted to tell him the details.

She was gathering the frayed ends of her courage when he spoke, interrupting her thoughts. "I think you know about my leg," he said quietly. "But I haven't told you how it happened yet."

Mallory glanced at him, surprised at the change in subject. "You don't have to—" she began, but he interrupted her.

"No, it's fine. I want to talk about it."

His eyes were full of sincerity, so she nodded.

"We were out on a mission," he said. "It was one of those hot summer days, where the air shimmered and we felt like we were walking on the surface of the sun." His voice took on a faraway quality, and Mallory got the impression he was retreating into his memories.

"We were accompanying a platoon that had been sent to secure the house of a former Iraqi scientist. Intel suggested the man was attempting to sell some lab equipment and materials on the black market, so they wanted CBRN officers to scout the place so we could identify and collect any hazardous material after the raid. It was supposed to be a straightforward job, no big deal." He shook his head, and offered her a rueful smile. "Isn't that when things always go to hell?"

Mallory sensed the question was rhetorical, so she merely nodded.

"Anyway, my team and I were in the last Humvee in the caravan. At the time, it seemed like the safest place to be. After all, there were three trucks ahead of us, so if we were gonna trip an IED, chances were one of those leading would be the one to find it."

"That makes sense," Mallory said quietly. "I can't imagine how scary it must have been to be in that first truck."

"Those guys don't get the credit they deserve," Everest said. "Every time the platoon went out, they risked their lives. Most patrols were uneventful, but that was the day our luck ran out."

He paused and swallowed hard, collecting himself. Mallory reached over and placed her hand over his, wanting him to know she was here. He squeezed her fingers and took a deep breath.

"I don't remember the actual explosion," he said. "One minute, we were following the truck in front of us. The next thing I knew, I was on the ground, choking on smoke and dust, staring up at the sky and wondering what had happened."

He ran his free hand through his hair and shrugged, as if trying to shake off an unpleasant sensation. "I couldn't hear anything at first. The bomb had blown out one of my eardrums, and the other wasn't in great shape. But after a few minutes, I heard the screaming."

A shudder ran through his powerful frame, and Mallory's heart cracked as she imagined the scene. She'd seen news footage of the aftermath of an IED explosion, but the reality had to be a thousand times more horrifying. And to know the men you served with day in and day out were injured or possibly dying? A chill raced across her skin at the thought, and she scooted closer to Everest, wanting to comfort him.

"I was one of four guys in the truck," he said. "The driver was part of the platoon, but the other two men were under my command. The driver lived, but he was pretty banged up. My guys didn't make it."

"I'm so sor—"

"I didn't know that at the time, though," he said, talking over her. Mallory got the impression that if he stopped now, he wouldn't finish the story. "I was just lying there, marveling at the fact that I was cold in the middle of the desert. My men were dying feet away, and I did nothing."

Mallory couldn't remain silent in the face of his self-recrimination. "There was nothing you could have done," she said. "You were gravely wounded—having a leg blown off is not something you can will away, or push through. It's a wonder you survived at all."

"I know that now," he said. "When I woke up in the hospital and realized my leg was gone, I knew there was no way I could have helped them. But I still spent a lot of time blaming myself. Those were my men. It was my job to look after them, and I couldn't keep them safe."

"What would you have done differently?" she asked. "How could you have possibly saved them from a bomb?"

He shrugged and ducked his head. "I know it doesn't

make a lot of sense, but I was depressed. My brain wasn't exactly functioning properly."

"I can relate to that," she said softly.

"I told my fiancée to leave," he said, matter-of-factly. "I didn't want her to stay because she felt sorry for me."

"And she actually walked out?" Mallory couldn't hide her incredulity. What kind of woman left her injured fiancé when he needed her most?

"I wanted her to," he said. "I could tell she wasn't happy, and I had changed a lot. I didn't want her to stay and grow to resent me, and I figured it was better to be alone."

Mallory shook her head, marveling at his selflessness. Not many people would have considered the thoughts and feelings of someone else as they tried to adjust to life as an amputee.

"Did you ever contact her? After you learned to live with your injury?"

He leaned back, and she could tell by the way his eyes widened he was surprised by her question. "No," he said, shaking his head. "I didn't even think to reach out to Leah after I worked through my issues." He paused, clearly thinking. "I guess I figured she was a part of my past, not my future."

"That makes sense," Mallory said. She hesitated, debating on asking about his dating life since the injury. *Might as well*, she figured. This was one of those confessional conversations, the kind that happened only when two people really wanted to get to know each other. If he didn't want to talk about his love life, he wouldn't.

"Have you dated since your accident?"

He shook his head. "Not really. I've been out on a few dates here and there, mostly at the insistence of friends who set me up with someone they knew. But none of it ever led to anything."

"Are you... I mean, can you...?" Mallory trailed off, her skin heating as she asked such a delicate question. She'd assumed his injuries had resulted in amputation below the knee, but if she was mistaken and he'd lost his leg closer to his hip, it was possible he'd suffered groin injuries as well, which might affect his ability to experience a sexual relationship. Was that why he'd withdrawn from the dating world after returning home?

"Yes, I can," he said. Twin spots of pink appeared on his cheeks, and he nodded. "I was lucky enough to just lose my leg. Everything else functions properly, in all the ways it's meant to."

"Then why aren't you seeing someone?" It was a blunt question, but she had to know. He was such a good man; she didn't understand why he wasn't in a relationship.

He laughed, the sound booming in the small office. "You sound like my mother," he said. "Did she put you up to this?"

Mallory ducked her head, affecting a guilty expression. "She made me a good offer," she teased.

He laughed again, and her heart lightened. "I hope you'll split the profits with me," he said. He shook his head, and when he spoke again, his tone was more serious. "In answer to your question, I haven't found the right someone yet. Women aren't exactly lining up to date a man with one leg."

"Then they're idiots."

A spark of heat flashed in his eyes, and an answering thrill shot through her. "Don't feel too sorry for me. There is one woman I'm interested in."

"Oh, yeah?" She tried to sound casual, but her voice wavered a bit.

Everest nodded. "If she'll have me."

"I'm sure she will." Mallory paused a moment, collecting herself. "But you might not want me after you hear my story."

He leaned a little closer on the bed, and she felt the heat from his body warm the air between them. The urge to lean against him was surprisingly strong, but she didn't want to touch him while she shared her past. It was silly, she knew, but part of her feared that if she was physically connected to him in any way, the stain of her memories would mark him, too.

She pulled her hand free, and Everest frowned slightly. "Mallory," he said softly. "You don't have to tell me. If you're not ready to talk, it's okay. This isn't a quid pro quo thing—just because I told you about my injury doesn't mean you owe me your story."

His words made her heart swell and gave her the strength to cast out her lingering fears. Everest was the right person to share this painful secret with, and while a part of her would always be scared to talk about her rape, she knew it was time. Even though years had passed since the attack, her reluctance to talk about the event had given the specter of her rapist a degree of control over her life. For too long she had let that man affect her thoughts and emotions. She was ready to reclaim her power.

Starting now.

Chapter 17

Mallory took a deep breath, and Everest watched as the movement of her shoulders strained the fabric of her shirt. She was clearly mustering up the courage to talk, and he knew whatever she had to say was going to be hard for him to hear.

But this wasn't about him. He needed to push his emotions to the side and focus on supporting her. This wasn't going to be an easy conversation for her, and he got the impression Mallory had kept this secret for quite a while.

"I was raped."

She spoke quietly, but in the stillness of the room it may as well have been a shout. Everest tried not to flinch as her words slapped him. He'd had his suspicions, but hearing her confirm the worst made him want to throw up.

"It was my senior year of college. I'd just finished finals for the fall semester, and there was a party that night to celebrate before everyone left for winter break. I wasn't going to go, but my roommate talked me into it. She said I'd been working so hard I deserved to have a little fun."

Everest could picture it easily: a studious, serious Mallory who was so focused on her classes she didn't have much of a social life.

"The party was at one of the frat houses. I'd never been there before, but my roommate had attended a few parties during the semester and she knew a lot of the guys. They were really nice and friendly, and they made me feel welcome."

I bet they did, he thought. Mallory was a beautiful woman now; she had to have been stunning in college. He'd been eighteen once, and well remembered the effect a pretty face had had on his system. It was no wonder the frat boys were happy to see her.

"There was one guy who really seemed to like me. His name was Blake." Her voice was flat and unemotional, but Everest felt the mattress move as she shuddered.

He lifted his hand, then thought better of it. Given the memories Mallory was facing right now, the last thing she probably wanted was to be touched.

"He was handsome and charming, and I couldn't believe he was actually interested in talking to me." She shook her head. "I was so naive," she muttered.

Everest opened his mouth to respond, but she continued before he could say anything.

"We chatted for a while, then he offered to get me a drink. I let him."

Oh, no, he thought. He knew where this was going, and he wanted to stop her, to tell her she didn't need to give him the details. But he owed it to her to bear witness to her pain. So he said nothing.

"I started feeling off about ten minutes later." Her tone was dispassionate, almost clinical, as if she was a doctor evaluating a case. "Blake offered to let me rest in his room. I don't remember saying yes, but the next thing I knew, I woke up to him on top of me."

Mallory paused, and Everest saw the glint of tears in her eyes. He wanted to offer her comfort and reassurance, but he was at a loss as to what to do. Touching her was out of the question, and he didn't know what to say. But he had to try something. He couldn't just sit there like a frog on a log while she relived the worst moments of her life.

"Mallory, I—"

She waved her hand, and he stopped talking. "I need to get through this," she said, offering him a small smile.

Everest nodded, understanding perfectly.

She took a deep breath, then started again. "I tried to move, but my body wouldn't respond. I was so scared—I'd never experienced anything like it before. It's like I was trapped in my body and no matter how hard I tried, I couldn't defend myself." She shook her head. "I must have struggled enough, because Blake put his hand over my mouth and told me to hush. He said it would all be over soon. That's when I knew."

Her voice broke, along with Everest's heart.

"He was on top of me, and then...inside me." She drew in a quavering breath, and Everest's eyes stung as tears gathered. "He was right, though. It didn't last long."

Everest swore quietly and stood, his anger and sadness propelling him up off the bed. He began to pace the narrow confines of the office, feeling like a caged animal.

"I'll stop," Mallory said.

"No." He shook his head and turned to look at her. "Not on my account. Not unless that's what you want to do."

"You're upset."

"You're damn right I am," he said. "But don't worry

about me. I just need to move right now, if that's okay with you."

"Are you sure?" She sounded skeptical, and he realized he must look truly distraught.

Everest knelt in front of her and began to reach for her hands before he thought better of it. "You survived the hard part. The least I can do is listen."

She studied his face for a moment, her eyes searching his for the truth. She lifted one hand and gently pushed a few strands of hair off his forehead. He sucked in a breath at the contact, hardly daring to believe she actually wanted to touch him after what had happened to her.

Finally, she nodded. "The next time I woke up, he was asleep beside me. He felt me get out of bed, and he quickly got dressed and offered to walk me back to my dorm. I was so foggy and confused, I let him." She shook her head ruefully. "That was my biggest mistake."

"What do you mean?"

"It took me a while to figure out what had happened to me," she said. "I knew I had had sex that night, but the details were fuzzy. Once I finally realized I had been raped, I reported it. But there was no physical evidence. He used a condom, and by the time I reported it, the drug he'd given me was out of my system. It was my word against his. And there were witnesses who saw him walk me home that morning. He even kissed me goodbye at the door to my dorm building. Everyone watching thought we were parting on good terms. After all, what kind of woman lets her rapist walk her home and kiss her cheek?"

"Bastard," Everest said bitterly.

Mallory nodded. "One of the police officers was sympathetic, but she couldn't prove anything. She said the only thing they could do was keep an eye on him, see if he did this again."

"Did he?" While he hated the thought of another woman going through the same thing, he hoped Blake had been arrested and was currently rotting in prison.

"Probably. I doubt he suddenly grew a conscience and stopped. But as far as I know, he never got caught."

The injustice of it turned Everest's stomach and made him want to punch a wall. "You're so calm right now," he observed. "How do you not walk around screaming all the time about how unfair this is?"

Mallory's smile held more than a hint of cynicism. "What good would it do? I can't change what happened by yelling. Believe me—I've tried it before. All I got for my troubles was a sore throat and angry neighbors."

"You are such a strong woman," he said. In truth, *strong* didn't begin to describe her character, but it was the only word he could come up with on the spot.

Mallory scoffed. "Not really. I talk about the rape like it's an event I've put behind me, but the truth is, I think about it all the time."

"That's only natural," Everest said. "It's the same for me and the explosion. Not a day goes by that I don't remember the men I lost, or maybe even feel the phantom sensation of my missing leg." He sat next to her on the bed. "We both suffered a trauma. You don't just walk away unscathed from something like that."

"You don't understand," she said. "I haven't been with anyone since it happened. I don't even know if I can handle that ever again."

She sounded on the verge of tears, and Everest's anger flared again. It was bad enough that Mallory had been raped in the first place. It sounded like the event had permanently affected her ability to form relationships, which made things even worse. She probably thought about the attack every time she interacted with a man, and he mentally replayed their first meeting in the ship's gym, seeing her behavior in a new light. No wonder she hadn't dated anyone in the years since her assault. It had to be exhausting, to live in such a state of constant fear.

"You shouldn't be so hard on yourself," he started, but Mallory interrupted him.

"Don't you get it?" Her voice held an edge now, a thread of anger that hadn't been there before. "I like you, Everest. I think you're a good man, and in another time and another place, we might have had a relationship."

His heart tripped at her words, hope building in his chest even as she closed the door on any chance of them being together. "But not here and not now?"

She shook her head, her expression pure misery. "You don't want to be with me."

"I don't?" This was news to him. "Why don't you let me be the judge of that?"

Her head snapped up, confusion in her brown eyes. "Didn't you hear what I just said? I haven't had sex since I was raped. I don't even know if I can. It's not fair for me to ask you to deal with that."

"If it's all the same to you," he said, trying to keep his exasperation in check, "I can decide these things for myself."

"Everest—"

He held up his hand, cutting her off. "No. It's my turn to talk now. I think you are an amazing person. In fact, you're the first woman I've been interested in since I lost my leg. And while I'm not going to lie and say I've never thought about sleeping with you, I can say that is not my main motivation for getting close to you."

"I don't understand," she said slowly.

"That's because you think sex is the biggest part of a relationship," he said.

"Isn't it?" she challenged.

Everest shook his head. "No. It's important, don't get me wrong. But I'm more interested in building a foundation based on an emotional and intellectual connection. Being a true partner is what makes a relationship work."

"Do you really mean that?" She sounded shy and a little hopeful, as if she almost couldn't dare to believe him.

"Yes," he said firmly. "I'm willing to bet you haven't had sex since the attack because you haven't felt safe with anyone. Am I right?"

She nodded. "That's a big part of it."

"So we'll work on building trust between us first. The more we get to know each other, the more comfortable you'll feel around me. And I think as our feelings deepen and grow, you'll reach the point where you feel safe enough to try adding physical elements to our relationship."

Mallory bit her lip. "I am attracted to you," she said, sounding almost confessional. "And while I was initially a little scared of you, I'm not anymore. Kissing you is… really nice." There was an element of surprise in her voice, as if she couldn't quite believe her own reaction.

Warmth bloomed in his chest, and Everest smiled. "I'm glad to hear you enjoy it. I do, too."

Mallory's answering smile was a little shy. "When I'm with you, I want to get closer to you. I'm not thinking about Blake or the rape when you touch me. But I'm scared that if we try to be intimate, it'll all come roaring back and I won't be able to handle it."

"Maybe it will," Everest said honestly. "And maybe it won't. The only way to find out is to try. And I'm not saying that because I'm trying to talk you into bed," he added hastily. "I'm happy to let you set the pace when it comes to anything physical. But I don't think you should let fear of the unknown stop you from going after something you want."

Mallory snorted. "You sound like Avery and Olivia."

"No wonder I like them," he said, grinning. "But seriously, even if you and I don't amount to anything, I hope you'll find someone and take a chance on your happiness."

"You make it sound so easy," she said. "But what if I do try and I just can't do it? Are you really going to stick around in that case?"

Everest considered her question for a moment, debating on how to answer. "I don't know what the future holds," he said finally. "But if you're willing to work on this issue, I'm willing to be patient while we figure things out."

Mallory looked down, twisting her hands in her lap. Everest hardly dared to breathe, hoping he hadn't ruined things by speaking so bluntly. But it was important to tell the truth, especially now when they were on the verge of a decision that would drastically change both their lives.

His knees ached from kneeling on the thin carpet of her office. But he didn't dare move. Mallory was lost in thought, and he wasn't about to distract her.

After what seemed like a small eternity, she met his eyes. "Okay," she said softly.

His heart skipped a beat, and he sucked in a breath. "Okay?" he repeated. "Could you elaborate a bit on what you mean by that?"

The corner of her mouth lifted, and a tendril of hair slipped free from her ponytail to follow the curve of her cheek. "Let's give it a shot. I'm willing to try if you are."

"I am." A sense of relief filled him, along with a heady feeling of anticipation that made him a little light-headed.

She patted the mattress next to her, and Everest pushed

himself off the floor and sat. Their arms brushed, and Mallory leaned against him until her head rested on his shoulder. Moving slowly, he curled his arm around her to anchor her into place. Her warm weight nestled against his side, and for the first time in a long time, Everest felt content.

They sat quietly for a few minutes, leaning on each other in companionable silence. Finally, Mallory let out a soft sigh. "We have to find the guy who drugged me," she said. She sounded tired, as if the thought of mounting such a search exhausted her.

"We will." Everest debated telling her his suspicions but decided against it. They both needed to rest, if only for a few hours.

"Just try to relax now," he said, running his hand over her hair. "We'll get him tomorrow."

"You sound pretty sure of that," she said.

"I am," he said softly. "I will find him. Trust me."

Mallory was quiet for a moment, and when she spoke again, there was a note of wonder in her voice that touched his heart.

"I do."

He wasn't sure how long they sat, leaning against each other in the stillness of the room. Everest would have been happy to stay like that indefinitely, but reality came creeping back into his thoughts.

Mallory hadn't said anything yet, but he knew she probably wanted to see her friends. And he was certain Olivia and Avery would want to know that Mallory had emerged from her drugged state. Grant would likely want to examine her as well, to make sure she was well and truly fine.

"What are you thinking?" Her voice was soft, but it

startled him all the same, and he jumped. She chuckled. "Sorry. I didn't mean to scare you."

"It's fine," he said, wondering if the woman was a psychic. "I just realized we need to tell your friends you're awake."

"Oh, yes," she said. A note of excitement entered her voice, and he smiled.

"I haven't talked to them since..." She frowned, clearly trying to remember. "...two nights ago?"

"You haven't seen them, but they stayed by your side for hours after I found you unconscious. Logan and Grant had to practically pry them off the chairs and force them to go rest, and they only agreed to leave because they knew I'd be here with you."

"That sounds like them," she said, a smile in her voice.

"They really love you," he said, happy to know she had the two women in her life. Friendship was important, especially considering everything Mallory had been through.

"We look after each other," she said simply. "That's what friends do."

Everest slid off the bed and reached for Mallory's desk phone. "Want me to step outside so you can talk to them?"

She shook her head. "No. I have no secrets from you anymore."

Her simple statement touched his heart and filled him with warmth. He sat next to her and ran his hand down her back as she dialed and talked to her friends.

Mallory hung up a few minutes later. "They're coming to the clinic." She sounded a little bemused. "I told them to stay in their rooms and rest, but they wouldn't listen."

"I'm not surprised," he said. "You'd do the same if one of them were hurt or sick."

"That's true," she said. She gave him a shy look from under her eyelids. "But I was kind of enjoying having you all to myself."

Everest smiled and leaned in, wanting to kiss her. Just before his lips found hers, he stopped himself, remembering just in time.

"Sorry," he said sheepishly.

"Don't be," Mallory replied. She leaned forward and reached for him, her intentions clear.

Everest let her guide her mouth to his, wanting her to claim ownership of the kiss.

She didn't disappoint.

Her lips were soft and supple against his, her tongue warm as it stroked his mouth. He let her take control, happy to follow her lead as the world faded around them.

Everest had enjoyed their earlier kisses, but this one felt different somehow. Now that Mallory knew about his leg and his past with Leah, he felt freer than ever before. He hadn't been conscious of holding part of himself back, but he realized now that he had been guarding his heart. He'd enjoyed the physical aspects of kissing Mallory, but this time he let himself get emotionally involved, as well.

Suddenly, she pulled away. Cool air hit his lips, and he froze, his breath catching in his throat. Was she having a flashback? Talking about her rape had probably stirred up all kinds of unpleasant memories—it was only natural she might feel overwhelmed at the idea of a physical connection right now.

"Did you hear that?" she said softly.

He tuned in to the ambient noise in the room and picked up on the sound of voices, growing steadily louder. He let out a sigh of relief. "Oh, thank God."

Mallory eyed him curiously. "You okay?"

He nodded. "I was worried you were having a flashback or something."

She shook her head, a smile curving her lips. "No. I just don't feel like kissing you in front of an audience."

As if on cue, an insistent rapping started on the door. "Mallory?" That sounded like Olivia, her voice muffled through the wood. "Can we come in?"

Mallory levered herself off the bed, swaying a bit as she stood. Everest reached out to steady her, but she waved his hand away. "I'm good," she said softly.

He stepped back, but kept a careful eye on her. Fortunately, she didn't have to go far to reach the door.

As soon as she opened it, Olivia and Avery came tumbling into the room.

"Are you okay?"

"What are you doing out of bed?"

"How long have you been awake?"

The women talked over each other as they took up positions on each side of Mallory. They moved as one, half carrying Mallory back to the bed, urging her to sit and then to lie back on the gurney.

Mallory was good-natured about the attention, putting up no resistance as her friends fussed and fretted. She answered their rapid-fire questions as best as she was able, though they didn't give her much of an opportunity to get a word in edgewise.

There wasn't much room left in the office, so Everest slipped out the door to find Grant and Logan standing in the hall.

"Hey," he said.

Logan gave him a friendly nod, and Grant craned his neck to see inside the room. "Hey. How long has she been awake?"

"Maybe half an hour?" Everest replied.

Grant nodded, as if he'd expected that answer. "Did she have a hard time waking up?"

"A little," Everest said. He decided to keep the details to himself, out of respect for Mallory's privacy. "She was confused at first, and it took a few minutes for her to understand where she was."

"That's to be expected," Grant said. He glanced into the room, then back. "Think they'll let me get close enough to examine her?" he asked wryly.

Logan clapped Grant on the shoulder. "I believe in you."

"Good luck," Everest added.

Grant squared his shoulders and took a deep breath, then stepped forward. The din of conversation didn't alter when he stepped into the room, and Everest had to wonder if the women even noticed he was there.

Logan cleared his throat. "Any new developments?" he asked quietly.

Everest shook his head. He'd already shared his suspicions about Wesley when he'd arrived earlier in the evening to watch over Mallory. "No. But do me a favor?"

"Name it," Logan said.

His instant acceptance reminded Everest of the men he'd served with, and their ready willingness to do whatever it took to help each other out. He'd already had a high opinion of Logan, but now it went up another notch.

"Make sure you guys get off the ship tomorrow in Philadelphia. I've got a friend coming on board to help us figure out some stuff, and I think it would be best if you guys weren't around."

Logan narrowed his eyes. "I take it this 'stuff' is dangerous?"

"It's a distinct possibility," Everest admitted.

"Do you need help? I could send the ladies with Grant and stay behind."

Everest considered the offer for a moment. It would be nice to have an extra set of eyes around, but he didn't feel comfortable asking Logan to put himself in danger. He'd served with Peter and knew how the man thought, how he moved and how he acted under pressure. And while he liked Logan and figured the DEA agent had a cool head and steady hand, there was no telling how he might react if it turned out there was radioactive material on board. The threat of radiation hit people in the gut, making them respond unpredictably. He and Peter had gone through a lot of training so that they could suppress the instinctive panic that struck when faced with a radioactive, chemical or biological threat. And as much as he liked Logan, he simply couldn't take a chance that the other man would panic if the news wasn't good. The last thing he needed was for the situation to get out of control.

"I appreciate it," Everest said. "But I'll feel better if you stay with the group. I think Peter and I can handle things on the ship."

"What about Mallory?" Logan said. "Should she come with us, as well?"

Everest glanced at the open door. From this angle, he could see Mallory's face in profile as she talked with her friends. As if she sensed his gaze, she tilted her head to the side and gave him a small smile before turning back to the group.

His personal preference was to get her as far away from the ship as possible. If Wesley really was the one behind the attacks on Mallory, he didn't want her anywhere near the man. But he knew she was too stubborn to leave. She'd been the one to first see the dangerous possibility of the mysterious putty, and he knew there was no way to convince her to walk away just as they were about to learn if her suspicions had merit.

"I'll keep her with me," he said. "Besides, short of carrying her off the ship, I doubt you'd be able to talk her into going with you guys."

"Fair enough," Logan said, a knowing grin playing at the corners of his mouth. "I figured as much, seeing as how I recognize the look of a stubborn woman. Just thought I'd offer, in case you could convince her to take a little time off."

Everest lifted one eyebrow, and Logan laughed. "You never know," he said. "Maybe she'd listen to Avery or Olivia."

"Anything is possible," Everest murmured. But as Mallory turned to glance at him again, he knew she wasn't going anywhere.

And deep down inside, he didn't want her to.

A drop of sweat trickled down the valley of Mallory's spine as she and Everest made their way down the gangplank. It was still morning, but the sun was already bright in the sky, promising a scorcher of a day.

"Do you really think he's here already?" she asked, glancing around at the throng of people busily going about their work. Docking a cruise ship and helping passengers disembark was a highly coordinated process that required a lot of moving parts. It would be difficult to find just one person in the crowd, but Everest seemed confident his friend would be there to meet them as soon as the stepped off the ship.

"Peter's not the kind of guy to wait for ideal conditions," Everest said, raising his voice so she could hear him over the din. "He's not one to let a little crowd stop him."

"If you say so," Mallory muttered. Everest had said his friend was eager to get onto the ship so he could check out the mystery material for himself, but it would have been easier to find him if he'd been willing to wait until a little later in the day.

She scanned the crowd, though she knew it did little good. Everest had given her a basic description of Peter, but there were several men who were tall and had short, dark brown hair.

"That's it?" she'd said, unable to hide her exasperation with Everest's bare-bones sketch.

He'd blinked at her, clearly at a loss. "Uh, he has green eyes?"

Mallory shook her head at the memory and returned her attention to the activity on the pier. She wasn't close enough to see the color of anyone's eyes, so that wasn't exactly a helpful bit of information.

"Maybe we should stay on the gangplank," she suggested. "It might be easier to let Peter come to us, instead of us trying to wade through the crowd to find him."

"Good point," Everest said.

They drew to a halt and stepped to the side so people could walk past them. Everest glanced at his phone and frowned. "I texted him a few minutes ago, and he said he's here. Hopefully he won't have any trouble getting to us."

As if on cue, a shout rang out. "Everest!"

They both turned in time to see a man step from the crowd, waving as he approached. Everest walked down the stairs to meet him, and the two of them clasped hands and pulled each other close, slapping each other's backs in the characteristic embrace employed by men everywhere.

Mallory watched for a moment, enjoying the sight

of Everest and his friend. The two men appeared genuinely happy to see each other; both sported wide smiles, and she could tell by their relaxed body language they enjoyed each other's company. Everest was usually so serious—it was nice to catch a glimpse of him relaxed and truly at ease.

After a moment, Everest led Peter to the stairs and they climbed onto the gangplank. Everest gestured to her with a smile. "Mallory, this is my friend Peter MacKenzie. Peter, this is Dr. Mallory Watkins."

Peter's gaze was friendly but assessing as he stuck out his hand. "Nice to meet you," he said.

"Likewise," Mallory replied. Before she could think better of it, she grabbed Peter's hand. From the corner of her eye, she saw Everest's eyebrows shoot up in surprise. She was shocked herself, but after talking to Everest last night, she was done letting fear rule her life. She wasn't going to be able to cast aside all her worries overnight, but every time she overcame an obstacle, no matter how small, she was making progress.

Shaking Peter's hand was a little thing, but it symbolized her new attitude. It felt strange to touch a man she didn't know without the creeping dread that normally accompanied introductions like this. Maybe it was Everest's presence that made her feel safe. Or maybe it was the fact that he was friends with Peter, and part of her knew he must be a good man to have earned Everest's regard. Either way, she was happy to meet him.

"Thanks for coming so quickly," she said. "We both appreciate your help."

"My pleasure," Peter replied. "I'm always glad to have an excuse to see Everest. How long has it been, Mountain Man?"

"A year, I think," Everest said, as they started to walk back to the ship.

"Mountain Man?" Mallory echoed. "I didn't know you had a nickname."

Everest blushed, and Peter laughed. "That's what we called him when he was in the army. Fits, don't you think?"

"Is it just because of his name, or did his height factor into it, as well?" Mallory asked.

"Both," Peter replied. "Along with the fact that Everest was always so stubborn. He took his time when making a decision, but once he did, there was no changing his mind. You'd have better luck trying to move a mountain."

"You say that like it's a bad thing," Everest said.

"Not at all," Peter said easily. "Just warning the good doctor here, in case she didn't know that about you yet."

Mallory was beginning to like Peter and his easygoing manner. Too bad they weren't meeting under better circumstances. She'd enjoy the opportunity to pick his brain about Everest. He probably had some good stories from their time in the service together.

Mallory and Everest flashed their ID badges to the security guard standing at the entrance to the ship. "This is my guest," Everest said, nodding at Peter.

"No problem, sir," the guard said. He moved to the side to let the three of them pass, and Everest led them to his office. Once they were inside, Mallory and Peter took a seat while Everest closed the door to give them privacy.

"So tell me more about your mystery material," Peter said. He was all business now, his earlier friendliness banked as he turned his attention to the reason for his visit.

"You pretty much know everything we do," Everest said.

"I haven't heard from you, yet," Peter said, turning to look at Mallory. "Everest told me a bit about your patients and suspicions, but can you give me a little more detail?"

"No problem," Mallory said. She told Peter everything, starting with her first patients and their GI symptoms and sunburn-like rash. The steady trickle of patients over the last few days made her even more convinced they were dealing with radioactive material.

Peter listened intently, interrupting only to ask a few questions here and there. He was particularly interested in Danny's injuries after touching the material.

"I'd love to get a look at his hand," he remarked.

"I might be able to arrange that," Mallory said. "I can call his supervisor and ask to have him report to the clinic for a follow-up."

"Please do," Peter said. "I'd really appreciate it."

"Why don't you try to do that now?" Everest suggested. "We have some time to kill while we wait for the passengers to disembark for the day." He turned to Peter. "The material seems to be concentrated in cabins, and it will be much easier to show it to you when the rooms are empty."

Peter nodded. "Makes sense. I'd rather not have an audience while we do this."

Everest turned his desk phone around so Mallory could access it easily, and he handed her the contact sheet that listed phone numbers for the different managers on board. It took only a moment for her to locate the correct extension, and a few minutes later, she hung up with a nod.

"Danny's on his way to the clinic now," she said. "I'll head over there and talk to him to make sure he's comfortable with you guys examining his hand. I'll page you if he agrees to it," she said.

She stood, and Everest did the same. He looked worried, and unless she missed her guess, he didn't like the idea of her going to the clinic alone.

"I'll be fine," she said. She appreciated his concern, but it was important she get Danny's consent before giving Everest and Peter the green light to come to the clinic. If Danny walked in to find the men waiting for him, he'd likely feel defensive and overwhelmed. It would be much easier to talk him into letting Peter look at his hand if she was alone when she asked.

Everest nodded, but he didn't look happy. "I'll be watching you." He nodded to his computer monitor, which displayed a grid of footage from various security cameras mounted throughout the ship.

"I won't take long," she promised. "I'll see you both in a few minutes."

She set off for the clinic, a warm feeling in her chest at the knowledge that Everest was watching over her. He might not be physically close to her, but she knew he would keep her safe.

Chapter 18

Peter waited until the door clicked shut behind Mallory, then turned back to face Everest with a speculative gleam in his eyes.

"You didn't tell me there was anything going on between you and the doctor."

"I didn't?" Everest said with mock innocence. He watched the video feeds on his monitor, tracking Mallory's progress to the clinic. Only when she was safely inside did he relax enough to breathe fully again.

Peter raised one eyebrow, his mouth slanting in a familiar smirk. "How long have you been fraternizing with a coworker?"

"You make it sound so scandalous," Everest said.

Peter laughed. "You're the one who was always such a stickler for the rules. I'm just surprised, that's all." He paused, his expression turning serious. "Does she know about your injury?"

"She does," Everest said simply. He debated a split second on telling his friend more about Mallory's own troubles but decided against it. She had trusted him with her secrets, and he wasn't going to betray her confidence. It would be nice to hear Peter's take on things, and Everest felt like he could use some advice regarding how to best support Mallory as they tried to build a relationship. But he wasn't going to risk their fragile bonds of trust unless it was absolutely necessary. If he had to talk to someone, he'd ask her friends Avery and Olivia first. They knew all about Mallory's rape, and could probably offer insights and advice if he needed it.

"That's great," Peter said sincerely. "Is she the first woman you've dated since Leah?" Peter was familiar with the circumstances surrounding their breakup, and he also knew how reluctant Everest had been to date in the years following his injury. He sounded genuinely pleased, and Everest had to admit it felt good to have his friend's support.

"Yes. But it's still early days," he cautioned. "We're not sure how things are going to work out, but we're hopeful."

"Better make sure you leave the toilet seat down, then," Peter joked. "Seriously, though, I'm happy for you. I've been a little worried about you. A lot of the guys have."

"What do you mean?" It was a little unnerving to learn his life had been an issue of concern for his friends, and Everest reflexively rocked back in his chair.

Peter shrugged. "You've been single for a while," he pointed out. "It's not healthy to be alone."

"I'm fine," Everest said, waving away the words as if they were pesky flies.

"Everest." Peter sounded suddenly serious, and Everest's stomach flip-flopped. Peter leaned forward, his gaze heavy. "You went through hell in the war. You have a lot of scars, and they're not all physical. I know you're doing pretty well, but I'm glad you seem to have found someone special. I hope you'll let her help you with your demons."

Everest nodded, his throat too tight to speak. He and Peter had known each other for a long time, but Peter usually kept things light and humorous. For him to speak so frankly now about such a serious topic told Everest just how much his friend had been worried about him. He was touched to find his friend cared to such an extent, but he wasn't altogether surprised. Friendships forged in the service were unlike those made under any other circumstances. It was nice to discover the intensity of their bonds hadn't diminished simply because they no longer served together.

They were both quiet a moment, a silent understanding passing between them. Then Peter leaned back and crossed his arms over his chest. "So where do you keep your bird?"

"My bird?" Everest echoed, confused. What the hell was he talking about?

Peter nodded. "Yeah, you know. Your parrot."

"I don't have one." Understanding began to dawn, and Everest shook his head.

"That's a shame," Peter said. "You have all the makings of a pirate—a peg leg, an accent, a ship. Why not get the bird and just complete the picture?"

Everest gave him a droll stare. "Ha, ha," he said drily. "And I do not have an accent."

"You do sometimes, *padna*," Peter said, adopting a thick Cajun accent. "Seriously, though, how does it feel to go from being an officer in the greatest army in the world to being a squid?"

"I didn't join the navy," Everest protested with a laugh. "I'm not that much of a traitor."

"Oh, yeah?" Peter said, his voice thick with doubt. He cocked one hip off the seat of the chair and dug in his pocket. "Prove it." He slapped his hand on the desk, revealing the challenge coin given to their unit upon return from Iraq.

The gold surface gleamed on the desk, shiny and ostentatious in Everest's drab office. The challenge coin rules were simple: when presented, the others in the area had to show their own coins. If they came up emptyhanded, the challenger was treated to a drink by the losers.

Everest stood and patted his pockets, pretending to search for his coin. Peter smirked. "That's what I tho—"

A metallic clang cut him off as Everest slapped his hand on the desk. Peter stared at the coin for a moment, his smug expression fading into a sheepish grin.

"You were saying?" Everest asked pointedly.

"Just making sure your loyalties are still in the right place," Peter said. He retrieved his coin and returned it to his pocket, and Everest did the same.

"Always," Everest assured him. "We can head to the bar later so you can buy me my drink."

"Fair enough," Peter said.

The pager on Everest's hip buzzed to life, and he checked the display: He'll talk to you.

Well done, Mallory, he thought, proud of her for getting her patient to cooperate.

"She's ready for us to come to the clinic."

Peter stood, all traces of teasing gone as he picked

up his backpack. "That didn't take long," he remarked, slinging the bag over one shoulder.

"She's very persuasive," Everest said, pulling his office door closed behind them. "Let's hope this guy can tell us something helpful."

"Are you sure I'm not in any trouble?" Danny shifted on the bed, clearly uncomfortable.

Mallory offered what she hoped was a reassuring smile. "I'm quite sure. Mr. LeBeau and Mr. MacKenzie aren't interested in causing problems for you. They simply want to look at your palm."

Danny frowned at the bandages on his hand. "Do you really think they'll learn anything by looking at my welts and blisters?"

"I hope so," she said. It was a long shot, but Peter was an expert on radiological material. Presumably he would recognize any injuries that resulted from contact with the toxic stuff.

Danny still seemed nervous. *Please don't back out on me now*, she thought.

Mallory caught his gaze and leaned forward a bit. "I know you're worried," she said, her tone serious. "But I will do everything in my power to make sure your job is not at risk. What happened was an accident. I'll vouch for you."

He smiled, but it was strained. "Thanks. I can't afford to get fired. Not with one kid in college and another about to be."

"I understand," she said. "And I don't think it will come to that."

The door to the clinic swung open, and they both jumped. Mallory turned to see Everest and Peter walk in, their expressions serious.

Danny shrank back against the gurney, and she tried to see the pair through his eyes. They were both large men, tall and broad through the shoulders. They carried themselves with an air of confidence and projected a no-nonsense vibe that she had to admit was a bit intimidating.

Everest noticed Danny's response and offered him a friendly smile. "Hello," he said, as he and Peter reached the gurney. "My name is Everest LeBeau, and I'm head of security for the ship."

"I'm Peter MacKenzie, a consultant working with Everest and Dr. Watkins." His green eyes were kind as he regarded Danny. "We really appreciate your willingness to talk to us."

Danny nodded, his body relaxing a bit. "Dr. Watkins said you're trying to figure out what that putty is," he said. "I hope I can help you. I don't want anyone else to get hurt."

"Can you tell me about your experience?" Peter asked.

"Sure." Danny described his encounter with the substance in the bathroom he'd been cleaning. Mallory had already heard this story, but Everest and Peter listened intently to Danny's descriptions.

"When did you notice the effect on your hands?" Everest asked.

"Almost right away," Danny said. "My skin began to tingle and then it started to hurt, like I'd scraped my palms raw. I tried to wash my hands, but I didn't help. My palm turned red and big blisters popped up, along with some welts."

"Do you mind if we take a look?" Peter said.

Danny wrinkled his nose. "It's pretty nasty, but go ahead."

Mallory stepped forward and gently removed the bandages on his palm, revealing the damaged skin underneath. Peter and Everest both leaned forward, studying the cracked and oozing mess as if it were a fine painting. She was a bit surprised at their reaction—she'd expected some degree of shock and revulsion, but now she realized they'd probably seen much worse in their time at war.

Peter nodded to himself, and he and Everest exchanged a knowing look. "How have you been feeling since you hurt your hands?" Peter asked.

Danny frowned, considering the question. "Well, to be honest, I'm not at one hundred percent."

"How so?" Everest said.

"I feel tired and run-down. And I've had some…bathroom issues," he said, his cheeks flushing a dark pink.

"Why didn't you come back to the clinic?" Mallory said.

Danny shrugged. "I couldn't afford to take the time off. And when I finished my shift, I was too tired to bother."

"Are you still feeling sick?" She reached for the digital thermometer and ran it across his forehead. His temperature was normal. Probably no infection, then…

Danny hesitated, and Mallory could tell he was weighing his response. "Please be honest," she said. "If you're not feeling well, I need to know so I can help you."

"I can't afford to miss any more work," he began.

"You're entitled to sick pay," she interrupted. "And I'll speak to your supervisor myself to make sure you aren't unfairly punished for taking time off."

He nodded slowly. "I do still feel bad," he said softly.

Mallory gestured for one of the nurses to come over, and she gave instructions for medications. "We're going to start an IV," she told Danny. "Hopefully some fluids will help perk you up."

"Thanks for talking to us," Peter said. He gave Danny's shoulder a pat. "You've been a huge help."

Danny looked relieved. "Really?"

Everest nodded. "Yes," he confirmed. "Get some rest now." The two men stepped away, giving the nurse room to work.

Mallory issued a few more orders, then joined Everest and Peter. She could tell by the looks on their faces they had something to say. "My office?" she suggested.

She led them to the small space and gestured to the chairs she and Everest had returned this morning after wheeling the gurney back into the main body of the clinic. Not much time had passed since their conversation in the small hours of the morning, but it felt like a lifetime ago. She caught his eye as they both sat, and he gave her a small, private smile that triggered a rush of warmth in her chest. It seemed she wasn't the only one remembering their earlier chat.

"What do you think?" she said, eager to hear what Peter and Everest had to say now that they had seen Danny's injuries.

"I feel bad for the guy," Peter said, shaking his head. "He can't be comfortable with his hand like that."

"He's probably not," she said. "But he'd never admit it."

"I wish I'd insisted on seeing him earlier," Everest said. "I would have been more forceful with the captain if I'd known."

Mallory's stomach sank. "So you think he's suffering from radiation burns, as well?"

Peter shrugged, but his gaze was serious. "It's definitely possible. You know better that most that it's difficult to determine the cause of a burn simply by looking at it. But his wounds are consistent with radiation damage, and his continued symptoms certainly fit the clinical picture, as well."

"That's what I thought," she said softly.

"We won't know for sure until I can examine the material," Peter continued.

Everest glanced at his watch. "It's late enough that the passengers should be off the ship for the day. We can get started, if you're both ready."

Mallory nodded and stood, feeling both anxious and eager to learn Peter's thoughts after he saw the mystery substance. She still held out hope that this was a false alarm, and that Danny's injuries were due to some kind of chemical exposure. Better to discover she had overreacted than to find the ship was loaded with radioactive material.

They decided to start in Jeff's former cabin, since they knew for certain it would be unoccupied. The sight of the bed brought back memories of the masked man who had drugged her, and she shuddered involuntarily. Everest had told her how he'd found her lying there unconscious, and how he'd tried to rouse her. She could picture the scene all too easily, an echo of the attack she'd suffered in college. *At least this time I wasn't raped*, she thought darkly.

Everest must have picked up on her discomfort because he moved to stand close to her. He didn't touch her, but she could tell by the look in his eyes he wanted to. It was thoughtful of him, the way he respected her personal space after hearing her story. He'd assured her that he would let her take the lead when it came to the physical side of their relationship, and she could tell he'd really meant it.

She brushed her hand down his arm, a light touch of acknowledgment to let him know she felt his support and appreciated it. It would take time for them to learn how to move around each other, but she had no doubt he was worth the effort.

Everest tilted his head to indicate the black box mounted high on the wall. "That's the communications hub I was telling you about. The material is inside." He pushed a chair over and made to stand, but Peter stopped him.

"Let me take a look," he said. "I brought a few things, just in case this does turn out to be dangerous."

He set his backpack on the bed and pulled out a clear face shield, a pair of gloves and a small gray device that was a little bigger than a cell phone. He quickly donned his gear, and Mallory held her breath as he climbed onto the chair and removed the cover of the hub.

Peter swore a blue streak, and Everest's body tensed. "What's wrong?" he said urgently.

Peter stepped down and turned to face them, his expression grim.

"Is it radioactive?" Mallory asked. She hadn't heard any sound from the detector he was using, but maybe the model he was using didn't make noise.

"I don't know," he said.

"What do you mean you don't know?" Everest asked. He sounded a little testy, and Mallory realized the degree of his worry matched her own. "What's the problem?"

If Peter was ruffled by Everest's tone, he didn't show it. He cocked his head to the side and gave them both a level stare. "Sorry to disappoint you, but I don't feel comfortable using a digital detector when there is a brick of C4 attached to the lid of the box."

"What?" Everest's face drained of color so fast Mallory thought he might faint. She placed her hand on his arm, but he didn't seem to notice her touch.

"C4?" Mallory asked. A growing sense of horror filled

her as she pieced together what Peter was saying. "Isn't that—"

"Yes," Everest confirmed. She could tell by the look on his face that his shock was fading, and his expression morphed into one of determination.

"It's a bomb."

Chapter 19

Mallory made a small sound of distress, and Everest gave her hand a squeeze. He wanted to offer her more reassurance, but there simply wasn't time.

"You're certain it's C4?" It was a stupid question, and he knew it. Peter was one of the best CBRN officers in the army—the odds that he would misidentify a hunk of C4 were so low as to be almost nil. Still, Everest had to ask. Maybe, just maybe, a trick of the light had convinced his friend one of the hub components was something else…

Peter lifted one eyebrow, not bothering to reply.

Everest nodded and held up a hand. "I know, I know. But you can't blame me for being hopeful."

Peter stepped away from the chair, making room. "Have a look yourself."

Everest wasted no time climbing onto the seat. He gingerly lifted the lid of the box, and sure enough, a brick of C4 about the size of a deck of playing cards was affixed to the plastic. A few wires connected the detonator to the explosive material, and there was a small blinking display that flashed intermittently.

Everest was no stranger to explosives, but being so close to a bomb like this never failed to turn his guts to water. He carefully lowered the lid, climbed down and ran a hand through his hair as he tried to figure out what to do next.

"I'm guessing that wasn't there when you guys did your survey for the other material?" Peter asked.

"No."

"There's really a bomb in the hub?" Mallory asked. She sounded hesitant, as if she didn't dare believe it.

"I'm afraid so," Peter said.

She frowned, looking up at the box. "But it's pretty small," she said. "I thought bombs had to be bigger."

"Not always," Everest said. "Usually, bigger bombs make for larger explosions. But even a little C4 can do some real damage."

"Oh." Her features tightened with worry. "What do we do?"

"We disarm it," Everest said simply. He turned to Peter. "I don't suppose you have some wire cutters in that bag?"

"No. But I do have this." He dug in the bag and produced a small multitool, which he handed over.

Everest unfolded the device and examined the different fixtures: a few screwdriver heads, a couple of blades, a file and a small pair of scissors. It wasn't his first choice for defusing a bomb, but it would have to do.

"Okay," he said with a nod. "This'll work." He turned to Mallory. "I think you and Peter should leave while I do this. The mechanism doesn't look very complicated, but if I make a mistake I don't want you two in the room."

Her eyes were wide as portholes. "I'm not leaving you." She sounded offended that he had even asked.

"Mallory—" he began.

"I'll stand in the bathroom if that will make you feel better," she said grudgingly. "But I won't leave you to do this by yourself."

He turned to Peter, hoping to appeal to his friend. Peter merely shrugged. "I'm not going anywhere. You might need some help."

Everest sighed, knowing better than to waste his breath arguing with the two of them. "Fine."

"Are you sure you know how to do this?" Mallory moved to stand next to him, placing her hand on his arm. He read the concern in her eyes and felt a rush of warmth suffuse his chest. It had been a long time since a woman had cared enough to worry for him. And while he wished the circumstances were different, it was nice to feel like he was important to Mallory.

"I'll be fine," he said, injecting confidence into his voice.

Peter spoke up. "Everest was the best in our squad at defusing bombs," he said. "The instructors were so impressed with his skills they offered him a job teaching other CBRN soldiers."

"Really?" Mallory sounded impressed. "I didn't know that."

Everest shrugged. "It didn't seem important." Safe handling of explosives wasn't exactly the kind of skill he'd thought he would use once he left the army. It had been years since he'd had to defuse a bomb. Hopefully the process was like riding a bike...

He climbed up on the chair again, tool in hand, then turned to look at Mallory. "Bathroom?"

She nodded reluctantly and walked into the small room, closing the door behind her. Everest turned back to the box and took a deep breath. His palms were sweating, so he ran his hands down the front of his pants to dry them.

"You've got this," Peter said quietly.

Everest shot his friend a grateful smile and nodded in acknowledgment. Then he turned his focus to the box, blocking out the world around him as he concentrated on the bomb in front of him.

It wasn't a complicated job, as far as these things went. But even though the bomb was small and the wiring was simple, Everest knew better than to take anything for granted. Complacency led to mistakes, and an error while working on a job like this was what got people killed.

It didn't take long to separate the wires and identify the ones responsible for connecting the detonator to the C4. Working carefully and methodically, Everest clipped the wires, severing the connection between the detonator and the explosive. Once that was done, he gently pried the detonator free. C4 was fairly stable on its own, so by removing the detonator with its explosive charge, he'd effectively neutralized the bomb.

He climbed down, his hands full of the bomb components. He laid them on the bed, and he and Peter bent over to study them, hoping to glean some useful information from the bits and pieces.

"Nice work," Peter said, clapping him on the back.

"Thanks," Everest replied drily.

Mallory must have been listening at the door because she flew out of the bathroom and ran into his arms. "You're okay," she breathed, clutching him tightly. She leaned back and kissed him hard, and he realized in that moment how scared she had been. He'd been a little nervous himself, but thanks to his army training, he'd known how to handle the problem. Mallory didn't have that advantage, though, and he felt a pang of guilt for not taking more time to reassure her.

He wrapped his arms around her and ran a hand up and down her back. "I'm fine," he said, pressing his mouth to her ear. "You're not getting rid of me that easily."

"It's not funny," she said. She pulled back, and he saw the glint of tears in her eyes. "Do you have any idea how much you scared me just now?"

"I'm sorry," he said, and he meant it. He truly hadn't wanted to upset her, but he'd been so focused on disarming the bomb he hadn't stopped to think about how his actions might seem to her.

She held his gaze for an endless moment, then nodded. He squeezed her hand, and together they turned to examine the bomb components spread out on the bed.

"Looks like pretty standard stuff to me," Peter mused. "What do you think?"

"I agree," Everest said. "Basic blasting cap, remote detonator. Probably runs off a cell phone trigger." But he couldn't see it from here. He'd need to dig a little deeper to know for sure.

"Then why didn't it explode?" Mallory asked. "The passengers all have cell phones, and they've been using them regularly. Wouldn't one of their phones have set things off?"

"Not necessarily," Peter said. "You usually have to specifically call the phone associated with the bomb in order to detonate it. Presumably, whoever placed this one here isn't ready to set it off quite yet."

Everest picked up the bundle of C4, drawing it closer.

Mallory let out a soft gasp and took a half step back. "It's okay," he said absently. "C4 is a stable explosive."

"What does that mean?" she said, sounding unconvinced.

"It means it won't go off in his hands," Peter said helpfully.

Everest peeled back a corner of the tape and began to unwrap the bundle. The explosive material was covered in a thin plastic wrap, and attached to one side he found a small, flat circuit board with protruding wires that he had clipped earlier to detach them from the detonator.

"Here's our trigger," he said, tossing it back onto the bed. He felt a small surge of satisfaction at being right, but the sensation didn't last long. He may have figured out how the bomb was going to be detonated, but that didn't solve the mystery of who had placed it there and why.

"What is that?" Mallory asked, leaning forward to peer at the panel.

"It's the guts of a cell phone," Peter said. "And now that the bomb is no longer a threat, I'm going to do the job you brought me here to do." He reached for his acrylic face shield and digital Geiger counter and climbed back onto the seat of the chair.

Everest held his breath as his friend extended the probe toward the gray putty in the box. The detector let out a shrill beep of alarm that needed no translation.

The material was radioactive.

Wesley paused in his journey down the hall, startled to hear a muffled, but still audible, beeping. It sounded like it was coming from Jeff's old room, but surely that wasn't possible...

He walked up to the door and leaned close. Yes, the

noise was coming from inside the room. Was it the bomb? His stomach grew queasy as he considered the possibility. The instructions for arming the bomb had been simple, but Wesley didn't know enough about explosives to determine if there was a problem. He'd pressed the small buttons in the correct sequence and had been rewarded with the appearance of a blinking light, but what if something had gone wrong? He'd placed the first bomb in this cabin, to take advantage of the uninterrupted privacy. Everything had seemed fine at the time, but perhaps one of the wires had worked loose?

Not that he could do anything about it, if that was indeed the issue. He had no desire to try to troubleshoot a problem with the explosives—carrying around a backpack full of the stuff was enough to make him break out into a cold sweat. Given his nerves, he was likely to touch the wrong thing and set the charge off. It wasn't worth the risk. He had no intention of dying in the upcoming blast. He was going to be safely on shore, watching the show from a safe distance.

Still, he needed to do something. If the noise continued, the passengers on either side of the cabin would complain, and someone would be sent to check the room. If the bomb was discovered before the ship docked in New York City's harbor, it would be disastrous.

Wesley fumbled in his pocket for the key card. Maybe he could tape a pillow over the hub, to further muffle the sound. It was worth a shot...

Just as he pulled the card free, the noise stopped. He breathed a sigh of relief; the less time he had to spend around the armed bombs, the better.

He turned to continue down the hall when another sound in the room caught his attention. Voices.

The hairs on his arms stood on end as he pressed an

ear to the door, straining to catch snatches of conversation.

"...have to go to the captain..."

"...evacuate the ship..."

Wesley drew back, his heart pounding in a panicked rhythm as he realized his mission had been compromised. For a brief second, he considered running off the ship and detonating the bombs he'd already planted. But he realized it wouldn't do enough damage. He still needed to place the larger charges in key locations, to maximize the spread of the radioactive material. If he pulled the trigger now, it would only wreck a plan that had been years in the making.

A sense of determination filled him, pushing aside his anxieties. He wasn't going to let this little hiccup prevent him from avenging his brother. Ryan deserved better than that.

That left only one option.

Wesley knelt and unclipped his gun from its holster at his ankle. It wasn't a large weapon, but it didn't need to be. Guns were prohibited on board the ship, so whoever was inside the room would be unarmed. One or two well-placed shots were all it would take to fix this problem.

The thought made him hesitate. He'd never killed anyone before. Never fired a gun at an actual person, for that matter. Did he have what it took to look someone in the eyes and shoot the person?

His hands began to shake. He took a deep breath and closed his eyes, picturing Ryan's face. The image of his brother in his khaki desert fatigues steadied him. Ryan had been a brave soldier; he could be, too. This was a war. Maybe not one fought on a field of battle, but it was a war all the same.

Feeling better, Wesley stuck the key card in the slot and listened for the click of the lock. He pushed the door open and stepped inside to finish his job.

Chapter 20

"We need to evacuate the ship," Peter said. "How long do you think that will take?"

Everest opened his mouth to respond, but a sound across the room caught his attention.

Someone was unlocking the door.

Acting on instinct, Everest grabbed Mallory and practically threw her toward the entrance to the bathroom. "Hide, now!" he whispered urgently. The only people who had any business in this room were with him. That meant anyone who was trying to come in now was suspect.

To her credit, Mallory didn't argue with him. She ducked into the dark room and hid behind the door, leaving it open a crack. Everest didn't like seeing her exposed even a little bit, but perhaps it was better this way. It would look more suspicious if the bathroom door was fully closed, like they were trying to hide something.

He turned back just as Wesley walked in the room.

He carried a backpack over one shoulder, and his other hand was down by his leg. He kept his hand obscured as he moved, which told Everest he was armed.

Everest's heart sank at the confirmation that his second-in-command was behind the attacks on Mallory and perhaps even the bomb they had found in this room. Wesley had always seemed like a dependable, trustworthy young man.

So much for appearances.

"Wesley," he said, striving for a tone of pleasant surprise. "What's going on?"

Wesley glanced from Everest to Peter, clearly sizing them up. "I heard noises coming from this room and thought I'd check it out. Is it just the two of you here?"

"Yes," Peter said, giving him a slightly puzzled look, as if he was wondering why Wesley would ask such a patently obvious question.

Thank you, Everest thought. Wesley might not have believed the denial coming from him, but he didn't know Peter, and so had no reason to think Peter would be trying to protect Mallory.

"Where's the doctor?" He sounded suspicious; maybe he hadn't believed Peter after all.

Everest shrugged, trying to make it look casual. "As far as I know, she's in the clinic. Why? Do you need to talk to her?"

"Maybe later," Wesley said evasively. He stepped farther into the room, and Everest moved toward Peter, trying to subtly guide Wesley so he was standing with his back toward the bathroom door.

"Have you met my friend Peter MacKenzie?" he said, gesturing toward the other man.

"No. Why is he here?" There was an edge of hostility in his voice that Everest had never heard before. It seemed Wesley was no longer interested in maintaining a pleasant facade.

"Everest asked me to come aboard and look at a few things," Peter said easily.

Wesley glanced from them to the bed, taking in the material strewn across the fabric of the bedspread. "I see you dismantled the bomb," he said flatly.

"Yes," Everest said calmly. "We did. Want to tell us why you put it there?"

Wesley shook his head. "How many have you found?"

Terror seized Everest's heart with a vise-like grip as all the pieces fell into place. Of course. Why hadn't he seen it before?

The radioactive material was distributed all over the ship. He was willing to bet that all the communication hubs were also now sporting small bombs like the one he'd just dismantled. Obviously, the plan was to blow up the ship, scattering radioactive debris all over the city.

Wesley had turned the ship into a floating dirty bomb.

"We found all of them," Peter lied smoothly, betraying no trace of nervousness or unease. "So why don't you take this opportunity to explain what's going on? I think there have been a lot of misunderstandings going on—it would help if we heard things from your perspective."

Wesley shook his head. "I don't think so. And I don't think you found all the bombs either. Did you get the one in the aft gym?"

"Yes," Everest said.

The young man's grin was full of malice. "I didn't put one there."

Wesley took a step forward, lifting his hand to reveal his gun for the first time. It was a small black revolver, the kind that fit in an ankle holster. He'd likely had no trouble smuggling it on board, especially considering his role as a security officer.

Everest glanced from the gun to Wesley's face. The man looked nervous, but determined. Had he even fired that thing before, or was this going to be his first time using it?

"Is that really necessary?" he asked quietly. "We're no threat to you."

"Yes, you are," Wesley said, a hint of emotion creeping into his voice. "I have a job to do, and I'm not going to let you interfere."

"Who put you up to this?" Everest asked. This plan was too sophisticated for Wesley to have implemented by himself. Someone else was pulling the strings. Were they on board, as well? Or were they directing things from afar?

"That's not important," Wesley said.

"What's your plan, young man?" Peter asked. "Are you just going to shoot us and leave us here?"

Wesley tilted his head to the side, as if considering the suggestion.

"Yeah, actually. That's exactly what I'm going to do."

Mallory crouched in the bathroom, breathing as quietly as she could while she watched events unfold in the room.

She hadn't been surprised to see Wesley walk in. Something about him had always rubbed her the wrong way, and it seemed her instincts had been right. Seeing him move now, she realized he'd been the one to drug her earlier. No wonder he'd worn a mask and a robe and had refused to talk—she would have recognized his voice immediately.

Anger surged in her chest as she stared at his back.

He'd attacked her twice. God only knew what he would have done to her if Everest hadn't found her when he did. She'd probably be dead at the bottom of the ocean if Everest hadn't tracked her down so quickly.

And now here Wesley was, threatening Everest and Peter because they had dared to interfere with his psychotic plans.

She saw the gun in his hand, and the rational part of her brain knew she should feel afraid. She didn't like guns; she'd tended to the aftermath of their wounds far too often to ever take pleasure in shooting, even if it was just target practice. But the sight of Wesley pointing his small revolver at Everest didn't scare her.

It enraged her.

This ends now.

She rose to her feet and glanced around the room in search of anything she could use as a weapon. The towel rack on the wall caught her eye, and moving carefully, she quietly pulled the rod free from the wall anchors.

Maybe it was foolish to go charging toward an armed man with nothing more threatening than a hollow metal tube, but Mallory couldn't afford to doubt herself. She pulled open the door, and before she could think twice, she rushed into the room, the rod held high above her head.

Wesley began to turn as she reached him, but she hit him before he could bring the gun around to point it at her. A jolt went up her arm as the rod made contact with his head, and Wesley let out a cry of pain.

Mallory lifted her arm and hit him again, taking a perverse pleasure in the solid thunk that sounded as the rod landed against his body. She hadn't gotten justice for her rape, but she wasn't going to let Wesley get away with hurting her.

She hit him over and over again, her arm moving under its own power. It was only when someone reached out and wrenched the rod from her grasp that she stopped, her body shaking as she tried to catch her breath.

"It's okay, Mallory." Everest pulled her close. "He's down."

She blinked, surprised to find she was crying.

Peter knelt and checked Wesley's pulse, then nodded. "He's alive. You conked him pretty good, though." He tilted his head to the side and studied her. "Who's Blake?"

The name sent a shock wave through her system, and her knees threatened to buckle. "What?" she whispered hoarsely. How did he know? Had Everest told him?

She twisted around, trying to see Everest's face. He shook his head, denying her silent question. "You were yelling," he said softly. "You called out his name while you hit Wesley."

"Oh."

She glanced down to find Wesley crumpled on the floor, unconscious. There were red welts on his skin where the rod had hit him, and a large bump had already formed on the side of his head. Mallory studied him, knowing she should feel guilty for continuing to beat him after he'd collapsed. But she was hollow inside, and for a brief moment, she feared that if Everest squeezed her too tightly, her body would shatter into a million tiny pieces.

All of a sudden, the scene before her blurred and she realized she was being moved. Someone guided her down until she sat, and then Everest's face filled her vision.

"It's okay," he said soothingly. "You're fine now."

"I should check on him," Mallory said, her voice wooden even to her own ears. She sniffed, her nose feeling congested thanks to her tears.

"Peter is with him," Everest said. "He knows first aid. Just rest now."

She stared into the depths of his blue eyes, using his gaze as an anchor to keep her mind from slipping away into the past. "I didn't mean to hurt him so badly," she whispered. "I just got so angry because I know he's the one who drugged me. I couldn't stand letting another man get away with hurting me..." She broke off and shook her head, her throat closing up.

"It's okay." Everest stroked her hair, his hand large and warm. She leaned forward, burying her head against his shoulder. His arms came around her, strong and sure, and she breathed in his comforting scent.

"It's okay," he said again. "You're safe now."

"Don't let me go," she said desperately. "Please don't let me go."

His hold tightened. "I won't," he promised softly. "I never will."

Chapter 21

It seemed to take forever before he saw Mallory again, but in reality, it was no more than a few hours.

After making sure Wesley was incapacitated, he and Peter had called the police and informed the captain. It hadn't taken long for officers from several different agencies to arrive and for bomb squad officers to board the ship. The evacuation had been relatively straightforward, thanks to the fact that most of the passengers were participating in excursions in the city.

Everest, Mallory and Peter had been separated, each taken to different rooms in a hastily commandeered office building close to the docks. The police, ATF, FBI and Homeland Security couldn't seem to decide who should have jurisdiction, so a rotating cast of suit-clad agents had visited him in a steady stream throughout the afternoon.

He'd answered the same questions over and over again, until his patience had worn thin.

"Don't you guys talk to each other?" he'd asked, after repeating himself for what must have been the hundredth time.

He understood the need for careful questioning, but he wasn't the bad guy and he wanted to see Mallory. She'd seemed so fragile in his arms, and he wanted to make sure she was okay.

Finally, after a last round of questions and admonitions to stay in town in case they thought of something else to ask him, the last batch of agents released him from the small room.

"What about Peter and Mallory?" he asked.

The man in the black suit shrugged. "I'm sure they'll be done shortly."

So Everest found a chair in the lobby of the office suites and sat, drawing on his self-control to keep his butt in the seat when what he really wanted to do was find the room Mallory was in and stay with her while the agents interrogated her. This had to be difficult for her—he imagined the last time she'd been questioned by the police was in the aftermath of her rape. And since her encounter with Wesley had stirred up those memories, he hated to think how scared she was right now.

He stood and began to pace, unable to remain still. Mallory needed him; there had to be something he could do.

He glanced at the closed office doors. He wasn't sure which room she was in, but it didn't matter. He'd go room to room until he found her.

The agents wouldn't be happy, but too bad. They'd taken long enough.

Just as he took the first step, one of the doors opened and Mallory stepped out, followed by two agents. They said something to her and she nodded, but as soon as she saw him, she ran forward.

He opened his arms and gathered her close, burying his nose in her hair. "Are you all right?" he asked quietly.

"I am now," she said.

The second door opened and Peter emerged. "I know, I know," he said. "You want me to stay in town. I hate to break it to you boys, but I'm expected back at my post in two days. So if you have any more questions for me, better think of them soon."

The agents in the room began to protest, but Peter shut the door firmly and walked over to join Everest and Mallory.

"Heck of a way to spend the day," he commented mildly.

"This wasn't exactly how I thought things would go when I called you," Everest said. He felt a little bad that Peter had gotten caught up in such a mess, but at the same time, he was glad his friend had been by his side.

"You okay?" Peter asked Mallory kindly.

She nodded, not loosening her grip on Everest. "Yes. Thank you."

"Thank *you*," Peter said. "If it wasn't for you, Everest and I would be in much worse shape right now."

"Do you really think Wesley would have killed you?"

Everest nodded. "He would have tried." And as close as Wesley had been standing to them, he probably would have succeeded in killing at least one of them.

Peter clapped Everest on the back. "Well, this has been fun. It was good to see you, Everest. Always an adventure."

"Where are you going?" Everest asked.

Peter shrugged. "I figured I'd find a hotel and spend tomorrow sightseeing. Then I'm headed back to post."

"Sounds like a plan." He let go of Mallory for a second so he could embrace his friend. "Thanks for everything. Let me know if you need help smoothing things over with the brass." Peter's unsanctioned use of army equipment for civilian purposes wasn't something his commanding officer would look kindly on. But since he had been instrumental in averting a large-scale terrorist attack on domestic soil, Everest hoped Peter wouldn't face any disciplinary action.

"Are you kidding?" Peter grinned. "When this is over, I'll have them thinking the whole thing was their idea. Might even get a medal out of it." He winked, and Everest and Mallory both laughed.

"It was nice to meet you," Peter said to Mallory.

To Everest's surprise, Mallory threw her arms around Peter and hugged him tightly. Peter's shocked expression made it clear he hadn't been expecting the gesture, but he returned her embrace, if a bit more gently.

"You take care of yourself," he said, sounding a little gruff.

"You, too," she said.

Mallory snugged back into Everest's side, and together they set off for the exit. "What do you want to do now?" he asked. They stepped into the fading afternoon light and waved goodbye to Peter as he flagged down a taxi.

Mallory considered the question for a moment. The wind whipped a few strands of her hair free from her ponytail, and he reached over to brush them out of her face. She smiled up at him, her eyes bright and clear, and he realized with a sense of relief that she was going to be fine.

"I can't think of anything in particular," she said.

"Me neither," he admitted.

Her smile turned a little mischievous. "It usually takes

a while for a couple to reach this phase of the relationship, or so I hear."

"Well, we've packed a lot of emotion into a short period of time," Everest said. A thrill shot through him at her use of the word *couple*, and he grinned. "I hope this doesn't mean you're already bored with me."

"Never," she said. She leaned her head against his shoulder and let out a contented sigh he felt in his soul. "This is only the beginning for us."

Epilogue

Three months later...

"I now pronounce you husband and wife. You may kiss your bride."

Mallory let out a happy sigh as Logan and Olivia leaned in to share a kiss. They were such a handsome couple—Logan in his charcoal suit and dark green tie, Olivia in her ivory sheath, clutching a small bouquet of pale pink roses.

Next to her, Everest leaned in close. "They look so good together." His breath was warm in her ear, and she leaned into his side, snuggling against his solid length. It was so nice to be with him again; their jobs had kept them separated for the past few weeks, and they'd both arrived in Virginia today for the wedding. They had the next few days together, and Mallory intended to make the most of them.

"They're perfect for each other," she said.

Olivia and Logan turned to face the small group, both grinning widely.

"Congratulations," said the judge, reaching out to shake their hands. "I'll sign your marriage license and then this will all be official." He stepped to the side to do just that, while Avery, Grant, Mallory and Everest surrounded the happy couple.

Mallory engulfed Olivia in a hug. "You're such a beautiful bride," she said, blinking back tears. "I'm so happy for you."

Avery held her arms open wide. "Mrs. Murray," she said, smiling broadly.

Olivia laughed. "It does have a nice ring to it, doesn't it?"

They glanced over at the men, who were shaking hands and slapping backs.

"It was a lovely ceremony," Mallory said.

"Short and sweet," Olivia said. "Just like we wanted it."

The judge handed the marriage license to Logan, and the group walked into the lobby of the courthouse, where several other couples sat, awaiting their turn to be joined in marriage.

"I must say," Avery remarked, "this was a great way to get married." She sounded thoughtful. "What do you think, Grant? We could duck out to the courthouse and be back at work in a matter of hours…"

"Oh, no," Grant said, rolling his eyes as he pulled her close. "You know I'll marry you anytime, anywhere. But we are not going back to work afterward. We're taking a break and going on a honeymoon."

"Speaking of," Mallory said. "We should head to the

restaurant so we can start lunch. We don't want these two to miss their flight."

Olivia and Logan were leaving for their honeymoon later that afternoon. The couple was headed to Maine to enjoy a quiet week at a quaint B and B. Mallory had seen their itinerary, and she knew it was going to be a wonderful trip, filled with good food, quiet afternoons by the fire and amazing views of the foliage, which was just beginning to turn for the fall. It was exactly the kind of restful vacation Olivia and Logan deserved, and Mallory was thrilled for her friends.

She glanced at Everest, and her heart swelled as a rush of feeling hit her. They'd spent the past two months getting to know each other very well, and the more she learned about him, the more she wanted to know. Unfortunately, they'd both been assigned to different cruises in the wake of the *Abigail Adams* voyage, and so they hadn't been able to see each other as often as she would have liked. But they still found ways to connect with each other every day—texting, talking on the phone and videoconferencing in the evenings. They'd spent countless hours talking about anything and everything, and Everest had quickly become Mallory's chief confidant, her cheerleader and her rock. He made her laugh, he lifted her spirits when she was having a bad day and he was a great sounding board when she needed to talk through a decision. Never in her wildest dreams had she imagined feeling so emotionally close to a man, and she reveled in the comfort of their relationship.

They sat side by side during lunch. Everest was left-handed, so their arms and hands brushed continuously throughout the meal as they both ate. Every time she felt his skin against her own, a tingle shot up her arm and her stomach fluttered. Mallory tried to pay attention to the conversation, but being so close to Everest was distracting.

At the end of the meal the couples said their goodbyes. Malloy hugged Olivia tightly. "Have a wonderful trip," she said. "Send us a postcard."

"They won't have time for that," Avery said, a knowing smile on her face. "I'm sure they'll be busy."

Olivia laughed. "We'll have to come up for air sometime," she said, her eyes sparkling.

Mallory turned to Logan, reaching out for a hug. Surprise flashed in his green eyes, and he smiled. He hugged her gently. "Take care of yourself," he said softly in her ear.

"I will," she promised. She could tell by his reaction Olivia had told him about her past assault. Once upon a time, she would have been bothered to know more people were aware of her rape. But now that Everest was in her life, she no longer felt vulnerable when she thought about the incident. It was a horrible thing that had happened to her, but Everest's support had helped her reclaim her power, so that she was no longer controlled by her memories. Their relationship seemed to have helped Everest as well—he'd told Grant and Logan about his leg, and he didn't seem so self-conscious about his injury anymore.

They all waved as Olivia and Logan drove away, headed back to their house so they could change clothes before their flight. Avery turned to Mallory. "We're going to head into DC and do a little sightseeing. Want to join us?"

Mallory shook her head. "Thanks, but Everest and I were thinking about going to Mount Vernon. Maybe we can meet up for dinner somewhere?"

"That would be nice," Avery said. They all exchanged

hugs, and then Avery and Grant started walking in the direction of the Metro station.

"I didn't know you wanted to see Mount Vernon," Everest said, a note of surprise in his voice.

"I don't," Mallory replied. She raised one eyebrow, and realization dawned in his eyes.

"Oh," he said. His Adam's apple bobbed in his throat as he swallowed, and Mallory got the distinct impression he was nervous.

That makes two of us, she thought wryly.

Their hotel was only a few blocks away. In a matter of moments, Everest shut the door behind them, leaving them alone for the first time in weeks.

"Hi." His voice was a low rumble that she felt as much as heard, a light brush against her skin that made her shiver.

"Hi yourself," she replied. She took a step toward him, needing to get closer.

He matched her movement, his eyes never leaving hers as together they closed the distance between them.

"I've missed you so much," he said softly. He lifted his hand and ran it gently down her hair. His touch was like a benediction, and Mallory closed her eyes, savoring the contact.

"I've missed you, too," she said.

She reached up to link her hands at the back of his neck, drawing him closer until her body flattened against his. It was a heady sensation, feeling every inch of his powerful frame pressed against her. The visceral reminder of his strength was overwhelming, but she wasn't afraid. Instead, she felt safe.

After a moment, she leaned back so she could press a kiss to his mouth. He tasted of coffee from lunch, and his lips were warm and soft against her own.

He hummed softly in his throat and ran his hand down her back, anchoring her against him. She didn't know how long they stood there, wrapped in each other's arms. Being so close to him was intoxicating, and her head spun as she breathed in the warm scent of his skin.

Need rose in her chest, urging her to seek more from Everest. She took his hand and led him to the bed, where they both sat. She reached for the buttons on her shirt and began to unfasten them, but Everest placed his hand over hers.

"Mallory," he said softly. "Are you sure?"

She met his eyes and saw a mix of emotions there—need, concern, hope. And love.

"Yes." She nodded, watched the relief flash across his face. "I'm ready. It's time."

The breath gusted out of him on a sigh, and he traced the line of her cheekbone with her fingertip. "Okay. How do you want to do this?"

"I—I'm not quite sure." Now that the moment was here, Mallory didn't know exactly how to proceed. What was the protocol for seducing one's boyfriend?

"That's fine." His smile was sweet and a little shy. "We'll just figure things out for ourselves."

He took her hand and placed it against his chest. "You're in charge," he said simply.

Mallory allowed her hand to roam across the planes of his chest and stomach, tracing the ridges of muscle through the fabric of his shirt. It was nice, but she wanted to feel his skin against her own. She tugged at the hem of his shirt and gave him a quizzical look.

"Can I—?"

In lieu of a response, Everest pulled his shirt off and tossed it to the side. "Pants, too?" he asked, a smile in his voice.

"Yes, please." Mallory felt her cheeks heat, but any embarrassment she felt soon faded as she got her first good look at Everest's body.

Her hands were pale against the golden glow of his skin. Dark blond hair dusted his chest and tapered into a line that bisected his toned stomach. She traced the lines of his thigh muscles, and was rewarded with the sound of a strangled laugh.

"Ticklish?"

"A little." Still, he let her continue to explore his body, offering no objections even when she bent to examine his prosthesis.

It fit just below his knee and appeared to be a no-nonsense contraption consisting of a sleeve, a metal pole and a prosthetic foot. This was the first time she'd had occasion to examine one so closely, and she studied it curiously.

"Do you want me to remove it?"

Mallory glanced at Everest, trying to gauge his feeling. The last thing she wanted was to make him uncomfortable.

"Only if you want to." She reached for his hand and squeezed gently. "This isn't all about me, you know."

He leaned forward and kissed her, hard. "I trust you," he said. "With all of me."

Mallory blinked back tears as Everest unfastened his prosthesis and removed a fabric sleeve, revealing a stump that was shiny with scars. She reached out to touch his leg, but drew up short before she made contact.

Everest took her hand and placed it on his knee. "It's okay," he said. "Like I said, all of me."

Mallory leaned forward to examine the site, her professional interest sparked. "Whoever operated on you did a nice job," she commented. She traced one of the longer scars and nodded appreciatively. "Looks like it healed well."

"Um, Mallory?"

She looked up to find Everest watching her, an amused expression on his face. "Do you think you could maybe sound a little more like my girlfriend and a little less like my doctor? You're going to give me a complex here."

"Oh! Sorry," she said, feeling sheepish.

"It's okay," he said, reaching for her. He drew her up the length of his body and kissed her again. "Where were we?"

"This feels familiar," she murmured against his mouth. Her heart pounded hard against her rib cage, and she gathered her courage. It was her turn to bare herself to his gaze.

She pulled back and unbuttoned her shirt, shrugging it off and dropping it to the floor. Everest sucked in a breath, and his blue eyes flashed with arousal. "Pants, too?" she asked teasingly.

"Oh, God, please, yes," he breathed. "If you want to, that is."

Mallory laughed, enjoying herself more than she'd thought was possible. She was beginning to realize that her rape had been more about violence and power than sex. Now she just had to hold on to that knowledge as she and Everest took this next step.

She lay back on the bed, raising her arms over her head so that Everest could see her fully. His eyes roamed over her body, his expression almost reverent as he studied her.

"Are you going to touch me?" she asked softly.

"Can I?" His voice was a little strangled, revealing the intensity of his need.

"Please." She needed to feel his hands on her body,

needed his touch to burn away the invisible marks of Blake's aggression.

His hands were big and warm on her skin, his movements in turn gentle and teasing. He angled himself over her and kissed her again, triggering a zing of sensation in her chest that shot down her torso to settle in her core.

His hands stroked her, followed by his lips. He worked his way down her body, and she gasped as the intensity of her arousal built. She felt like she was headed toward something, her body stretching in pursuit of a goal she couldn't quite see.

Everest's clever fingers seemed to know exactly where to touch her, how to move to bring her pleasure. She gripped his shoulders, holding on to him as her world spun and she lost herself to sensation.

Dimly, she felt his weight settle over her. Panic slammed into her, hard and fast, and she fought to breathe.

She must have made some sound, some noise of distress. In the next instant, she felt a gust of cool air on her body and realized Everest was sitting next to her.

"I'm sorry," he said, his eyes bright with concern.

"It's okay," she said. The tight band around her chest eased, and shame flooded her. Her worst nightmare was coming true, and she didn't know what to do about it.

Everest placed a finger under her chin, turning her head until she faced him. "Don't worry about it," he said. "We knew this might happen."

Tears filled her eyes, and she shook her head. "I'm sorry."

"Don't apologize," he said. "You never have to apologize to me."

"I really want to make love to you," she said, a sense of despair settling over her. "But I don't know how."

He was quiet for a moment, his expression thoughtful.

"Why don't we try something different?" he suggested. He lay flat on the bed, assuming her earlier pose. "I think you should be on top."

She eyed him, her appreciation for his body growing as she took in his length. "That might work," she said, feeling the faint stirrings of hope in her chest. If she didn't feel restrained, she might not experience that rush of fear.

"Let's see if we can recapture the magic," he said, reaching for her.

She went willingly, covering his body with her own. Gradually, her panic subsided as her sense of need returned, ushered in by Everest's soothing murmurs and careful strokes.

Finally, she could stand it no longer. She needed to feel Everest inside her, needed to join with him in this most basic and most profound way. She threw her leg over his hips, straddling him.

He clearly sensed her impatience. "One second," he said hastily.

She paused, taken aback. But her confusion dissolved as she watched him quickly don a condom. "Ready when you are," he said with a grin.

Mallory took a deep breath and lowered herself onto him. She braced herself for the jolt of panic, the hit of disgust. But it never came. The ghosts of her past were quiet; it was only the two of them in bed right now.

She nearly cried with relief, her eyes stinging with tears.

"Mallory. Look at me."

She opened her eyes and found Everest staring up at her with a look of naked yearning on his face. "Stay with me," he said, moving under her.

"Yes," she whispered, her heart swelling with love for

this man and the life they were building together. "Only with you. Always."

For the first time, Mallory shared her heart along with her body. Her connection with Everest strengthened as they explored each other, touching, moving, giving each other pleasure. She'd thought they were close before, but now that she felt him move inside her, heard him gasp and tasted the salt of his sweat on his skin, she realized what they'd been missing. Everest made her feel whole again. He was her missing piece, her safe place, her true match. She clung to him, reveling in the knowledge that he was hers and she was his. With every thrust, every caress, their bond grew stronger, cementing the connection between them.

Afterward, they lay together, limbs tangled and skin flushed and damp with sweat. Everest idly ran his finger up and down her arm in a gentle caress.

Mallory turned and snuggled into his side. "Thank you," she said quietly.

He chuckled softly, his chest vibrating against her ear. "That's my line."

They were quiet a moment, then he spoke again. "Are you okay?"

She took a moment to consider the question. She had expected to feel all kinds of emotions in the wake of her first sexual encounter after the rape, but in truth, she felt pleasantly spent, empty of worries or concerns.

"I'm more than okay," she said, lifting her head to smile at him. "I feel amazing."

Relief flashed across his face, and she realized he had been worried about her reaction. "I'm so glad," he said sincerely. "Does this mean you'll sleep with me again?" He lifted one brow teasingly, and she laughed.

"Ready for round two so soon?"

"No, not quite," he admitted. "But I do hope you'll give me another opportunity to show how much I love you."

His words made her heart soar. She stared at him, unable to contain the grin spreading across her face. "You love me?" she said softly.

"I do."

She kissed him, then leaned back and laughed, unable to contain her joy. "You love me!"

He smiled and ran a hand down her side. "I'm glad to see that makes you happy."

"Of course it does!" She kissed him again. "And it just so happens, I love you, too."

Warmth filled his eyes, and he wrapped his arms around her. "I had my fingers crossed," he whispered into her hair. "It's nice to know the feeling is mutual."

"Most definitely," she assured him. "You're all mine, Everest LeBeau."

He grinned. "Does this mean you're mine, Mallory Watkins?"

She nodded, drinking in the sight of him, etching this view in her heart so she would remember it always.

"Yes."

* * * * *

If you enjoyed this thrilling romance,
don't miss the first two volumes of Lara Lacombe's
DOCTORS IN DANGER *miniseries:*

ENTICED BY THE OPERATIVE
DR. DO-OR-DIE

Available now wherever Harlequin books are sold!

#1955 CAPTURING A COLTON
The Coltons of Shadow Creek • by C.J. Miller
Declan Sinclair never intended to like the Colton family, but
with his best friend marrying into it, he suddenly can't resist
Jade Colton. Her notorious mother is still on the loose and out
for revenge—against Jade! As Declan and Jade grow closer,
danger draws nearer and they realize they're in for the fight of
their lives...

#1956 CAVANAUGH ENCOUNTER
Cavanaugh Justice • by Marie Ferrarella
Luke Cavanaugh O'Bannon is determined to find the serial killer
targeting women through an online dating service. He wasn't
expecting help from Francesca DeMarco, a fellow homicide
detective struggling with her own demons. And neither one
of them expects the sparks to fly when they begin working
together to bring a killer to justice!

#1957 DETECTIVE DEFENDER
by Marilyn Pappano
A ghost from Martine Broussard's past dredges up long-held
secrets and hurts, putting her in danger. With her friends dead
or missing, she has to set aside her animosity for Detective
Jimmy DiBiase—the man who once threatened her heart—and
work with him to avoid becoming the killer's next victim.

#1958 RESCUED BY THE BILLIONAIRE CEO
Man on a Mission • by Amelia Autin
Jason Moore is a billionaire CEO by day, but by night he runs a
covert rescue organization. One of his secret missions brings
him into close contact with Alana Richardson, the woman who
might just help him fulfill his dreams—if they can shut down a
human trafficking ring first.

"Want to come in for a cup of coffee?" Jade asked.

If he went inside with her, he would have a hard time
tearing himself away and going home. "I have a meeting in
Odessa tomorrow. I have to leave early in the morning to
make it in time."

"On a weekend?" Jade asked.

"Unfortunately," Declan said.

The disappointment in her face was unmistakable.
"Another time, then."

Jade stepped out of the car and Declan followed her up
the steps to her front door. A gentleman walked his lady to
the door, a simple and kind gesture to ensure she was safe.

At the door, Jade turned.

"I'll ask again. Want to come in?" she said.

She turned and unlocked her door. Declan followed
her inside, pushing the door closed and locking it. He had
declined her offer, but he wanted to be with her. He should

keep a travel bag with him. It wasn't like the bed-and-breakfast was home. He was living on the road.

The air-conditioning cooled his skin, the humidity of the air disappearing inside the house. In a tangle of arms and legs, they stumbled to the couch. The couch was good. Better than the bedroom. Being in the bedroom would lead to one thing. As it was, this was inviting. Declan pivoted, pulling Jade on top of him.

He had several inches on her, but their bodies lined up, her softness fitting against him. The right friction and pressure made Declan want to peel her clothes away and finish this the right way. But he would wait.

She leaned over him, bracing a leg on the floor. Her hair swung to one side and he ran his fingers through it. Her blue-and-white dress was spread over them and lifting the fabric of the skirt ran through his mind.

Jade sat up. "Did you hear something?"

Declan shook his head. "Nothing." His heart was racing and his breath was fast.

"Like a creak on the porch. Like the wood shifting beneath someone's feet."

Worry speared him. Declan moved Jade off his lap and rolled to his feet. "I'll walk the perimeter and have a look."

Jade fisted his shirt in her hand, stopping him. "Maybe that's not a good idea. My mother has no compunction about killing or hurting people. I could be next. We could be next."

Don't miss
CAPTURING A COLTON by C.J. Miller,
available August 2017 wherever
Harlequin® Romantic Suspense books
and ebooks are sold.

www.Harlequin.com

Reward the book lover in you!

Earn points from all your Harlequin book purchases from wherever you shop.

Turn your points into *FREE BOOKS* of your choice
OR
EXCLUSIVE GIFTS from your favorite authors or series.

Join for FREE today at
www.HarlequinMyRewards.com.

Harlequin My Rewards is a free program (no fees) without any commitments or obligations.

3 1270 00810 8963

MYR17